THE LEATHER SUIT CASE

A Pegasus Investigations Mystery

By Brian D. Eyre

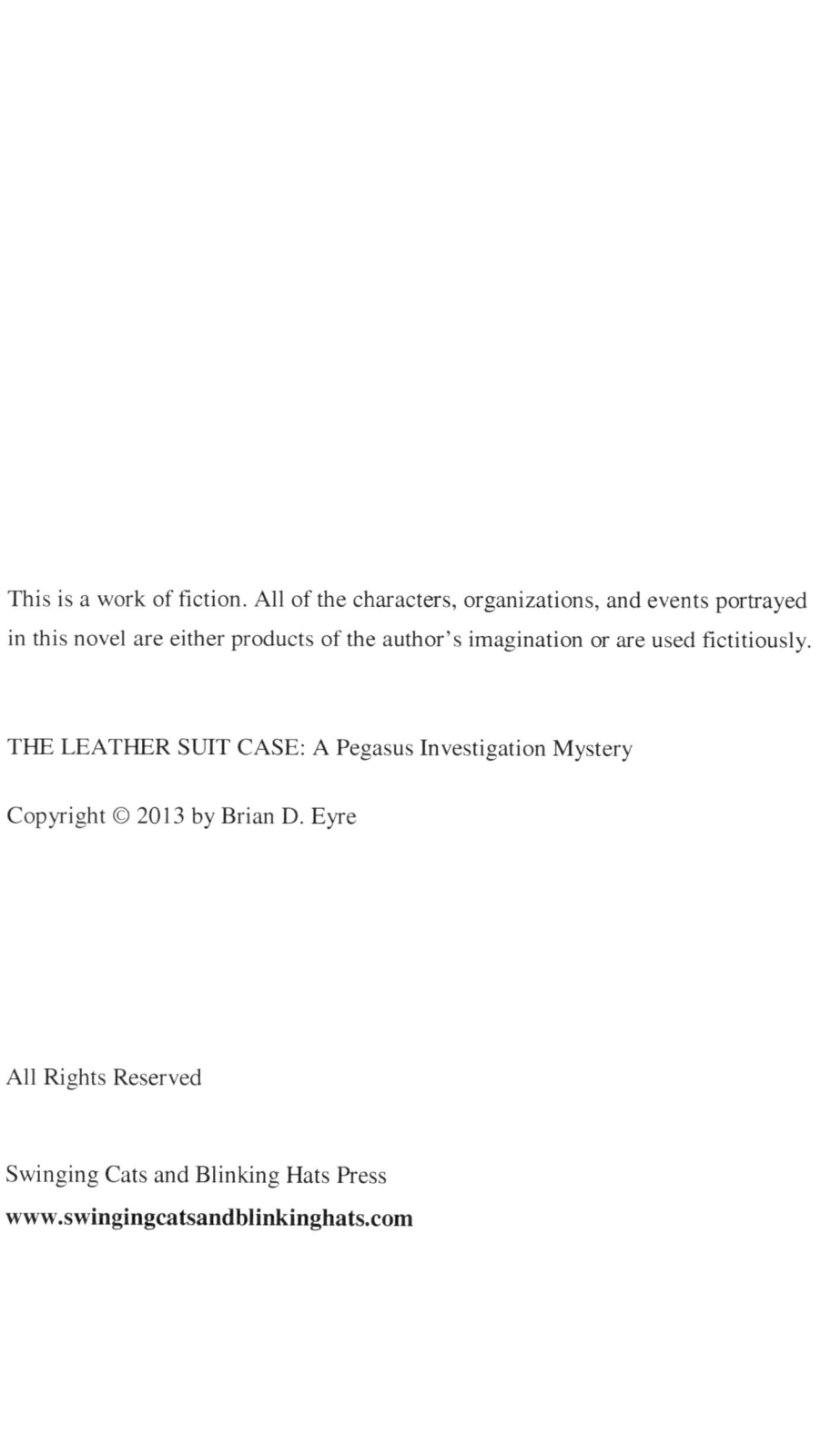

This is a work of fiction. All of the characters, organizations, and events portrayed in this novel are either products of the author's imagination or are used fictitiously.

THE LEATHER SUIT CASE: A Pegasus Investigation Mystery

Swinging Cats and Blinking Hats Press
www.swingingcatsandblinkinghats.com

Prologue

Her marriage of inconvenience can not continue. She knows that more certainly than she's ever known anything in her life. She never cared for the marriage when it was actually convenient. Now it is so inconvenient as to be completely intolerable.

Ten years ago, she and her friend, Caroline, had opened up a house of domination. The money was good, and the work was easy and often quite enjoyable. Still, it wasn't the type of income that one mentions in the social circles that such an income allowed her to join.

A few years later, Mistress Caroline suggested that she find a husband who would allow her to move with the social elite without having to answer questions about her source of income. The idea intrigued her greatly, and she immediately began her search.

A few months after that, she'd found the perfect candidate. He wasn't a good man, but he was disinclined to ask uncomfortable questions. He also lacked the confidence it would take to stand up to her or cheat on her. Unfortunately, it hadn't worked out. The son of a bitch somehow developed a backbone.

Last year, she discovered that her husband was not only asking questions and standing up to her; he was also having an affair. She'd probably already be out of the marriage if it hadn't been for the incident. As she thought of the incident, she also thought about the client currently getting dressed in the changing room.

Six months ago, he'd come to her to live out his fantasy of being bound, suspended and whipped. Since then, he'd become one of her favorite clients. His endurance and ability to withstand pain impressed her even more than his generosity as a tipper.

Hours ago, she'd bound him as usual for a suspension session with a gag and a rubber ball for him to hold. A gagged client can't use a safe word, so clients drop the ball to signal an end to the session. A few minutes ago, the client had dropped the ball. It was the longest suspension session any client of hers had ever endured.

When he came out of the changing room, he thanked her politely as he always did. She asked him if he wanted to schedule another session. He surprised her by saying that wouldn't be necessary. He surprised her even more by shooting her in the head with a 9mm Glock.

Her marriage officially ended, but the inconvenience had just begun!

Part 1 – Texas Wedding

"The candlesticks are burning low now
The walls are weighted down with flowers
I watch her shake the hands of three hundred happy people
And her dress gets whiter by the hour.

You stand beside her like a shadow
Echo her smile when her teeth start showing through.
Your hand rests gently on the small of her back.
But you hold my gaze across the room."

EmmeLine
'Not That Girl'

01 Cancelled Plans

"I do," she said and then she kissed me.

With that formality out of the way, the Reverend Ezekiel James pronounced us man and wife. I turned and shook hands with my best man, Carl Jennings, while April hugged her maid of honor, Bobbie Jo Nottingham. Carl's wife, Emily, stood a few feet away talking to Lisha McDonough who surprised us all by coming to the wedding.

Bobbie Jo's girlfriend, Mandy, stood beside them trying to pretend it didn't bother her as Bobbie Jo embraced a girl more beautiful than even she could hope to be. Emily noticed Mandy's discomfort and quickly ushered April and I back into each other's arms. Emily's always had a gift for preventing awkward moments or at least minimizing the awkwardness. Since Carl never even notices them, even when he's the cause, he's lucky to have her around.

Bobbie Jo took Mandy by the hand, and they walked over to talk with Lisha, one of the few guests without a date. April and I started mingling. More accurately, April mingled; I walked around with April as she mingled. Our wedding had less people than my funeral a few years ago, but Lovers Lane Wedding Chapel was packed.

Over the next hour or so, I shook hands with more men than a politician and politely hugged more women than I used to hit on in a typical night in Deep Ellum back in my single days. Two of my best friends from the Deep Ellum days, Rachel and Sam the Man were there together, and I talked with them for a little while before April squeezed my hand and we moved on.

"You do know she still wants you, don't you?" April asked.

"I never knew for sure if she wanted me when she had me, but you may be right. Sam wants you, too. I guess that makes it even."

"I guess it does," she said smiling. "I didn't know he ever wanted me. He never mentioned it."

"He never does; he thinks he has the ability to project an aura that the women he wants will pick up on. Apparently, you never picked up on it."

April kissed me and flashed me her million watt smile. "Lucky for you, I didn't."

I nodded toward Sam and Rachel who were holding hands and trying not to look out of place. "Lucky for Rachel, too," I said.

"Think they have a chance to make it?" April asked.

"No," I answered honestly, "but they do make a cute couple."

April looked back toward them; Sam stands 6'10" with dark chocolate skin and a completely shaved head. He wore a rented suit that he obviously hated. Rachel is about 5'6" with ivory skin, green eyes and curly black hair. She wore the always appropriate little black dress, except that even on her small frame, her little black dress was so little it would be more appropriate at Plush or The Ghost Bar than at a wedding.

"Of course they do, dear. Of course they do," April said. "Tell me Sam's real name again, in case I need to know it for their wedding."

"It's Osalumense, but I doubt if you'll need it. Rachel might be the marrying type, but he's not."

April smiled again, the smile that always tells me that we're talking about something she knows more about than I do. I see that smile often. "Just in case, I'm going to learn to pronounce it."

"Why do you say that?"

"She's positively glowing. Nobody can beam like that at her ex's wedding unless she's on her way to the altar herself."

I smiled. "Maybe you don't know everything about all my friends, after all. Miss Rachel, or perhaps I should say Mistress Rachel, just landed her dream job."

"Oh really, and what's her dream job? I never knew she wasn't happy at the costume shop."

"She's going to be a dominatrix at one of our local dungeons."

For one of the few times since I'd known her, April looked surprised. She asked, "One of our local dungeons? How many dungeons does it take to serve all the men who are willing to pay to be tied up and whipped?"

"Don't be sexist; it's not just men who pay to use the services professional dominants provide. To answer your question, I don't know how many. I do know Rachel applied to at least four because that's how many called me as a reference. Apparently, after I shut down the revue, she missed the sensation of whipping people. Now she'll get to do it to her heart's content."

Our discussion of Rachel's new career was interrupted when my Godfather slapped me on the back. Larry Joe McCoy, the most infamous defense attorney in North Texas, practically raised me after my parents died, and has been my friend and attorney for all of my adult life. He also has the most practiced, and profitable, fake Texas accent of anybody not named Larry Hagman.

"Well, Pardner, looks like you done got hitched. I reckon I'll have grandkids to be wetnursin' purty soon."

April put her hand up in Larry Joe's face using a gesture Carl calls giving the Heisman. "Don't count on it, Mister. I'm a career woman. I may

3

only be the office manager for Pegasus Investigations at the moment, but I expect to be a partner by the time I'm thirty."

Actually, neither one of us wants children, but her well-rehearsed answer always changes the subject politely. It also avoids any mention of the uncomfortable fact that I am already closing in on my expected lifespan. If we have children now, April will most likely end up raising them alone.

I inherited Congenital Analgesia from my parents, who both died young because of it. The condition can be both a blessing and a curse. Without it, I'd almost certainly already be dead, but with it, I'm not likely to live past thirty-five. I have to admit though, that not being able to feel physical pain allows me to pull off some really cool tricks. I can do stuff for real that Penn and Teller wouldn't even try to fake.

Larry Joe knows all about my condition. "Ah figured that, Missy. Ah just reckoned Ah was s'posed to say somethin' like that seein' as how Ah'm about the oldest cowpoke at this here rodeo. Now that Ah done my part, you lovebirds should be gettin' to your honeymoon. I rented this here chapel by the hour. If y'all don't mosey on, Ah'll be in the poorhouse before Ah clear this room."

The Pope will endorse second trimester abortions before Larry Joe ever has to worry about going broke, but heading to our honeymoon seemed like a good idea to me. April and I said our goodbyes and walked out to April's Mitsubishi Eclipse. I opened the driver's side door and kissed her again as she got in. I closed the door behind her like a true gentleman, then jumped over the hood like a twelve year old boy and got in on the passenger side. I don't have a driver's license, so April is accustomed to doing all our driving. She's also used to me acting like a twelve year old at inappropriate times.

"Viva Las Vegas," I said as I closed the car door behind me, looking forward to our honeymoon. We weren't going directly to Vegas, since April insisted on taking the scenic route. Being from Australia, April wanted to see the Grand Canyon and Carlsbad Caverns on our way. I've seen them both without being impressed, but I knew I'd enjoy it more with April.

"We can't go, Freak. You know that, don't you?" April didn't start the car.

She calls me Freak because Freak Show was the name I was using when we first met. Nobody else calls me by my real name, so why should my wife? "Why can't we? We're legally married now, and we've been planning this honeymoon for months."

"We can't leave now. Woodbury is in jail, you know?"

4

"I know that, darling; that's where they put men who murder their wives."

"It's also where they put innocent people. You, of all people, should know that."

"I know that, dear. I also know my godfather made himself rich by making sure innocent, or plausibly innocent, people get released when that happens. He's already told Woodbury he won't take the case. That means something to me."

We were still parked in front of the chapel, and April still hadn't started the car. She called me by my given name, "Franz, Larry Joe didn't take the case because he doesn't like Woodbury. That has nothing to do with whether Woodbury killed her. Lisha's going to hire Pegasus to look into it, and I'm staying in town to help. If you want to go to Vegas without me, get somebody else to drive you. I'm sure Sam and Rachel would love to go."

I thought about the last time I'd gone to Vegas and left somebody who loves me here in Dallas. I knew I was going to lose control if I kept thinking about it, so I got out of the car. I love April with all my living heart, but some of my heart died years ago when Katherine Elizabeth died. I closed the car door gently, so April would know I wasn't mad at her.

April knows and accepts that I sometimes need to be alone when I start thinking about Katharine Elizabeth. She has her own memories like that. A wedding day isn't a good time to have to be alone, but I did. I just started walking east on Lover's Lane without paying attention to where I was walking; I was just trying to not think about Katherine Elizabeth or the lunatic who murdered her and our unborn son.

As I got near Inwood Road, I thought about how Detective Woodbury's partner planted false evidence, attempting to frame me and several of my friends years ago. I thought about how Woodbury took credit two years later when Carl and I caught a serial killer, which helped Woodbury get promoted to Sergeant. I also thought about how happy he always seemed when I saw him with his girlfriend, Lisha, and how miserable he seemed around his late wife.

April wanted us to get him out of jail, and I liked that he was in jail. When I told Carl that April and I were getting married, he asked me if I was ready to start doing things I hate to do, just because somebody else wants me to do them. I'd assured him that for April, I'd be happy to do things that I hate. It never occurred to me that the first opportunity would be our wedding day.

I turned around to walk back toward the chapel and April's car. April was walking toward me. When she saw me turn around, she broke into a run. As we embraced she said, "I'm so sorry. I wasn't thinking about

5

what you've been through. Let's go to Vegas and see if I can make it up to you."

"Screw Vegas," I told her. "Let's find out who really killed the biggest bitch I've ever had the displeasure to meet. If it turns out to be Woodbury, I'll make Larry Joe take the case, and at least get the charges reduced to justifiable homicide."

April smiled again, "Or unlicensed extermination. That woman was definitely a rat."

02 Public Defender

April started the car and put it in drive, "Where to, Miss Daisy?" She's used to doing all our driving, and I'm used to her teasing me about it.

"Let's go home. I'm not doing any detective work until I get out of this monkey suit."

While April drove, I made a couple of calls to see if I could get in to see Woodbury. By the time we got home, I'd spoken with his court appointed attorney, Janice Reynolds, and had an appointment to meet her at Lew Sterrett at three o'clock.

I took off the suit pants, tie and jacket, but left on the white dress shirt. I slipped into a pair of Social Collision pants that I bought at Hot Topic shortly after I became a detective. Carl claims they look just like Dockers. He's wrong about that, of course, but it definitely was the right look for visiting a lawyer and her client at Lew Sterrett.

April's wardrobe was still in the guest room where we moved it when she started spending more nights here than at her apartment. She still has a few months left on her lease, but our plan was to move the rest of her stuff in right after the honeymoon. Plans change. We both learned that the hard way years ago. She was still in the guest room when I finished changing and went downstairs.

"What color pants are you wearing?" She called down to me.

"Black," I answered glancing down to confirm it. "Why? Does it matter?"

She made a sound that may have been a laugh. Obviously it matters to her, so it matters. I plan to learn everything I can about how to make April happy, but I know I'll never learn everything about how she thinks. I waited patiently in the living room for her to choose her outfit and come down.

A few minutes later she descended the stairs wearing a conservative gray pinstripe business suit and blue pumps. The skirt came down just past her knees and only the top button on her blue blouse was open. She frowned when she saw my pants, "Pinstripes? You said, 'black'. Don't you know the difference?"

I looked down at my pants again and noticed the thin white stripes for the first time. "I guess not, should I change?"

She put her arm around my waist and walked us to the full length mirror in the downstairs' bathroom. She looked at our reflection for a few seconds before saying, "No, we're fine. But thank you for understanding."

She put her arms around my neck and kissed me while I wisely chose not to mention that I really didn't understand. We walked arm in arm out to her car, and headed toward Lew Sterrett. April drives like a race car driver until she reaches the speed limit then slows down.

Her V6 Eclipse has frequently proven it can go from zero to fast in a few seconds flat, but it never gets the chance to show off its maximum speed. I mentioned once to her that her driving style isn't ecologically green or particularly cost efficient. I don't plan to mention it again.

At two-fifty, April and I pulled into the parking lot at Lew Sterrett. We held hands as we walked across the parking lot, but when we entered, we let go. We may be newlyweds, but we're also professional detectives, key word being professional.

April's title at Pegasus Investigations may be Office Manager, but she's every bit the detective I am. In fact, she's probably more of a detective than I am. She helped solve more cases while she was a bartender than I have since I've become a detective. We've been doing this together long enough that the switch from lovers to working partners is usually seamless.

I saw Janice sitting against the wall and steered April in that direction. Janice stood and shook my hand. She looked at April the way most women do when first meeting her, with a combination of jealousy and awe. "I don't believe I've had the pleasure."

I made the introductions, "April, this is Janice Reynolds. Janice, this is April Rose; she works with the agency."

"I'm sure she'll be a big help recruiting some real detectives if Carl ever decides to quit hiring amateurs."

April smiled politely, apparently ignoring both insults. "I'm sure Mr. Jennings can hire whomever he decides to hire without needing me to recruit them. He's running a detective agency, not one of those big law firms that have to go all out to recruit the latest honor roll grads from the Dedman School of Law." April left unsaid that public defenders seldom came from the ranks of SMU honor role grads.

"I guess he can, at that." Janice forced a smile and turned to me, "So, is this a one-time personal visit or are you hoping he'll hire you."

"We already have a client," I told her, "but we expect Woodbury will want you to cooperate with us. That means we'll need a letter authorizing us to visit whenever needed."

"Of course, as a Public Defender, my clients don't usually have private detectives on the case, but I'll cooperate. Wait here, I'll check on our visitation."

As Janice walked away, April smiled at me, "She's kind of a bitch, isn't she?"

8

"Like everybody else who goes to law school, she expected to start out at Baker and Botts making a six-figure salary. The county pays her about half of that and she's not getting to work with the city's most respected lawyers or the most prestigious clients. Besides, you must be used to less attractive women acting bitchy around you by now."

"Sure, but it usually doesn't happen when I'm with you."

I resisted the urge to kiss her. Janice returned escorted by a uniformed deputy who I thought I recognized from the last time I'd been a guest of the county. When he got close enough, I read the name Matheson on his name tag, and remembered that he'd been very friendly during my stay.

He also remembered me. "Freak, how the Hell are you? Good to see you in the just visiting square for a change. I heard you were getting married." He looked at April trying hard to be subtle about it and almost succeeding. "Does your new bride know you're escorting a doll like this to visit a murderer?"

After a short, possibly uncomfortable pause, Janice answered, "Mr. Scholes is a private investigator. The young lady is his associate, Ms. Rose. Mr. Woodbury is accused of a crime he did not commit, and should not be referred to as a murderer. Your job is to escort us to the interview room, not rehash old times or speculate on how Mr. Scholes' bride might react to the fact that his associate is a beautiful young woman."

Matheson's relaxed attitude ended. He said curtly, "Please follow me." He turned and led us through the labyrinth that is the Lew Sterrett Justice Center until we finally reached a small white room much like many I've sat in talking to my lawyer over the years. I was a little surprised that Woodbury wasn't in this one.

Matheson led us inside. "Wait here, your client will be brought in shortly."

Janice stood at the door, as Matheson went to get Woodbury. "I presume you don't wish me to be here while you interview Woodbury. I also presume you're on his side, so I won't balk. I don't want to hear anything that would make it harder for me to represent him." She tapped her cell phone as she turned toward the hallway, "I'll be in the lobby if you need me."

April smiled, "Thank you, Ms. Reynolds. We appreciate your consideration."

Janice smiled back, "I don't know which is more pathetic; that Matheson is stupid enough to refer to a man awaiting trial as a murderer, or that you two plan to spend your honeymoon trying to keep the accused man from being going to trial."

03 Murderous Intent

"How's Lisha holding up?" Woodbury asked the question before his uniformed escort even left the room and locked the door on us. His priorities were self-evident.

April answered, "She's doing as well as can be expected. She'll be doing even better when we get you out of here."

Woodbury made a sound that might have been meant to be a derisive laugh. "She can forget about that. She'll be an old lady before I get out, if I ever do."

April turned to me, "Well, I guess we can go on our honeymoon, now. I thought maybe we could help, but I guess not." She stood up and took my hand as she faced Woodbury. "Was it worth it? Did you enjoy killing her as much as you're going to hate being in prison instead of being with Lisha for the next twenty years?"

As April and I stood up, Woodbury sat down. "You know I might have. God knows I've thought about it at least a thousand times. I thought about how to do it; what steps to take to make sure I got away with it; what to do with the body. I thought about how much I might enjoy it, and what might happen if I got caught."

"I thought about all of that every day for at least the last three years. It just never occurred to me that somebody else would kill her and pin it on me. Now, all I think about is who's going to take care of Lisha and why didn't I kill her."

"Lisha can take care of herself," I said with more force than I intended. "My guess is you didn't kill your wife because you're just an asshole, not a murderer. Of course, I've been wrong before."

Woodbury's face turned red, "Thanks, I think. Too bad you're not going to be on the jury. Not that it would matter, with Janice as my lawyer, I wouldn't like my chances even if the evidence against me wasn't overwhelming."

"You don't trust her?"

"Oh, I trust her. I trust her to question witnesses in a thoroughly professional manner that will bore the jury to tears. Kenth calls her the most competent ineffective lawyer he's ever had the pleasure of defeating in court. I think she's also the only attorney who's never won a case against him."

Kenth is the incompetent D.A. who wanted to try me for Katherine Elizabeth's murder. He's also the closest thing Carl has to an enemy. If Janice had never won a case against him, I didn't like Woodbury's chances very much, either.

"Is Kenth prosecuting your case?"

"Of course, he takes all the high profile slam dunk cases."

I tried to keep my smile to myself. I knew with Kenth prosecuting, it wasn't going to be hard to talk Larry Joe into taking the case if necessary, regardless of how much he might despise Woodbury. Nobody inspires hatred the way Douglas (Dougie) Kenth does.

"So what makes this such a slam dunk case?"

"You mean other than the fact that a husband who is known to be having an affair is real easy to convict when his wife's dead body is found naked in their back yard?"

April smiled, "She was found in your backyard, but it's been established that she was killed elsewhere, hasn't it?"

Woodbury looked at April, "Good to see you taking a more active role in Pegasus Investigations. I've always believed you have more brains than either of your associates. It has been established, but unfortunately that doesn't help my defense very much. Kenth will argue that I brought her back to the house intending to dispose of the body in the woodchipper."

"He'll also mention that I bought the woodchipper right after I got my promotion, which was well after my relationship with Lisha began."

"The promotion you earned by shooting a killer in the back instead of letting me shoot him in the heart?" I asked.

"I look at it as not letting him shoot you, but have it your way. Either way, Kenth will have a field day with the fact that I bought a woodchipper that's hardly been used since I bought it. Janice will counter that there is no law against owning a woodchipper without using it, and that the evidence is purely circumstantial. She'll mention it competently. Later on, when Kenth brings up movies like 'The Wood Chipper Massacre,' she'll object in a professional manner. But none of that will matter, because the jury will have already made up their minds."

"Why did you buy the wood chipper?" April asked.

Woodbury smiled at her; then turned and stared at me. "You know why I bought it. Why don't you tell her?"

As he kept smiling, I realized that I knew exactly why he bought a woodchipper, and I knew why it hadn't been used much. I returned the stare, and thought about the first time I stared into the eyes of Katherine's killer. Woodbury's eyes were different, but not markedly different. The biggest difference seemed to be that Woodbury's eyes still showed a little fear. I knew exactly what that meant.

I took April's hand in mine, and we locked eyes. "He bought the woodchipper to throw his wife in after he killed her. Once he killed Arrington, he figured he could kill again, so he started figuring out how to get away with it. Disposing of the body is the hardest part of getting away with murder."

April never looks shocked, but she opened her beautiful big eyes a little wider than normal. "Like a snake that goes from being fed dead rats to getting to eat live prey, huh?"

"Maybe," I answered without mentioning that snakes generally can't do that. "Or maybe like a pit bull that tastes blood for the first time."

She addressed me as if Woodbury wasn't even in the room. "Interesting, how much of an idiot would that dog have to be to let the victim's naked body be found less than 30 yards from the very device he purchased just to destroy the evidence?"

I liked her idea, so I also pretended Woodbury wasn't in the room. "He'd have to be pretty stupid, but he is a cop. We both know how stupid cops are capable of being."

April smiled, "That's true, but Woodbury's not a typical stupid cop. Other than a really bad marriage choice, and a complete inability to hide the fact that he's having an affair, he seems pretty smart or at the very least, a little bit clever."

I knew several examples of Woodbury not using great intelligence, but I chose not to mention them. "So why do you think an intelligent cop would leave his murder victim intact in her own backyard waiting to be discovered only a few yards from the woodchipper he bought for the express purpose of getting rid of her body?"

Woodbury remained silent as April and I discussed his intelligence, or lack thereof, and pretended to think about the question. After a long silence that would have made Carl proud of April and me, Woodbury spoke. "It doesn't fucking matter; no jury is ever going to think it out that far. I'm toast and everybody knows it. Even McCoy knows it, and he's freed more guilty clients than Johnnie Cochran. If I had a chance in Hell, he'd have taken the case."

April turned toward him, "Lisha doesn't know it. She's sure you didn't kill your wife, and she thinks Pegasus Investigations can prove it."

"No, she hopes I didn't kill my wife, and she figures Pegasus will at least take the case seriously and not just charge her by the day until I get convicted or she runs out of money."

"Speaking of money," I interjected. "Why are you using a public defender? I know McCoy said no, but there are other lawyers you could hire. You're not exactly indigent, are you?"

"Not exactly, but most of my money is actually our money. I can't touch it as long as I'm a suspect in her murder. I thought McCoy would take the case knowing he'd get paid as soon he got a not guilty verdict. I don't know any other attorneys with his confidence. What money I do have of my own is for Lisha. She's going to need it to start a new life when I get convicted."

April shook her head fiercely, "You just don't get it, do you? Lisha loves you! She loves you totally and unconditionally. If you go to prison, she's going to waste her life away baking you cakes with files in them. The only thing she wants from you is for you to love her in the same way."

I noticed a tear in Woodbury's eye, but declined to comment on it. April continued as if she hadn't noticed.

"It's all she's ever wanted from you! She didn't give a damn that you were married, and she doesn't give a damn about the money you put aside for her in that stupid safe deposit box. If you go to prison, she can't buy a new life. You are her life."

If somebody told me five years ago that I'd see Officer Richard Woodbury, the self proclaimed High Sheriff of Deep Ellum, crying like a broken hearted sorority girl, I would have assumed it would be the high point of my life. At that moment, as I actually watched it, I felt nothing but sadness.

As Woodbury tried to pull himself together, Janice and Matheson came back in the room. I asked them to give us a few more minutes. Matheson held up three fingers and mouthed the words 'three minutes' as they walked back out.

When I turned back to Woodbury, he stared at me. Only the fear was left in his eyes, "Get me out of here, Freak. Even if she will wait for me, I can't live without her for the next twenty years."

I had no idea how to respond to that, but even if I had, I never got the chance. April reached out her left hand and turned Woodbury's face toward her. "We'll get you out of here. But, I promise you, if you ever cheat on Lisha like you did on your wife or mistreat her in any way, I'll make sure you spend the rest of your life wishing you'd died in prison."

Woodbury's head was on the table as Janice and Matheson entered the room, and April and I left. I didn't know if we could keep April's promise to keep him from going to prison. I did, however, know that if it came to it, April would definitely keep the second part of the promise. I hoped for Woodbury's sake that he loved Lisha at least as much as April liked her.

04 Mixed Feelings

"You couldn't have missed your flight because you're driving to Vegas, and you didn't forget anything since neither of you ever forgets anything and you packed days ago. You're together, so you obviously haven't decided getting married was bad idea, so what are you doing here?" Carl didn't even turn from the computer screen in front of him as he asked why we were at Pegasus Investigations' office instead of driving on our honeymoon.

April answered, "If you've mastered that Sherlock shit well enough to know it's us without turning around, you have to know why we're here instead of on I-20."

Carl turned around smiling, "Sherlock shit? I like it. Maybe, we should change our business cards to read 'Pegasus Investigations, Masters of Sherlock Shit.' Unfortunately, the only Sherlock shit I've mastered is staring out the window as y'all parked the car."

Carl has mastered much more than he ever lets on, but staring out the window in the virtual fortress which is our office is something we both do often. All the windows are made of bullet-proof glass. Even the window which covers most of the wall separating the waiting room from the main office is bulletproof. It is also one way see through and impossible to detect from the waiting area. On the side in the office, there's a panel which slides over it, so few people even know it's a window.

I smiled, "Were you looking for something out the window or just checking out the ladies going in and out of Neiman Marcus?"

"Just staring like I usually do when I don't have a clue how to even get started on a case. Are you going to answer the question, now?"

April answered it for us, "We're here to help you solve the case. We've already started. We just came from Lew Sterrett. Woodbury's not optimistic, to say the least."

"I can't blame him. Has he hired a lawyer, yet?" As he spoke, he left the computer and walked over and sat at our conference table. April and I joined him there.

When we were all seated, I answered. "He's going with a public defender, a lady named Janice Reynolds."

Carl laughed. "No wonder he's not optimistic. Kenth will eat her alive. I presume Kenth is prosecuting?"

"Of course, doesn't he always take the high profile cases?"

"Not as much as he once did. Now, he only takes the ones he thinks he can win."

14

April asked, "How does he decide which ones he can win?"

Carl looked at me as he answered, "Nobody knows for sure, but he hasn't prosecuted a case against anybody Larry Joe represented in a long time."

"McCoy's out on this one, so I guess we're dealing with Kenth." April frowned, "That means we have to find a way to save Woodbury without relying on McCoy."

Carl looked at me, then back to April. Nobody said anything for a few minutes, and I decided I wasn't going to be the first to speak. If April talked too soon, Carl could chalk it up to her inexperience. As the apprentice, I'm supposed to know the trick by now.

The next noise in the office was Carl's laughter. "The old man would be proud of us all. He taught me the value of being silent, and you two obviously have learned it well. Somehow, I don't think this is the right occasion for it."

"Probably not," I agreed. "But, you also taught me that it's best to listen until you have something to say. If I knew anything to say, I wouldn't have packed a suitcase. I expected to be in Vegas celebrating my honeymoon while you solved the case."

Carl gave me a hard look, "So why aren't you? You know, I am capable of running this agency for two weeks without your help. I managed to solve cases for many years on my own before you decided you wanted to be Philip Marlow when you grew up."

April answered, "Relax, Carl. We're back because of me. Maybe I've decided I want to be Kinsey Millhone when I grow up. Besides, this is an important case, and we'll have a better chance of solving it if we all work on it."

Carl smiled, "Okay, we all want to be detectives, so let's start doing it. The evidence against Woodbury is pretty convincing. He definitely had motive. With no way of knowing exactly when or where she was killed, opportunity will be assumed. Since he's a police officer, and she was shot, he also clearly had means."

April objected, "But, they've confiscated all three of his guns, and none of them match the bullet found in her head."

"Really, did he tell you that this afternoon?"

"No, it's in the police report."

Carl looked a little surprised that April had read the police report, but he knew better than to say anything. "True, so they don't have a murder weapon to show the jury, but that's something for his lawyer to use. We're in the investigating business. There are several things for us to investigate, but I don't know where to start on most of them. We could look for the murder weapon, but what if when we find it, we also find that Woodbury's prints …"

I could tell Carl thought we were tilting at windmills, so I stood up quickly. He stopped in mid-sentence and looked up at me without rising. "Yes?"

"Our client is sure her boyfriend didn't kill his wife. She hired us because she trusts us. If any of us think he's guilty, we need to either put it out of our mind or withdraw from the case."

April smiled, but not with her megawatt smile, "Well, you two are from the country that invented 'innocent until proven guilty;' is it just a phrase or do you believe it?"

I sat back down as Carl looked at April. "In this town, it's been pretty much just a phrase for at least half a century. In this office though, we believe it. Okay, Woodbury's innocent of everything but adultery until it's proven otherwise."

"Which means if we find the murder weapon, it will do more to exonerate him than to convict him, so let's find it." I probably sounded more excited than I meant to as I said it.

"Where do you plan to start looking?" Carl always asks the right question.

"I don't know; you tell me."

"I don't think we can find a murder weapon until we find out where she was killed. I suggest that we investigate the victim to find out everything we can about her. That way we'll know where she might have been and where she might have been expected when she died. That might help us find other suspects and the murder weapon."

"Aren't the police already doing that?" April asked.

"Maybe, but I doubt they'll be aggressive about it. They think they've got their man."

This time April smiled with the smile that's been known to kill, "But we know they don't; advantage us! Where do we start?"

Carl sighed. "You two can start by getting Woodbury to tell you everything he knows about his wife's habits. I start by flying to Virginia."

05 Travel Plans

"Virginia? Mr. 'I don't leave Texas' is flying to Virginia?" To say I couldn't have been more shocked would be an understatement. "Why are you flying to Virginia?"

"Because, my young associate, you don't fly. Therefore, you two will have to handle things here, while I look into things there." If Carl noticed that I didn't know what he was talking about, he didn't acknowledge it.

"Okay, we'll handle things here. That still doesn't explain why you're flying to Virginia."

"Oh, that," Carl sighed. "I thought you read the police report. Trudy Woodbury, nee Gertrude Lund, was born and raised in Norfolk, Virginia. If we're going to learn everything about her, we'll need to start with her formative years. As the three of us learned all too well recently, when somebody gets murdered, everybody's past can be relevant."

"April read the report, I didn't. I suppose I better since we're obviously taking the case. When do you leave?"

"I leave Monday at 1:15 on flight 682 out of DFW. Emily took the day off; she's going to drop me off."

"You already booked your flight? What would you have done if Freak and I had gone to Vegas for our honeymoon?"

"I never gave that any thought. Emily said you wouldn't go, so I knew you wouldn't go."

April squeezed my knee under the table. "I told Emily I wanted to work on this case. I guess she presumed that you'd agree. I probably should have told you first, but I didn't want it to affect our wedding."

I laughed, "Of course not, only the honeymoon is expendable. Weddings always have to be perfect. If you've booked a flight, I presume you have a plan. What do we do while you're gone?"

"Like I said earlier, you need to find out what you can about the victim: who she knew, what she liked to do, where she hung out. Find out anything you can. Anything we know will be more helpful than not knowing anything. Since Woodbury didn't kill her, somebody else did. I think we can rule out random act of violence."

I nodded, "I agree this definitely wasn't random. So once we find out who she knew, we investigate each one to see who might have had a reason to kill her. It sounds like we might be billing Lisha for a long time without finding anything."

April disagreed, "Actually I think as soon as we find out who she knows, we'll have our suspect. Anybody who's ever met her had a reason to kill her; we'll just have to learn which one had the means and opportunity."

"Maybe," I said, thinking out loud. "Or maybe, we just need to find somebody who would want her dead and would want to frame Woodbury for it. I guess that narrows it down to everybody who's ever met them both."

"Not everybody," Carl interjected. "The one person with the best motive to kill her is the one person on earth who wouldn't have wanted to frame him for it."

"Of course," I agreed. "Our client is the suspect in waiting. If we prove Woodbury didn't kill his wife, she'll be the next suspect, unless we prove it by finding the killer."

"Exactly, that is why I'm flying to Virginia to learn everything I can about the girl who eventually became Trudy Woodbury. It's also why you two are going to learn everything you can about what she's been up to since she left the Commonwealth of Virginia to migrate to the Republic of Texas and marry Detective Woodbury."

"Actually," April said. "I believe she was Mrs. Woodbury long before he became Detective Woodbury."

"I think that's probably true. I'm sure you'll know that for sure and everything else before I get back from Virginia." Carl stood up as he talked and was obviously taking his leave. "Call me if you need any advice or find anything that might be helpful."

"You're leaving now?" I asked incredulously. "You're flight out is on Monday."

"That's true, but my flight back isn't even scheduled. Emily and I are going to miss at least one Tuesday date night and probably more. I'm going to make sure I spend the weekend before I leave for the state that claims to be for lovers with my lover. I wouldn't even have to go if you weren't the only detective since the Wright brothers' little experiment at Kitty Hawk who won't take a plane ride."

Carl hates leaving Texas and Emily, every bit as much as I hate the fact that my condition makes it very dangerous for me to fly. That's why I'd been so shocked that he even planned to go to Virginia. I could have reminded him that it wasn't that I don't want to fly, but I saw nothing to be gained by that.

"Give Emily my love; any advice?"

"Use your wisdom, guided ..."

I joined him for the conclusion, "by your experience." He's been giving me that borrowed advice since before I even had any experience.

Carl was out the door before I thought of a suitable comeback. Once he was gone, I quit trying to think of one.

April took my hand. "Is he like that often? I've never seen that side of him."

"Cut him some slack. He's doing the thing he hates most to try to free a man he really doesn't like."

"You hate Woodbury more than Carl does, plus you missed your honeymoon. Why aren't you acting like a brat?"

I answered honestly, "I guess I got that out of my system walking on Lovers Lane. Once I turned around and saw you there, I was over it. When Emily drops Carl off at the airport, he'll be over it, too. That's how love works."

April smiled. "Yes, it is! This is supposed to be our honeymoon. Wait here a minute."

April pulled her cell phone out of her purse as she hustled into my office. I wasn't sure what she was doing, but I suspected I was going to like it. After about three minutes, April came out of the office smiling.

"Our honeymoon is officially rescheduled. You ready to go?"

"Of course, where are we going?"

"We're booked in the honeymoon suite at the Gaylord Hotel. We can dine and dance at The Glass Cactus, then consummate our marriage in style. Check out time is 8 o'clock Sunday night."

"I didn't even know the Gaylord had a honeymoon suite, and how do we have a night time check out time?"

"Every hotel has a honeymoon suite if you know the right people. We know the right people, so we have a honeymoon suite with a night time check out."

"You know the right people. Except for you, I mostly know the wrong people. Let's go have the best twenty-four hour honeymoon in history."

April took my hand, and we went to her car. I don't know if we had the best twenty-four hour honeymoon of all time, but it had to be top ten. We saw very little of the Glass Cactus and almost all of the honeymoon suite. I then spent the next day meeting more of the wrong people.

06 Young Love

"Do you really expect me to believe that this is all you know about your late wife? I know more than this about women I went out with one time."

I'd spent an hour talking to Woodbury trying to learn more about his late wife. So far, I had learned that he met her at a Dallas Museum of Art mixer before he joined the police force.

"I can't make you believe anything you don't want to believe. We've led separate lives since the honeymoon ended. Don't you think I'd tell you if I knew anything else?"

I sighed, "I guess you would. Let's try something different. You guys drifted apart a long time ago. Why don't you talk about how you ended up together in the first place? I know you met her at the Dallas Museum of Art. Take it from there."

"What the Hell do you expect that to accomplish? That was years ago. I don't like thinking about those days, let alone talking about them."

"I don't blame you, but I don't like the idea of telling Lisha that we can't take the money she's paying us to investigate because you're withholding information."

"Is that a threat?" He glared at me as he asked the question, but his famous glare faded quickly. "Never mind, you're right. I don't have anything better to do than talk to you."

I slid my Phillips PocketMemo 9350 a little closer to him, a purely symbolic gesture since it records every sound in the room. "You've got nowhere to go and this thing will record for 3 more hours before I need to change memory cards. Why were you even at a Dallas Museum of Art event? You don't strike me as the type."

Woodbury laughed. "No, I'm not the DMA type. I never was. But, I've always liked getting paid. I worked for NorTex Security back then, and the guy who normally worked the DMA events couldn't make it, so I got the assignment."

He didn't continue, so I needed to prime the pump. "So, were you in the habit of hitting on girls while you worked your security job, or did she strike you as so special that you made an exception at this event?"

"Honestly, back then I was probably in the habit of trying to hit on girls every place I went, but I didn't hit on Trudy. She was with three friends, all of whom were drunk, but she was by far the drunkest. They ended up calling for a cab, but Trudy needed help getting to the cab. The ladies asked me to help her out. Since my job was to ensure the safety of patrons, I did."

"What did you think of her at the time?"

Woodbury didn't answer immediately; he actually thought about it. "I remember thinking two things. First, she was the drunkest person I'd ever encountered who didn't just reek of alcohol. At the time, I assumed she'd gotten drunk on expensive vodka, since it usually doesn't reek. The second thing I kept thinking was that a woman with her money might be able to help me land a better job than security guard. That's why I didn't mind that she kept trying to kiss me and grope me as I got her in the cab."

"How did you know she had money?"

"DMA events aren't attended much by the middle class, at least they weren't back then. Also, she wore designer clothes. I don't remember exactly what she wore, but I knew they were expensive. Her shoes alone probably cost more than the car I owned at the time."

"Okay, so you decided she might be sugar mama material? Did you get her phone number as you carried her to the cab?"

"No, I was going to ask the guy who normally worked the DMA events to try to hook me up. He'd done it for other guys, and we were friends."

"What's his name?" I asked.

"You know, I don't remember. Everybody called him Duckie, but I don't know why. I'm sure I knew his real name back then, but I don't remember it. It doesn't matter, anyway."

I didn't agree with his assessment that it wasn't important, but I let it slide. I knew there were better ways to learn Duckie's real name than trying to get Woodbury to suddenly remember it. I also wanted Woodbury talking about his late wife, not his ex-coworkers.

"You said you were going to ask Duckie to hook you up. That means you never asked him. Why didn't you?"

"I never got the chance. The next morning, I was working a day shift at a bank, when she walked in. She never even pretended to be there on business. She walked straight to me, thanked me for saving her life. She really put it that way; then she kissed me. Even if I didn't think she had money, I would have been interested. How could I not be? Have you ever had a good-looking woman you've only met once show up at your workplace and kiss you?"

I didn't see anything to be gained by telling him how frequently that used to happen to me during my performing days. Instead, I continued my Chuck Woolery impersonation. "She kissed you and piqued your interest. What happened next?"

Woodbury blushed. "Let's just say things moved very fast. We started dating and being together all the time. When I'd get my schedule from the company, I'd call her to tell her. Then, she'd call me back with ideas for things we could do whenever I wasn't working. When I worked a night shift, she'd make plans for a breakfast or brunch date. On the days I had a normal shift, we'd always do something at night. We'd go to movies or plays or just go to the mall and walk around."

The way Woodbury talked, he sounded like the people you see on commercials for online dating services describing their relationships with the ones they met online. His sad, bitter eyes didn't match the tone, but I now knew for the first time that he had once really loved his wife.

He had quit talking, so I asked, "How long did it go on like that? Was everything still perfect when you proposed?"

"Actually, I didn't propose. I couldn't believe how great things were, and I didn't even consider doing anything that might change things." Woodbury paused and gave me his hard glare, again. "You damn well better not tell Lisha any of this, or let her hear that tape."

"I won't," I promised. "Lisha loves you enough to hire Pegasus to save you. Telling her things that might make her think you used to be a loser won't benefit us in any way."

"I guess I have to trust you, and I won't even deny that I was basically a loser back then." Woodbury paused. I think he was hoping I'd either deny that he'd ever been a loser, or accuse him of still being one. I chose to do neither and remained quiet.

Eventually, Woodbury continued. "About three months after we started dating, Trudy asked me if I'd ever dined at Antares. Of course, I hadn't. Hell, I didn't even know that it was the rotating restaurant in the ball at the top of Reunion Tower. She laughed when I told her I'd never heard of it. When she quit laughing, she asked me to make reservations for dinner."

"Did she let you know how much the dinner would likely cost?"

"No, but since she paid, I don't guess that matters. She also proposed that night and I accepted. That night was basically perfect. It's been all downhill from there."

"What changed?" I asked.

"I don't know. I probably didn't even notice the change until we'd been married for a couple of years. When I did notice it, I also noticed that it had been going on for a long time. Basically she quit asking me to do things and started telling me. When I told her I was going to the police academy, she tried to stop me."

"Apparently, she failed." Carl says I have a knack for stating the obvious. I don't think he means it as a compliment.

Woodbury smiled. "She failed, and I passed. The funny thing is, I probably wouldn't have made it through the academy if she hadn't been so against it. I'd never succeeded at anything else before then. It's possible that I'm only a cop, because she didn't want me to be."

"Do you know why she was so against it?"

Woodbury thought for some time before answering, "No idea, but I don't think it matters at this point."

I agreed with him, but we were both very much wrong.

07 Security Guard

Duckie isn't a common nickname. I felt confident I'd find somebody who remembered him from a decade ago. My confidence waned quickly when I learned that Nortex Security had closed shop three years ago. I called my friend, Jeff, to see if he could help."

Jeff works for Secure Investigations, so I normally call him at the office. I was hoping this would just be a personal favor so I called his cell phone."

"Hey, Freak. What's up?" he answered.

"I need a small favor. Is this a good time?"

"Sure, I'm just staring at my screensaver waiting for Pat to assign me a case. It's been kind of a slow summer."

I didn't mention that we'd been pretty busy. "I'm trying to locate someone who worked for NorTex Security about ten years ago. Do you know if any of their principles are still in the business?"

"Aha, of course Woodbury would hire you. You're the ones who made him famous. For the record, we did help you on that case."

"Yes, you did, and you got paid for your help. What makes you think Woodbury is our client?"

"NorTex Security, he used to work there. Back when he used to try to intimidate everybody with that goofy stare of his. Some guys started calling him Officer NorTex."

"Not that it's any of your business, but Woodbury is not our client. Will you help us?"

"Of course, even though I don't believe you, I'll help. The two of us are kindred, honest souls striving in a soulless world to stay whole. Tell me who you want found, and I will ask around."

Jeff occasionally waxes poetic for no reason, but he's a good friend and a better investigator. "Thanks, I don't know his name; I just know his nickname back then was Duckie."

"Duckie," Jeff said confidently. If the word 'Duckie' has ever been said that confidently before, I can't imagine why."

"Do you know him?" I asked hopefully.

"No, but I suspect I know who gave him the nickname. Are we an expense account item or is this a favor?"

Before I answered, I thought about how fast Lisha might run out of money if Woodbury didn't get acquitted, "A favor if you don't mind. If you have to bill, send the bill to my house, not the office. You know I'm good for it."

"Damn, I guess Woodbury isn't your client. I'd have bet my paycheck he was, but I guess I'd have lost that bet. I'll make some calls and get back to you."

Jeff called back less than thirty minutes later. "Who's your hero?"

"Since you're asking, I'll presume you are. What've you got?"

"As I suspected, your boy 'Duckie' got his nickname from Glenn 'Sharky' Sharp. Glenn's been working security gigs around here since before I can remember. He always gives people nicknames based on movie characters."

"Aha, so Duckie looks like Jon Cryer did when he was still young enough to costar in a high school romantic comedy."

"You're on the right track, but you don't understand the genius of 'Sharky'. He doesn't rely on physical characteristics; that would be too obvious. No, young 'Duckie' had a major and unrequited crush on the redheaded secretary at Nortex security."

"Fascinating, does this help me find the man who once had a crush on redheaded secretary?"

"Probably not, but this does. His given first name is Ken and he plays drums for a Journey cover band, called Escape."

"That's original," I said sarcastically. "I guess Open Arms was taken."

"I guess so. Let me know if you need any more help finding him. The boss will probably insist we bill from here on out."

"If I need more help than that, I'll send our client to you. Thanks."

I didn't have to send Lisha to Secure Investigations. Even if you're not a trained investigator with contacts in the local entertainment industry, it's not hard to find a band member in this MySpace, Facebook and You Tube world. About twenty minutes later, I'd sent Duckie a message explaining that I was a private eye and would like to talk to him about his days at NorTex security."

His reply came late the next morning. "If it's about Woodbury, I probably don't know anything, but I'll talk with you. Call me." He included his phone number. I called right away, and he offered to come by the office after he got off work.

April sat at her desk pretending to be an office manager instead of an investigator until I hung up. When I did, she quickly turned and looked at me expectantly. "Is it him, is he going to help?"

"It's definitely him, and he'll be here tonight between 5:30 and 6:30. I guess I'll be putting in a little overtime."

"We'll be putting in a little overtime," she corrected.

"True, I guess we'll both be putting in a little overtime."

April walked as only she can walk and sat down on my desk. She leaned very close to me and said in a breathless whisper, "That, my darling boss, means we'll be earning a little comp time. We've got at least three hours before he'll be here. Let's go home and spend a few hours the way newlyweds should spend their time."

"You want to spend three hours sight-seeing and getting so drunk we take off all our clothes and sing karaoke off-key?"

April laughed at my joke, but not the way she laughs when she finds something funny. "You really need to quit patterning your life after the people who used to come to your shows." She took my hand. "Follow me, I'll show you how a honeymoon goes for normal couples."

I did.

She did.

If I missed a two week honeymoon with April in Vegas to save Woodbury, and it turns out he did kill his wife, the state might not get the chance to execute him.

08 Returned Affection

"Did he kill her?" Ken 'Duckie' Mathis knew exactly why I'd looked him up, and wasted no time starting the conversation as the three of us sat down at the conference table.

April answered, "The police think he did; our client thinks he didn't. We're hoping you can help us find the truth."

It was the perfect answer, since we had no idea how he might actually feel about Woodbury.

"I can't imagine how I can help. I haven't seen him in years. He was kind of a tool, but if he didn't kill her, I'd hate to see him fry for it."

"We appreciate your help," I said. "I'm surprised to hear you call him a tool. He made it seem like y'all were friends."

Ken laughed, "Friends, huh? No, we weren't friends. If Rick had any friends, I never knew about it. He might have thought we were friends, because I didn't razz him the way the other guys always did."

April asked, "What kind of razzing did he get?"

"Oh, it was mostly the usual, but it bothered him. It really got bad after Sharky got everybody calling him Dudley. Rick got mad, and threatened to kick his ass. Like I said, he was kind of a tool. Sharky always had nicknames for people and everybody went along with them. It was kind of a morale building thing. Anybody who didn't get a nickname probably didn't work there long."

"Why did he get so upset? Was the nickname offensive to him, or did he just not understand how it worked?"

Ken looked at April as if he didn't understand the question. "How should I know? Maybe both, maybe neither; I promise I never gave that question a single thought. Sharky named me Duckie."

April smiled sympathetically, "We know."

"Every day I went to work, I got called by the name of perhaps the biggest damn loser in the history of film, and I never complained. If he couldn't handle being called Dudley Do-Right, why should I care?"

His volume rose as he spoke, and reached a scream as he concluded, "Tell me that! Why should I have given a damn about Dudley freaking Woodbury?"

April smiled, "I don't know about that; maybe you shouldn't have. But for the record, I always thought Duckie was kind of cute in that movie. I might even have had a crush on him."

Ken calmed considerably, "Interesting, too bad you didn't work for NorTex at the time. I guess I should get over it. Nobody has called me Duckie for at least five years. Besides, unlike Duckie, I got the girl."

"What do you mean?" I asked.

"Since you already knew, I assume you know why Sharky named me Duckie?"

"I've heard one version, but that doesn't mean I know. Please tell us."

"Okay, wait, how does this help you find out if he killed his wife?"

"We won't know until we find out. All information is good information, once we know the answer; we can decide what information helped the most."

"I don't know what that means, but I said I'd try to help, so I will. About a week after I started working for NorTex, I became infatuated with Sara. She was an admin with long dark red hair, green eyes and a smile that just melted my heart. I started asking around about her. Sharky had nicknamed her Kate because all the guys thought she was an ice princess like the girl in 'The Cutting Edge.' She was always really nice to me, though. Despite what the guys said about her, I asked her out."

"Since Sharky didn't name you Blane, I'll presume she said no."

"She did, but worse yet, she continued to always be nice to me. Being called Duckie probably wouldn't have bothered me as much, except that it was so accurate. I lived for every conversation with her even after I realized she was never going to go out with me. I asked her out several more times, and she always declined, and she was always very polite about it."

"When NorTex shut down, I realized security wasn't the stable career field I'd been looking for to support my music career. I'd been messing around with computers since I was little, and my dad helped me get a job working on the website for Southwest Airlines. About six weeks after I got that job, there was a message from Sara on my answering machine. Several of the old NorTex guys had called asking me to help them get on at Southwest, so I just figured she was doing the same."

I asked, "Was Woodbury one of the guys who called?"

"No, I'm not even sure he was still at NorTex when it closed. I think he left for the police academy before… yea… he must have left before that, cause I never talked to him after NorTex closed, and I knew he joined the academy. Is that important?"

"Probably not," I conceded. "I just wondered. So, did Sara call for job seeking help?"

He smiled at the memory. "No, when I called her back, she asked me if we could meet for lunch. I agreed, of course, and we met at Jake's the next day. After about twenty minutes of small talk, mostly catching up on what we'd been doing, she asked me if I was seeing anybody. I told her that I wasn't."

"Were you?" April asked.

"Were I, I mean, was I what?"

"You said you told her you weren't seeing anybody. I just wondered if you were telling the truth."

"Oh, yes, I was telling the truth. You're right though, if I'd been seeing somebody, I might have lied about it. Fortunately, I wasn't. She explained that she'd always liked me, but that she had a firm rule against dating coworkers. We started going out, and we've been married now for over three years."

"Congratulations," April and I said in unison. April continued, "I just love happy endings."

"Everybody loves a happy ending. Unfortunately, not everybody gets one. Since we're here to investigate an unhappy ending, let's do it." I looked at Ken, "Why don't you tell us about Rick and Trudy's happy beginning?"

"I'd be glad to, but I don't think I know anything about it."

"We think you might, since he married a lady he met at the Dallas Museum of Art. I understand you're the one who normally worked that gig, and that he was filling in for you the night he met her."

"Woodbury married that Trudy? Holy cow, no wonder he killed her!"

09 Art Patron

"Technically, we're exploring the possibility that he didn't kill her. Since you obviously knew the future Mrs. Woodbury, tell me what you can about her."

"I don't know how much I can add. I didn't know her well. The only times I ever saw her were at DMA events. I doubt if I've seen her more than ten times total."

April smiled, "But they must have been ten dramatic meetings for you to say what you just said."

"Oh, it didn't take ten dramatic meetings. Any ten minutes taken at random would probably have done it!" Ken asked April, "Did you ever meet her?"

I answered for both of us, "We'd like to learn what you know. Some other time, we can discuss our relationship with the dearly departed. I wouldn't want to temper what you might have to tell us with our thoughts."

Duckie hesitated thoughtfully before responding. "You're good. If you ever decide not to be a detective, you should take up acting. I know the bitch, and you still damn near convinced me that you might miss her. Anyway, you want me to tell you about Trudy, not critique your lying ability. What do you want to know?"

"Anything or everything. Since you only met her ten times, let's go for everything. The first time you met her you were working security at a DMA event. Why don't we start there?"

"Sure okay, it was late fall, my first time working a DMA event. The event was for members only and by invitation only. My job was to work the door, check everybody's invite and membership card. Once everybody was in and the presentation began, I was supposed to just walk around looking like a security guard to make all the rich people feel safe. As security gigs go, DMA events aren't exactly high risk. If any of the guys have even needed his gun at one, I never heard about it."

I couldn't resist, "If anybody did, it would be Woodbury, and we haven't heard about it, so we'll accept that it hasn't."

"You got that right. Woodbury would show his gun if he was working as a crossing guard. Back then, he might have even needed to show it. But I guess he's gotten better if the Morning News is to be believed."

I declined to speculate on the believability of the local paper. "So, you've set the scene. You're working the door at the DMA trying to look official and not expecting any trouble. Pick it up again from your first encounter with Trudy."

"Everything's going like you would expect. A modest crowd of affluent, polite people are streaming through the door. Most of the people are older, some couples, a few groups of women, an occasional person alone. What everybody has in common is they're all sober, all dressed conservatively and they talk softly if they talk at all. Then Trudy shows up; more accurately Trudy's group shows up. Four women, talking loud and laughing like frat boys at a keg party."

"A little inappropriate for a DMA event, but not a capital offense," I suggested.

"Actually very out of place, but it gets worse. I asked them for their membership cards and invitations, politely of course, just like I'd been doing all evening. They started yelling at me, asking for my name and threatening to get me fired. As calmly as I could, I told them I was simply trying to do my job."

Ken sighed before he continued, "Trudy stepped to the front and stared at me like a cobra looks at a wounded bird. She said, 'Young man, your job is to do what your superiors tell you to do. You're not qualified for anything else, or you wouldn't be wearing that hideous uniform. I am your superior and I'm telling you to quit asking goddesses for common paper documents. Either let us in, or call your boss, and we'll have him let us in. If you choose the latter, I assure you that you will regret it for the rest of your pathetic life."

"Damn!" April seldom cusses, but I couldn't blame her. "What you'd do?"

"What could I do? I let them in."

"Did you get in any trouble?"

"That depends on your definition of trouble. The lady next in line smiled and told me to ignore them. 'Some people have more money than class. Don't let them get you down. Nobody ever gets fired from this job, and Trudy is all bark, anyway.' So no, I didn't get in any trouble with NorTex or the DMA, but there are different kinds of trouble."

I laughed, "That's the truth! What kind of trouble did you get in?"

"About an hour later, I was just milling around trying to look like a security guard. Trudy walked up to me and showed me her membership card and invitation. Then she smiled, 'A real man wouldn't have caved as easily as you did. You didn't even put up any resistance. None of the other guards have ever been that easy. I own you now.' Then she dropped the invitation at my feet. 'Never, ever ask me for anything else again, boy. Do you understand me?'"

31

"I leaned down to pick up the invitation and she put her foot on it. She just held it there for a couple of seconds; then she let me pick it up. 'I asked you a question,' she said. I answered her, 'Yeah, I get it.' She frowned and put her hand on my chin, pressing in my cheeks with her thumb and forefinger. 'Speak respectfully when you address a superior. Say yes, ma'am, I understand.' Embarrassingly, I did, and thankfully she walked away."

"Okay, she's a bitch. To be honest, we already knew that. How did she treat the other members and any other staff?"

"I tried not to pay much attention, but she often made it impossible not to notice. I doubt if there's a single person who attended those events or worked them who didn't get the bitch treatment at least once or twice from her. She really seemed to enjoy being hated by everybody."

"Why'd they put up with it?"

"Apparently, she was one of the most generous donors."

"That would explain them putting up with her. What about the harpies she was with that day? Were they always with her?"

"Not all of them, but none of them ever came by themselves. At least two of them came to most events. Trudy wasn't always one of them. She was the worst, but all four had their moments."

"What you can tell us about the other three."

"Nothing, I don't even know their names. The only reason I know Trudy's name is that she showed me her membership card. I never asked any of the others again."

He looked at his watch and stood up. "Hey, I've got to go. I promised Sara I'd be home by eight. If you need more, call me and I'll come by again. I really do want to help."

I stood and shook his hand. "Thanks, we'll let you know if we need anything else."

"Hey, if you can, could you try not to share this with Woodbury or any of the other guys? I don't want it to get back to Sara how that bitch humiliated me."

April took his arm and walked him to the door, "We won't tell a soul without asking you first, but it shouldn't matter. Sara's a lucky girl, and I'm sure she knows that. If she does find out about any of this, she'll just know you're not one of those dumb guys who thinks violence is always the answer. I sometimes wish my husband understood that better."

When April closed the door behind him, she said, "So I guess we can add every member of the DMA to our list of suspects."

"I guess we can, as well as all the staff. Why don't you tell me how often you wish I didn't think violence is the answer?"

"Darling, my job is to massage the male ego; your job is to find clues and shoot people if the need arises. If you need your ego massaged again, let's go home and do it properly."

On the way home, I worried to myself that having the entire membership of the DMA as suspects might not actually be a good thing. After we got home, April and I spent the third night of our honeymoon giving no thought to the DMA or Trudy Woodbury's death. On Wednesday morning, the possibility that somebody associated with the Dallas Museum of Art killed Trudy Woodbury decreased dramatically.

10 Hate Crime

As soon as I got to the office, I started reviewing my notes from our interview with Mr. Mathis and entering them on the computer. We'd learned a great deal about Mrs. Woodbury, but I didn't know if any of it was useful or particularly eye-opening. Duckie certainly wasn't the only witness who could testify that she could be a bitch. I hoped the fact that she had enough money to be a major donor to the Dallas Museum of Art might be relevant, but I doubted it.

At 9:30, the office phone rang and April answered, "Pegasus Investigations."

After a short pause, she said, "One moment, please." To me she said, "Janice Reynolds on line one."

I didn't mention that we only have one line. I just picked up the phone. "What can I do for you, Ms. Reynolds?"

"We need to talk. Would you prefer to come to my office or shall I come there?"

Carl's always stressed the importance of home field advantage. "Why don't we meet here? What time would you like to be here?"

"I'll be right over." She hung up before I could object.

I looked at April. "She's on her way over. This can't be good."

April agreed, "Doesn't sound like it. What do you think she wants?"

"I have no idea, but we'll know soon enough."

While we waited for Janice, my cell phone rang. I looked at the caller I.D. and saw it was my doctor. "Hey, babe," I answered it. "I'm a married man now; you really need to quit stalking me."

She laughed. "I'm not stalking, darling. I'm calling with my concession speech."

In addition to being the best pain specialist in the southwest and my personal physician, Cynthia Faulk is also a very attractive lady in her mid-forties with a great sense of humor. If laughter really were the best medicine, she'd never lose a patient. Unfortunately, it's not that easy.

"I'm sure April will be happy to hear you're going to quit stalking me. Why did you really call?"

"I need…" She hesitated. "You need to come in again soon. When will you be back from the honeymoon?"

"Actually, we're still in Dallas."

"Thank god! Can you come in this week?"

"I don't think so. We stayed in town to work on a case. We're going to be pretty busy. Can it wait until next week?"

She didn't sound happy, "Okay. Come by Monday or Tuesday. Don't worry about making an appointment. I'll fit you in when you get here."

It's never a good sign when your doctor says she needs to see you soon without making an appointment. As we exchanged a few minutes of light banter, I tried not to worry about it. When she hung up, I decided not to worry about it until I knew what it was I needed to worry about.

Janice arrived just as my conversation with Dr. Faulk concluded. I joined her and April at the conference table. Janice looked at me as she asked, "How much do you know about the Round-Up murders?"

I wasn't sure how her question related to our client, but I saw no reason not to answer. "Not too much, just what I read in the paper. Obviously, somebody shooting two guys coming out of a gay bar for no apparent reason didn't reflect well on our city. Wasn't the killer convicted a couple of months ago?"

"Yes, Darryl Ray Robinson was convicted on April 11th of two counts of first degree murder. The jury took less than an hour to deliver a guilty verdict. They debated for two days before deciding against the death penalty, even though Robinson took the stand during the punishment phase and asked for the death penalty. Mr. Robinson should spend the rest of his life in Huntsville learning more about the homosexual lifestyle."

Janice clearly savored the thought, and probably overestimated the frequency with which prison rapes occur. Some people believe everything they see in movies. I chose not to dampen her enjoyment with facts. "Does Mr. Robinson's conviction have anything to do with our common objectives?"

"As of yesterday afternoon, it does. The lab boys have determined that the bullet which killed Mrs. Woodbury was fired by the same gun which killed George Murphy and Tommie Billings."

"Robinson's victims, how can that be? Isn't that gun still in an evidence locker somewhere?"

"It should be, but it isn't. When the lab boys came back with the ballistics results, they went to get the gun, and it wasn't there."

"How do you know all this?" April asked.

"I'm Woodbury's attorney; they have to share any evidence they plan to present against my client with me. It's the law." Janice smirked at April. "I know you're new at this, but you have seen 'My Cousin Vinny,' haven't you?"

April smiled at her, "I'm not really into modern American cinema, but I'm quite familiar with the justice system here. Perhaps you should explain how a missing murder weapon might be used in court as evidence that your client killed his wife."

"Of course, for one thing Woodbury was the arresting officer in the Robinson case. Secondly, as a police detective, he had access to the gun. Nobody else who might have wanted Mrs. Woodbury dead would have had access to it."

"I'm not sure about that," I said. "There's no shortage of people who might have wanted her dead, but I see what you're saying. Have you talked to Woodbury about this?"

Janice snorted, "I've talked to him; he has nothing to say. What are you going to do? Are you going to talk to him? Maybe you can get something out of him."

April said, "Maybe there's nothing to get. He either killed her, which we don't believe, or he was framed. If he killed her, this tells us where he got the gun. If he didn't, this tells us that the killer planned out the frame before committing the murder. This probably doesn't affect how we investigate, except that we now know more about the killer and how long he or she planned the murder."

Janice looked at April like she had just heard a parrot lecture on the finer points of quantum physics. "Ms. Rose, you're right. I apologize for my earlier comment. You have a keen understanding of your business. Please forgive me for underestimating you."

"Don't worry about it," April smiled and used a line we've heard Carl use many times. "Being easy to underestimate is one of my greatest assets."

"Somehow, I doubt that, but thank you." Janice stood, "I'll get back to being a lawyer and let you guys continue your investigation. Let me know if I can help."

As we watched Janice walk back toward the county courthouse, April locked the office door and asked me, "Did I say something that brilliant, or was Janice just patronizing me?"

"Probably neither, but you said something Janice hadn't considered, which she took to mean you must be brilliant, since she has this crazy idea that she's brilliant."

"Well, she does have a law degree. She must be pretty smart."

"She is, but there's a huge difference between pretty smart and brilliant. I can play the guitar pretty well; Stevie Ray Vaughn was a brilliant guitarist. Janice got a law degree; Larry Joe McCoy is a brilliant attorney."

April flashed her million watt smile, "I see. So where do we rank as detectives?"

"I don't know, but if the brilliant Mr. McCoy can't be persuaded to defend him, Woodbury better hope we're pretty damn good."

"Then I suggest we either prove we're brilliant, or you convince your godfather to take the case. I don't want to watch Lisha cry because the jury came back with a guilty verdict. By the way, who called you earlier?"

"Oh, it was Dr. Faulk. She wants me to tell you that she's going to let you have me. I guess she'll just have to accept dying as an old maid pining away because she can't have me."

April laughed. "If she really wanted you, I wouldn't have had a chance. Why'd she really call?"

"She just wants me to come in for a checkup soon. She worries a lot for a woman as young as she is."

April knew I was lying, but she let it slide. Instead of pressing, she changed the subject "Hey, shouldn't we call Carl and let him know about the gun?"

I thought about it before answering. "No, let's wait on that. He might use it as an excuse to come back. I think it might be better if he has an uncluttered mind for the background check. Besides, the only calls he's going to want to take in Virginia are the ones from Emily. You do know Virginia is for lovers, don't you?"

She took my hand and led me into my office, "I do. I also know everything's bigger in Texas."

A small detective office in the heart of Dallas can't rival a beachfront villa in Hawaii as a honeymoon destination, but it has its charms. At least, it does for April and me.

11 Missing Gun

"I've got nothing to say to you, got it? Absolutely nothing! You got a lotta nerve even coming here to talk about it."

Any hope I had that the civilian clerk at the police property room might want to cooperate with me vanished as soon as he opened his mouth. Maybe if April were with me, he might be more willing, but she was busy reporting to our client. Carl seldom has trouble getting people to talk; maybe his famous silent act would get Robert Crawford to talk.

I sat across the desk from Crawford for several minutes, but he never started. As I looked at his decorations, I noticed a photo on the wall behind him of a college basketball team picture. The uniforms were white with an eagle drawn over the letters BC in maroon. Except for the fact the players were girls; it looked like some of the pictures of Carl back in the day that Emily had showed April and me.

While I waited for Crawford to talk, I wondered which of the players on the team his friend was. I know sports fans can be fanatical, but nobody has a women's college basketball team photo at his desk unless he knows somebody on the team personally.

There were fifteen girls in the picture, along with two older guys wearing coaching shorts, tee shirts and whistles. The only other guy was shorter than all the girls and wore a maroon polo and khaki's. Written on the picture in what appeared to be faded red were the words, 'Luv ya always, KC!' I suspected that if the letter 'i' had been in the phrase, it would have a heart above it.

When I glanced back to Crawford I noticed that he was paying less attention to me than I had been paying to him. While I'd been looking at his décor, he'd turned his entire focus to his computer screen. I chose not to ask about the photo.

Instead, I asked in what I hoped was a friendly, conspiratorial tone, "Downloading porn or playing solitaire?"

He glanced up at me with his dark gray eyes barely visible under his black bangs. From his eyes up, he looked like he could have fit into the Goth scene pretty easy. But his face wasn't made up to fit the part, and didn't look like it ever had been. I learned long ago, that Goth is more about attitude than having the right look to pull it off.

Robert Crawford may have been physically born with the ability to be Goth, but it wasn't in his character. At this moment, he looked more like the typical down-trodden government worker whose looks or potential looks no longer even matter.

He shrugged his shoulders without expressing much, "If you must know, neither. I'm looking over my résumé. You know anything about résumés?"

"Not much," I admitted, happy to have any form of conversation started. "I doubt if it's a good idea to work on it on your company computer, though."

"Yeah, I guess not, but it doesn't matter now. Your boy Woodbury done ended this gig for me."

I tried to steer the conversation away from Woodbury. "I'm sorry to hear that. When's your last day?"

"Oh, it'll take awhile. They're gonna work my ass off before they fire me. Hell, they already had me take a full inventory of everything in here, which is a major pain in the ass if you care. Of course the gun wasn't the only thing missing. Hell, it wasn't even the only weapon missing."

I asked, "Is that unusual?"

He pointed to the storage room, "Of course not. Look at the size of this place. There's no way anybody could keep track of everything here."

I smiled. "I'm sure that's true. Surely they understand that."

"I thought so, but after they saw the inventory, they made me do it again. They said they just wanted to be sure, but I don't trust them. They're probably just stringing me along until they finish all the paperwork. When they do, I'm history."

"That doesn't seem fair." I expected him to agree, but he just went back to staring at his monitor, so I continued. "Hey, maybe I can help. I've got a friend who's a headhunter; maybe she can help you with your résumé."

He looked up at me. "Really, that would be sweet. What's her name?"

I didn't actually know any headhunters, but I felt confident I could find one if needed. "Well, if I'm going to help you, I'd like you to help me first. If things are as bad for you as you suggest, talking to me won't hurt you."

"No, I guess not. This sucks though; this is a pretty good gig, or it was anyway. Why'd Woodbury have to steal a gun from here? If he wants to kill that bitch he married, I'm all for it, but why get me fired in the process? What did I ever do to him?"

"I don't know, why don't you tell me?"

"Nothing, that's what; I never did one damn thing to that prick. I just come in here and do my job. Then he decides to kill his wife, and he decides to screw up my career while he's doing it."

"I'm sure whoever stole the gun was more interested in using it to commit murder than to get you in trouble." I doubted it would calm him down, but it was worth a try.

"You're probably right. Hell, I don't even know if it was Woodbury or not. Could be somebody trying to cast doubt on the Robinson case for a possible appeal."

"If that's it, will it work?" I asked.

"I doubt it, from what I know of the case. But if it does, it will sure as hell end any chance I have of keeping this job."

I had to admire the way he never lost sight of his number one priority, himself. "I've got an idea. Why don't you help me figure out who took the gun, then I'll make sure you get the credit for it. As the guy who helped find the missing gun, you'll be a hero. They can't possibly fire you at that point."

He looked at me incredulously, "You'd do that? Wait! How do I know I can trust you? You could easily throw me under the bus after I help you."

"I suppose I could, but why should I? My client doesn't care about the gun. If we solve this, I get paid regardless of who helped find Robinson's gun. I do you a solid, and it's a win/win for everybody. I get paid; you keep your job; I've got a friend at city hall, and you've got a friend in the detective business."

"This ain't really city hall, and you've already got more friends there than you need." He stood up, "I need a cigarette. Come on, we can talk outside."

When he stood, I noticed that he wasn't as tall as I first thought. He probably wasn't more than 5'8", but he had a solid build like a collegiate wrestler. Any thoughts I might have had of him fitting in with the Goth crowd disappeared.

As I followed him outside, I noted that I could have easily slipped a piece of tape on the door jamb without him noticing it. In his haste to get his nicotine fix, he focused more on his cigarette package than making sure the door locked securely behind us.

When we got to the exit door, he already had the cigarette in his mouth. He lit up just as he got through the revolving door. He walked across the street to a red sports car, "Too hot to stand out in the heat."

I nodded agreement. He started the car, maxed out the air conditioning and barely cracked a window to let the cigarette smoke escape. If it helped, it wasn't noticeable. When I left the entertainment field, I'd hoped to spend less time smelling like a cigarette factory. Most days, it worked. This just didn't happen to be one of those days.

"Nice car, what is it?" I commented.

He beamed, "2006 Saturn Sky. It's one of the first ones ever made. I got it second hand, but the first owner took really good care of her."

I let him smoke for a little longer before asking, "What do you think of my offer?"

He took several puffs before answering. Even then, he started to say something, but hesitated. I thought he might be going to try to negotiate some kind of payment. Instead, he asked, "Is April as hot as everybody says she is?"

I wished again that April hadn't gone to see Lisha. "I don't know. I don't know how hot everybody says she is. Does that have anything to do with us working together to save your job and solve my case?"

He smiled, "No. I guess not. I've just been wondering about it ever since I started hearing the guys talk about her. I guess I can try to help. What kind of help do you think I can give you?"

"Did you know Mrs. Woodbury?"

He answered quickly, "No, why?"

"I just wondered; you did call her a bitch. I thought maybe you knew her."

"Oh that, well, she has a reputation. I assume you know that."

I smiled, "I've heard it mentioned. Feel free to call her a bitch if you wish. Everybody else does."

He smiled, "Everybody but Woodbury. He married her. I wonder what he called her before he killed her."

"If we're going to cooperate, can you for now presume with me that Woodbury didn't kill her?"

"Oh, sorry, I take that back. It's just that the evidence is pretty solid. I wonder what he called her before she died."

"Thank you. Since I'm operating on the theory that Woodbury didn't kill his wife, I have to believe somebody else stole the gun that killed her. Can you provide me with anything that suggests that others had access to the gun? The more people who had access to it, the better I'll like it."

"Well, pretty much anybody who knew about it could have taken it. All they'd need is access to the evidence room and the database that tells where it was stored. It'd be hard to steal it unless you knew where it was."

"What if you weren't trying to steal that particular gun, but just wanted to steal a gun?"

"Well, that'd be easier, but that gun wasn't near the door. Whoever stole it had to walk past several other guns, and that was the only one stolen. I did mention that I had to inventory the whole damn place, didn't I?"

"You did." I said as sympathetically as possible. "That had to suck, especially having to do it twice. Maybe the powers that be will appreciate your effort."

He took a long pull on the cigarette. "I doubt it, but they should."

"Okay, we'll assume the person wanted that gun. Who'd have had access to the database, and the room itself?"

"I really don't know who has access to the database, but it probably doesn't matter. If anybody wants to find something, they'd just need to call me. As long they're authorized, I'd tell them. That's what they pay me to do."

"Who would be authorized?"

He hesitated slightly before answering, "Officially, probably certain people on the police force or at the D.A.'s office. Really though, anybody who knows to call me and ask the right question would get an answer."

"That narrows down the field a little bit. What about getting into the room? Could the same people get in there?"

"Probably, but most of them would have to sign in. I don't sign the log, because I'm there everyday. But most people are supposed to sign in and out."

"Can you get me a copy of the log?"

He put out his cigarette in the ashtray and opened his car door. As we walked toward the building, he said, "I guess I could, if you bring April with you to pick it up. I should tell you though, that it's been doctored since the gun got stolen."

That surprised me, "Really? Who doctored it? When and why?"

"I did when I heard about the gun. Didn't I mention that I like this job?"

"So you doctored the log to save your job. How is that going to help?"

"Maybe I wasn't always as careful to make sure everybody signed in as I should have been. I've learned my lesson though. If you find that gun and save my job, I'll be the best damn property room clerk in the world."

I left it at that, and promised to bring April with me to pick up the doctored log. He didn't say anything about the headhunter. As I walked back to the office, I thought to myself that maybe we really could solve the case and save Crawford's job for him in the process. Carl sometimes tells me I'm too much of an optimist. He's often right.

12 Society Lady

At 10:15, April and I drove to Highland Park to talk to the only person on the Dallas Museum of Art's board of directors who agreed to discuss Trudy Woodbury. April parked her Eclipse in front of a large colonial style house, right down the street from an SMU frat house that used to hire us to perform about twice a year when I was the titular attraction of The Absolutely Incredible Freak Show Revue and Burlesque.

April would have been very popular at the frat house, but she was never part of the revue. Now, she's my wife and my associate in our detective agency. I hoped her being with me would help me feel at least half as comfortable in the home of one of Dallas' wealthiest women as I used to feel hanging from meat hooks in a frat house three blocks away.

I rang the bell and listened to the chimes. Before the chimes stopped, the door was opened by an attractive sixty something woman with light brown hair and a pleasant countenance. If I'd been expecting a servant to answer the door, I'd been wrong. This was clearly the lady of the house, Susan Loren.

"Yes?"

"I'm Franz Scholes and this is my associate, April Rose. We spoke yesterday on the phone. I thought we had an appointment?"

"Oh, of course, come in. I'm sorry. Don't take this the wrong way, but I guess I expected someone older, and perhaps less gorgeous. Maybe my expectation of detectives has been prejudiced by television programs like 'Matlock' and 'Murder, She Wrote'."

April answered, "If there's a wrong way to take that, we won't. Thank you for the compliment."

Ms. Loren escorted us into her den, and we all sat. "That's a relief. In this era of political correctness, I sometimes seem to offend people without even knowing it. Often, things I think are innocuous turn into big brouhahas."

"I understand," I said. "I do the same thing myself. Of course, in my business that isn't always a bad thing. I presume as chief fundraiser for the DMA, it usually is a bad thing for you."

"Yes, it is. Wait, how did you know I do most of DMA's fundraising?"

"I'm sorry. I thought I told you on the phone that we're professional investigators." I declined to mention that I only knew for sure that she did most of the fundraising because she had just confirmed it.

"Of course, I guess it isn't that big a secret. Since Ray, I mean since Mr. Nasher died, fundraising has been a far more important task. We used to know that if we needed money for a spectacular event, Mr. Nasher would come through. Now, we're on our own."

"My husband and I have always felt strongly that the DMA should be a big part of the culture of our city. We contribute what we can, when we can. But we're not in a position to simply sponsor every special event. That's why grassroots fundraising is so important to us."

"Was Mrs. Woodbury's membership a grassroots contribution?"

"Heavens no! She's a Patrons Circle member."

I made a mental note to look up Patrons Circle on the DMA website, but April saved me the trouble by asking, "What exactly is a Patrons Circle membership, Ms. Loren?"

"Please, call me Susan. I always feel like a school teacher when young people call me Ms. Loren. The Patrons Circle is a membership for our most generous donors. It costs $5000 a year. The first year she joined, she joined at that level, although it had a different name then. It surprised me very much that she did so."

April asked, "How so?"

"Well, for one thing, Trudy was in her twenties when she first joined. Even then, we had a junior program for people under forty that would have given her mostly the same benefits as the regular memberships for far less money. It's a marketing concept we borrowed from the country club model. If people join at that age, they generally stay and contribute for many years."

My dad had a junior associate membership in a country club before he died, so I sort of knew what we were talking about. "So, even though she qualified for the yuppie discount, she passed on it. Do you have any thoughts on why she did that?"

"I didn't at the time, but I do now. I just don't know if I should tell you or not."

I thought about how to convince Mrs. Loren to tell us more about Trudy. Nothing came to mind, so I was silent.

April answered, "You should, let me tell you why. First, Mrs. Woodbury is dead, so nothing you say can offend her now. Second, we're confidential. We won't repeat anything you tell us, unless you give us permission. Third, and most important, there's a killer out there who may get away with murder if we don't do something about it."

"Of course, you believe that. Most people, including me, think the killer is already in jail. However, you're right. I agreed to help, so I'll help. From the very first event, she was rude to almost everybody, including other members. She was especially rude to the Junior Associate Members.

She'd often say things like. 'Just because you scraped up $500, doesn't make you a real member' to younger members who attended events."

"Interesting, we'd heard she could be rude to staff. Were there any members to whom she was particularly nasty?"

"Young man, I know what you're thinking, and I don't like it."

I smiled. "If you really know what I'm thinking, you're at least one step ahead of me. I'm just asking questions. It's the only way I know to do my job. Honestly, April and our partner, Carl, do most of the thinking for the agency. I just ask questions."

Mrs. Loren smiled back at me. "I doubt that, but I did agree to answer questions. No, Mrs. Woodbury wasn't nastier to any particular members. She was always rude to everybody. Many of our minority members have accused her of being racist, and I've had to assure them that her vitriol was not racially motivated."

April asked, "Why did you bother with her? Couldn't you have refused her money and ended her membership?"

"We probably could have, and it was discussed on more than one occasion. In the end, we never did. The reason, quite frankly, was always the same, greed. We wanted the five thousand dollars each year. The thing is she seldom attended more than three or four events a year, so she didn't really have the impact that she might have otherwise."

"Did any members ever quit or decline to renew their memberships because of her?"

Mrs. Loren looked at me thoughtfully before answering. "No, at least nobody ever said that's why they left us. If even one person had, that would have probably changed our thinking dramatically. We had a few members who would leave events early because of her, but, of course, the events themselves don't generate revenue. I'm not proud that we put up with her actions simply for her money. But honestly, that's what we did."

She didn't look happy with herself. Hoping to cheer her up, I said, "Susan, it takes money to provide the service to the community that you provide. Don't feel bad for taking it from somebody who isn't nice. Her bad attitude doesn't make the money bad. Money that goes to a good cause is good money being well spent, regardless of who it comes from."

"Thank you, I don't know if that's true, but thank you."

"You're welcome. I believe it to be true." I stood. "I don't think we need to take up any more of your time."

April and Mrs. Loren also stood. As we walked toward the door, April asked, "Can you tell us the names of the members who would leave early when Mrs. Woodbury attended events."

She answered firmly, "Certainly not!"

"I understand you feel that way, but I wish you'd reconsider. We aren't going to harass them, just like we didn't harass you. We'd simply like to talk to them for a few minutes." April was born to be the good cop; it just comes naturally.

"I'm sure you won't, April. But I'm not taking any chances."

I hate when the good cop part of good cop/bad cop doesn't work. Especially when Carl is out of state, and I have to be the bad cop.

"That's understandable, but it's a real shame. It's going to be so much harder to do our job if we have to get a subpoena to pull the membership file and talk to every member."

"You wouldn't do that!"

"I will if I don't have a choice. I'm trying to find a killer and keep an innocent man from being electrocuted. What choice would I have?"

"What happens if I just destroy the list?"

"The system is generally unkind to people who destroy evidence in a murder case. You can take your chances if you wish, but I wouldn't recommend it."

"I see." She picked my business card off the end table and looked at it. "I'll email you the contact information for the people I know had issues with Mrs. Woodbury. I hope threatening old ladies isn't the way you normally do your job."

"It isn't." April assured her as we walked through the door Mrs. Loren had opened. "And we're very grateful for your help."

It may have assured Mrs. Loren, but it did little for me. By the time I got to the car, I felt like a thug.

"Are you okay?"

"Sure, why wouldn't I be? She's going to give us the names. You know she is. She probably even believes if she doesn't, she might actually go to jail even though she's wealthy enough to hire Larry Joe, and we don't even have the right to subpoena the list."

As soon as she had the car in gear and on the road, she took my hand. "You know good cop/bad cop only works if one of the actors plays the part of the bad cop. It doesn't make the actor a bad person. You've been performing since you were old enough to know what performing is, you know that."

"But that's on the stage; this is real life."

We'd just stopped at a light. April put the car in park, and looked at me fiercely. It was a look I'd seldom seen directed my way. "I saw you give a real life performance that left a man dead. Not only did you play your part, you wrote the script and directed the action to make sure he died, and you didn't."

I thought about what she was saying. As usual, she was right. "I guess the difference is that he was a psychotic killer, and Mrs. Loren is an innocent society lady."

"Are you sure? She had as much motivation to kill Mrs. Woodbury as anybody, maybe more."

She put the car back in drive and started driving. I only noticed that the car behind us had been honking when it stopped. "But if we need to play good cop/bad cop again to get her to confess, I'll let you be the good cop."

I've never seen her play the bad cop. For the first time, I realized that she'd probably be much better at it than I am. The realization scared me and comforted me at the same time.

13 Sincere Honesty

"Okay, the honeymoon's over!"

If I'd made a list of everything I thought April might say as we sat down to breakfast, 'the honeymoon's over' wouldn't have been on it. "What do you mean? What's wrong?"

"What's wrong is we've been trying to be newlyweds and detectives at the same time. If we keep this up, Woodbury will fry while we're still trying to be newlyweds. We need to be full-time detectives until we get the killer."

"Of course, what do you suggest we do as full-time detectives that we haven't been doing already?"

"Nothing, that's your department; my job is administration, morale and motivation. Right now, we need action and crazy plans. You're in charge of action and crazy plans, remember? When we get to the office, I can show you the org chart if you need to see it."

"I don't need to see it, and there's not one. When did you add motivation to your job description?"

"This morning while I was making pancakes. I decided you're too busy with our honeymoon, so I decided to motivate you."

We finished breakfast without talking, which isn't that unusual for us. We're not exactly morning people. As we were putting the dishes in the dishwasher, a thought occurred to me. "If she was a bitch to everybody at the DMA, why was she nice enough to Woodbury to get him interested in her?"

"Well, she was drunk at the time."

I turned on the dishwasher and gave April a quick kiss. "In all the years you were officially the hottest bartender in Dallas, how many people did you meet who were more likable when they were drunk than when they were sober?"

April gave me a much longer kiss. "See? I knew I could motivate you. Once you start thinking about the case, you immediately come up with the right question. How do we get an answer?"

"I guess we start by asking Woodbury. Mrs. Loren's too mad at us to answer, and Mrs. Woodbury is too dead."

"Actually, Mrs. Loren is mad at you, not us. If it comes to it, I can try her alone. If she does email us that list, we might learn something from somebody on it. Do you think she will?"

"She will, but while we wait, we can talk to Woodbury again."

I called Janice and told her we needed to talk to Woodbury. She called back in less than an hour. "Meet me at Lew Sterrett at 11:30. But he wants something."

"Of course he does; he wouldn't be Woodbury if he didn't want something. I don't know how to bake cakes, so I can't sneak him a file."

Janice laughed insincerely. "Actually, he doesn't want a file. Can you bring Lisha?"

"That's not a good idea. We need to talk to him without her being there."

"He may not agree, if you don't."

"Then lie to him. Surely they taught you in law school that the client's best interest is more important than the truth."

Janice was not amused. "They did not. The truth and the law go hand in hand. I'll talk to Woodbury. I'll call you if he chooses not to meet with you."

"He'll meet us," I told her confidently.

Around noon, Matheson escorted Woodbury into the room where April and I sat waiting. Janice had already left. "Where's Lisha?"

"She couldn't make it." April said softly. April always talks softly when she lies. Maybe, if she gets more practice, she'll get better at it.

"Why not? Is she okay? Is she mad at me?"

I interrupted before Woodbury's questions descended to complete blubbering, "She's fine. She's not here because I didn't invite her. We need to ask some more questions about Trudy, and I don't think you…"

"But Janice said she'd be here," he interrupted.

I guess Janice learned more in law school than she readily admitted. "Well, she must have misunderstood. We'll bring her next time if we don't get you out of here soon."

Woodbury relaxed, "Okay, what did you want to ask me?"

"You told us you met Trudy at a DMA event and that she was drunk, right?" He nodded and I continued, "But you didn't notice her until she was leaving? She didn't say or do anything that a security guard working an event might notice before they got ready to leave?"

Woodbury hesitated slightly before answering, "If she did, I didn't notice it. Have I mentioned that I might not have been the best security guard ever?"

"No, but that's been collaborated during the course of this investigation. For now, we'll accept it as fact. However, even bad security guards notice some things."

He let the insult pass. "What are you implying?"

"I'm not implying anything. I'm asking a simple question. During the course of the event, did you notice Trudy do or say anything, before you were asked to escort her to the cab?"

Woodbury looked down as if deciding if he needed to polish his shoes. After a few seconds, his look went from morose to defiant, "What if I did, but I don't want to talk about it? You can't make me."

He was right, of course. I thought about threatening to drop the case, but I'd already skipped the honeymoon, and Carl had already flown to Virginia, so I didn't want to take the chance that he'd call my bluff.

April handled it, "No, we can't make you. We don't even want to make you. We want you to want to tell us. Lisha's not here, and we aren't going to say anything to her."

"That's why you didn't bring Lisha, because you already knew. I don't know if I should be grateful or mad."

"You don't have to be either." I suggested, "Just tell us."

"Okay, I noticed she was being a complete bitch. I saw her berate almost all of the service staff, and she argued with and insulted several other members and guests."

"Did she insult or berate you?"

"No." He didn't look proud.

April picked up on the look. "You know why she didn't, don't you?"

"Because she could tell I was laughing with her as she was doing it. I thought it was hilarious. I wasn't even subtle enough about it to keep her from seeing that I thought it was funny."

Woodbury had more to say, but he was having a hard time saying it. If Carl's taught us nothing else, it's the value of silence. We didn't wait long.

"I guess I keep underestimating you guys. You now know my deep, dark secret. Trudy didn't turn into a bitch after I married her. When we got married, we were two of a kind. She was a bitch and I was a bastard, and we had more fun than any two people ever had a right to have. We'd go out, insult people, act superior, and we enjoyed it immensely. We were kindred spirits."

"So what changed? It sounds like a match made in heaven." I tried not to sound sarcastic, but I doubt if I succeeded.

Woodbury stood up, "You really want to know? Do you, Freak!? Do you really want to know?!"

I did when I asked the question, but now I wasn't so sure.

April said, "I do, Richard. I didn't know you then, and neither did Lisha. Whatever you were before doesn't matter, now. But what changed you might be important to the investigation."

Woodbury sat back down and looked at April like I wasn't even in the room. Since April is hotter than ninety-nine percent of the supermodels in the world, I'd seen men do that before. This time, the look was different, more resignation and less lust.

"Your husband changed it. When I joined the force, I requested the Deep Ellum beat so I could go prove how tough I was by controlling all the thugs down there and make it a safe place. I had that beat for over a year, and I might have stopped or contained ten brawls, and maybe I prevented five or six crimes. Every weekend I was there, I saw him diffuse at least two situations that could have become brawls or talk somebody out of committing a crime."

April looked at me and I shrugged. Woodbury's gaze never looked away from April. "And in that whole time, I never heard him raise his voice, or threaten anybody. I called myself the High Sheriff of Deep Ellum, but even I knew Freak was the king and his girl, Starlight, was the queen. One day I mentioned to my partner that Freak was doing more to keep Deep Ellum safe than we were. He told me not to worry about it, that he had a plan to change that. He did have a plan, and like the dick I was, I went along with it."

"We dropped a few baggies in a few places, or had people do it for us. Pretty soon, we were making more arrests in Deep Ellum than anybody else on the beat ever had. Then, I found out my partner had dropped a bag in Starlight's Corvette. She was the only person in Deep Ellum who was ever nice to us, and he tried to frame her like she was one of the thugs. After that, I couldn't even look at myself in the mirror long enough to shave without cutting myself."

April listened with her practiced intense interest, not unlike the way she used to listen to customers when she was a bartender. "So what did you do? How did you change?"

Finally, Woodbury relaxed and was talking to both of us again. "That's part of the public record. I talked to Internal Affairs, my partner went to jail, and I got taken off the Deep Ellum beat. Trudy, of course, noticed quickly that I wasn't any fun any more. I thought she might divorce me, and I wouldn't have minded. She never did, though. She pretty much decided that if we couldn't have fun insulting people together, she'd just get her fun insulting me whenever there were people around."

April asked, "Why'd you put up with it?"

Woodbury looked at April; then looked at me. He shook his head as he answered, "I guess because I deserved to be insulted, just like I deserve to be in jail."

14 Painful Memories

"It's not a coincidence, you know? It's actually pretty creepy." April was sitting at her desk and I was in my office with the door open.

"What's not a coincidence?" I asked.

"Woodbury and Lisha being a couple, he obviously thought the world of Katherine Elizabeth. Of course, as soon as he met a girl who looked just liked her; he'd want to date her."

"I guess you could be right." I said without being convinced. "Does it matter? Woodbury's in a sham of a marriage and he meets an attractive young lady who seems to adore him. We don't even know if she's the first mistress he took."

"I guess we don't, and I guess it doesn't matter. It's still creepy."

I agreed with her and went back to downloading and printing everything Google News could find on Mrs. Woodbury. Most of it related to her murder, but using the advance search features, I found some other things of interest.

One thing of interest I found was that Gertie Lund had been a witness for the defense in a murder trial in Virginia when she was a teenager. I thought about calling Carl to let him know, but decided it would be an insult to imply that I might have found something online that he might not find doing his style of investigating.

Around two o'clock, I was searching the archives of the Virginian-Pilot trying to learn more about the murder trial. I was also wondering if we were wasting our time. We'd already established that Trudy Woodbury was a bitch. More corroboration wasn't needed. Our background check might prove that everybody she ever met hated her, but it wouldn't give anybody a better motive to kill her than Woodbury's motive.

My negativity was interrupted by April standing behind me massaging my shoulders. "Thinking about Katherine again, huh? Is there anything I can do to cheer you up?"

I didn't realize I'd been looking that morose. "Actually, I'm thinking about the case. Even if we prove that everybody hated her, will it really help?"

April continued the massage. "We won't know that until we do it. We knew that before we started this case. What's changed to cause you to be depressed about this all of a sudden?"

As usual, April had asked a good question. It took me a few minutes to come up with the answer. Once I did, I answered, "I know he didn't kill her now, before I thought maybe he did."

52

"I finally convinced you, huh? I'm glad you're finally learning to trust my instincts."

I put my hands on hers as she continued to massage my shoulders. "Actually, Woodbury convinced me. There's no way he would have admitted to me that he'd been involved in the attempt to frame Katherine without also admitting to killing his wife if he killed her."

"How does that prove he didn't kill his wife? And why does he call her Starlight?"

"He always did. Everybody else called her by her name du jour, but Woodbury always called her Starlight. The thing is, he's right about how popular she was back then. If I told certain people that he'd tried to frame her, he'd be begging for the death penalty, rather than dealing with their version of justice."

April had moved to my desk and was still holding my hand. I hadn't noticed her moving. "Why aren't you one of those certain people? She was your fiancée. Aren't you the one who should be the maddest?"

"Probably, but I know the truth. Woodbury and his partner never tried to frame her. They tried to frame me. Katherine saw his partner plant something in my backpack, and moved the baggie to her car."

"Why did she do that?"

"She thought Woodbury was a decent man deep inside, and would do the right thing if properly motivated. I told her she was crazy, but she insisted. Of course, she turned out to be right. She was the only person in Deep Ellum who wasn't shocked when Woodbury got his partner convicted."

April slid off my desk into my lap and hugged me, "Maybe we shouldn't have taken this case. I had no idea how involved Woodbury's past was with yours and Katherine's."

Before I could reply, I heard the familiar, and incredibly irritating, sound of April's computer, "You've got mail."

April jumped up, "I bet that's Mrs. Loren's list."

As she got back to her desk, I called after her, "I bet it's spam."

April didn't answer, and I returned to my computer. As I was reading the Newport Daily News' account of the trial where Trudy had testified, April re-entered my office. She sat two sheets of paper on my desk. "You lose. Here are the names, addresses and phone numbers of eleven DMA members who had run-ins with Mrs. Woodbury."

She stood there staring at me as if I might contradict her. I had no intention of doing that. "You win, what do I owe you?"

"Sonny Bryan's, why don't you walk over and get us something to eat while I call these numbers and see how many will talk to us?"

I grew up here, so I'm pretty used to the greatness of Sonny Bryan's Barbeque, but April's only lived in Dallas a few years, so it still excites her. Usually, when I lose a bet to her, Sonny Bryan's is the payoff. Since I love barbeque, I don't really mind losing bets.

As I walked down Ervay toward the tunnel, I kept my thoughts on deciding what to order. Once I had two chopped ham sandwiches and one sliced beef sandwich with fries in my hand, my thoughts returned to the case. I hoped April was right to believe that we might find something helpful, but I had my doubts. As Carl would say, it's not a good sign when even the optimists are pessimistic.

"Good thing we cancelled the honeymoon," April said as I walked in. "We're going to have a busy weekend. All eleven people on Susan's list have agreed to meet with us. We've got four tomorrow; three on Sunday and four more on Monday. I hope the batteries are charged on that recorder of yours. Plus Rachel called; she and Sam want to treat us at Fogo de Chao tomorrow night."

"Sam may be the only person on earth who always gets the better end of the deal at a $50 all-you-can-eat restaurant, but if they're buying, it sounds good to me. I wonder how her first week working at The Castle went."

"Pretty good I guess, she sounded very happy. I'm sure she plans to tell us all about it. Maybe she thinks she might finally shock one of us."

I laughed, "She knows better, but she probably figures she'll shock enough eavesdroppers to make it worth her while. That pretty much covers our schedule for the weekend and Monday, what's left for tonight?"

April flashed her megawatt smile, "I'm sure we'll think of something."

Not surprisingly, we did think of something. The divorce rate in this country would be much lower if more nights were like the first night we spent after our honeymoon was over.

15 Dot-Com Millionaires

About three o'clock Saturday afternoon, April and I turned off White Chapel Boulevard in Southlake into a cul-de-sac for our fourth interview of the day. I don't spend enough time in Southlake to know if there's a non-affluent neighborhood in Southlake or not. If there is, we weren't in it. April parked in front of a white house that might have been a little bit smaller than The White House, but it might not have been.

I told April, "If you scheduled these appointments in reverse order of the value of the homes we'd be visiting, we're going to be visiting Buckingham Palace by Monday afternoon."

April smiled, "I'm from the Australian Outback. If I hadn't known we were still in Dallas, I would have thought the last house was Buckingham Palace."

April's upbringing in St. Mary's School for Girls is as far removed from the outback as Larry Joe McCoy's upbringing in Ithaca, New York is from Southfork Ranch, but they both loved playing to the stereotype.

"Sorry, I forgot. If we stumble across a crocodile, please don't kill it before we make sure it's not somebody's pet."

April looked at the house, then back at me, "Sure thing, Mate."

As we got out of the car, I checked the batteries in my pocket recorder. "Do you have yours with you, dear?"

"Of course, you told me if I want to be a real detective I should always have one with me. I never use it, but I always have it with me." She picked up her notebook and read aloud. "Isaac and Melissa Lawler have both been Chairman Circle members since the program was established. Susan said they're the only couple to be both committed at that level."

"I read Mrs. Loren's email, darling. They donate $500,000 a year to the DMA. They have money, and they use it. I did some research of my own. The Lawlers also give generously to the Dallas CAN Academy, the Austin Street Homeless Center, the Texas Food Bank and most of the other worthwhile charities in town."

As we got to the porch, April put her hands on my face and quickly kissed me. When the kiss ended, she looked me in the eye, "And if these two Angels of Mercy killed that bitch and framed Woodbury, they're going down for it. Don't lose sight of the prize, baby."

"Of course not," I said as I reached for the doorbell.

Before I reached the bell, the door was opened by an attractive brunette wearing a white blouse with a peter pan collar and a blue denim skirt that stopped just below her knees. I wasn't sure if that made it a miniskirt or not. I would guess her to be in her early thirties, but her outfit, especially accented as it was by wedge sandals, hoop earrings, and several gaudy rings made her appear closer to twenty-five.

"You must be the detectives, come right in. We've been expecting you."

If for no other reason than to prove we really were detectives, I gave her a business card as we entered.

"Thank you, I'm Franz Scholes, and this is April Rose. Thank you for admitting us."

"Certainly, for the record, neither one of us killed the bitch." She smiled as she said it. "Isaac is so proud of the monitoring system in the house."

"That's good to know, Mrs. Lawler," I said as if we'd been expecting her to hear us talking about them on the porch. "For the record, we don't think you killed her. The thing is, we also don't think her husband killed her. We're hoping you can help us find out who did."

A male voice in another room called out, "Bravo!"

I turned toward the voice, and saw a slightly built man in his late thirties wearing tan cargo shorts and a navy blue polo shirt enter the living room. The logo on his shirt read Trophy Club Country Club, which didn't surprise me.

"You should be in theatre, young man. That was positively spectacular, not even the slightest stammer." His tanned face positively beamed as he approached us and held out his hand. "I'm Isaac Lawler and, of course, I know who you are. I guess you're also more than simply co-workers, but don't worry about us saying anything. Melissa and I were also co-workers with a clandestine love.

He waved his arm slowly to point around the room, "But then, fortune came our way, and we no longer have to hide our love."

Carl taught me that it's always helpful to get someone talking about something they like. That way, you learn about the person, and you can usually transition the conversation to the less pleasant subjects. We'd only known the Lawlers for a few minutes, and I already had two things I figured I could get them talking about.

"Fortune seldom just comes anybody's way. Why don't you tell me about how you two lovebirds left the oppressive corporate world and became the Angels of Mercy you are today?"

I'd expected a long story with more lies and exaggerations than the memoirs Oprah typically recommends. Instead, I got an obviously packaged curt reply, not unlike what I'd read online when I googled the Lawlers.

"There's not much to tell. We got into the dot.com boom at the right time, and we got out at the right time. Occasionally, one just gets lucky. Perhaps, that's why we're so committed to giving back to the community. We know how blessed we are."

I half expected them to hug and smile for a nonexistent camera posing for a picture like the ones that recently graced the cover of D Magazine and the pages of many publications over the last few years, but they didn't. I hadn't believed that story when I read it, and I still didn't. Several of the investors who had filed suit against Isaac Lawler and his company obviously didn't believe it, either.

I tried again, "That monitoring system on the porch is totally cool. Since you also heard us in here, I presume it's throughout the house. I'd love to learn more about it. It might really help us to have that at our office. Can you tell me how it works?"

The beaming smile returned to his face. "Tell you? Hell, I can do better than that. I can show you, if you want."

"That would be awesome." I stood up as Mrs. Lawler sighed.

April said, "Boys and their toys. They never change. They just buy more expensive toys as they get older."

Mr. Lawler had stood up when I did. April and Mrs. Lawler followed suit. "Come with me, April; let's have some girl talk while the boys play with the toys."

I knew April was far more interested in the toys than the girl talk, but she went with Mrs. Lawler toward a breakfast nook that from my angle appeared to be about the same size as our entire office.

Mr. Lawler ushered me into the room I'd seen him come out of earlier. "This is the command center; check this out."

As he spoke, I saw a desk with three computers on it. Two were HP dual cores in metallic gray; the other was an older Dell with the legacy black case. Above them were six video monitors showing various parts of the house. Lawler explained to me how everything was tied together as I watched the screens.

As April and Mrs. Lawler appeared on the different screens, he'd flip a switch to allow us to hear what they were saying. As much as I love April, small talk is still small talk. I'd hoped April might be able to get more than that from Mrs. Lawler, but now that I knew their conversation was being monitored, I hoped April wouldn't even try.

As the ladies entered a small indoor garden, I heard Mrs. Lawler tell April, "This is my sanctuary. It's the only room in the house Isaac doesn't monitor. It took some convincing, but he finally agreed. A girl has to have some privacy, right?"

I didn't hear April's response because Lawler said, "Come on. Let me show you the equipment that makes all of this work."

As I followed him out of his command center, I slipped my recorder out of my pocket and hid it behind the Dell computer. Lawler didn't notice. He was right when he said I should be in theatre. What he didn't know is that I've been performing all my life. The first act is always easy. The hard part will be the third act when it's time to retrieve the recorder.

16 Unethical Behaviors

"Impressed?" Lawler asked me as we finished the tour back in his command center.

I answered him honestly, "Definitely!" His monitoring system blew away anything I'd ever seen in any club where I'd performed. Of course, I seldom performed in the best of clubs and the Lawlers lived in the best of houses, so I was impressed, but not surprised. I was, however, surprised by how much he shared. If Mr. Lawler had anything to hide, he either hadn't hidden it in this house, or he was confident that I wasn't sharp enough to find it.

"Thank you, but you guys didn't drive all the way out here just so Melissa and I could show off our house."

He flicked the remote, which caused the monitors to switch from room to room until he finally found April and his wife in the breakfast nook looking over the spacious backyard.. They each had a wine glass in front of them on the ornately tiled table. April's was almost full; Mrs. Lawler's was almost empty.

He flipped another switch, and said. "Honey, we promised these detectives we'd answer some questions, and we're due at the club in a little while. Perhaps we should get down to business."

As if they were talking face to face, she answered. "Of course, darling, we'll join you in the east den. I'm sure you were too caught up in your toys to offer him anything to drink. Ask him what he'd like."

He looked at me, and I said, "Nothing thanks. I'm fine."

We went to the east den which was considerably larger than my living room. He sat on a Victorian loveseat that probably cost about the same as April's car. I sat across from him in a matching, high-backed upholstered chair. The chair was more ornate than it was comfortable, but it was far more comfortable than many that I've rested on in the course of my unique professional career.

A few minutes later, April and Mrs. Lawler joined us. Both their wine glasses were full again. April carried a Dr. Pepper for me, while Mrs. Lawler carried a Blue Moon beer for her husband. She handed it to him, as she kissed him and joined him on the loveseat.

April handed me the Dr. Pepper and sat in a chair identical to mine. Nobody said anything, and I quickly decided this wasn't the time for Carl's silent act. I looked at the Lawlers, "Since we're going to be talking about a murder case, do you mind if we record the conversation?"

Lawler smiled, "I guess not. It's probably already being recorded, so you might as well record your own copy."

I turned to April, "Ms. Rose, can we use your recorder? I left mine back at the office." Act two is easier if the play has been rehearsed, but I trusted my co-star's improvisational skills."

"Of course," April replied. As she reached into her purse, she asked, "Why'd you leave it at the office, you always have it with you?"

"I added some memory to our Dell this morning. It fell out of my shirt pocket, while I plugged the cables back in. I just forgot to pick it up."

We don't own a Dell computer; I only wear shirts with pockets to weddings and funerals, and I have a better chance of living to a hundred than I do of adding memory to a computer. Also, April and I had been together all morning. I felt sure the second act was going smoothly.

April smiled at me as she set her recorder on the coffee table and pushed record. "Okay, but I like your digital one much better than this tape recorder, let's be sure to pick it up as soon as possible." She turned to the Lawlers. "For the record, do you both grant permission for us to record this conversation?"

They both agreed, and I began asking them the same questions I'd been asking all day. The answers were also the same answers I'd been receiving all day. I continued to confirm what I knew before she died, and what I'd learned from Mrs. Loren and others. Mrs. Woodbury wasn't just a bitch; she took great pleasure in being a bitch.

Shortly before five o'clock, Mrs. Lawler said something I hadn't heard. "Once, I actually saw Trudy try to be nice."

Even Mr. Lawler seemed surprised by this. "Did you, honey? Was I there for that?"

"I don't think you were. But even if you were, you wouldn't have noticed. She wasn't good enough at being nice to actually pull it off. I could tell she was trying though, and I wondered why."

"When did it happen? Tell us about it."

"One night we had an artist meet and greet with Jack Sorenson during an exhibit of his paintings. You'd have thought she was meeting Michelangelo. She wasn't just nice to him. She was nice to everybody for a change. I was sitting at the main table with the artist. I cringed when Mrs. Woodbury joined us, but as she sat down, I saw her name on the placard indicating that she'd paid for the right to join the artist for the meal."

"Had she ever done that before?" I asked.

"Not that I know of, but I don't attend every event. Susan can tell you."

I smiled, "She can, but I don't know if she will."

"I'll ask her to tell you," she said smiling. The Lawlers might not have been rich long, but Mrs. Lawler has certainly gotten used it.

"Thank you. Please, go on."

"She sat at our table and just gushed about what an honor it was to actually meet him. I remember her saying that she always felt that he painted the scenery of her youth even better than she remembered it."

"Pardon my ignorance of the art world," I interjected, "but what does Jack Sorenson paint?"

Mrs. Lawler smiled. "Sorenson isn't that well-known. Don't feel bad. His specialty is western art. He's called the Rockwell of the west."

"By the west, you mean the American west, like the west that Ansel Adams photographed, Ace Reid drew cartoons about and Edgar Arthur Tharp, Junior painted?"

"See, you're not ignorant of the art world. I'm not familiar with Tharp's work, but the other two are definitely western artists of a sort. Perhaps at the next meeting, I'll suggest an Ace Reid Cowpokes exhibition." She smiled before continuing, "I recall Mrs. Woodbury being particularly fond of a Sorenson piece called 'Rocky Mountain Spring.' She said it brought back the most pleasant memories of her childhood. She might have even bought it, but I'm not sure."

"But she clearly liked it, and she tried to be nice during the meet and greet. That's very interesting."

"Yes, it is. I thought maybe something about western art had a calming influence on her, so I was curious how she might act the next time we had a similar exhibit. A few months later, we had a Georgia O' Keefe exhibit. Mrs. Woodbury attended, but she was her usual bitchy self. Since I'm not a big fan of western art, I just quit attending those. I still don't know what caused her to try to be nice that one time."

Mr. Lawler cleared his throat to get our attention, "We really need to be getting ready to go. We'll be glad to answer any more questions if you need, just call and we'll make an appointment."

April said, "Sure, that's fine, but can you spare us just a few more minutes?"

Lawler looked surprised, "I suppose so, why?"

April looked at me, "Honey, you should really let Melissa show you the orchids in the garden, they're absolutely fabulous."

"Would you?" I asked Melissa.

She gushed, "Of course, but I'm not sure they're as fabulous as all that."

"I'm sure they are. April isn't prone to hyperbole."

As I followed Mrs. Lawler to the garden, I heard April say, "Isaac, boys aren't the only ones who love cool toys, why don't you show me your monitoring center?"

The third act was proceeding as planned, even without a script. As I gazed at the orchids I'd seen earlier on the monitor, Mrs. Lawler said. "Nobody misses her, you know? You don't have to keep investigating her murder."

She must have spoken freely because she did believe her husband didn't monitor her indoor garden. I knew better, but I played along. I just hoped April hadn't recovered my recorder and turned it off, yet.

"Yes, we do. It's what we do for a living. We have a client."

 "I could be your client. I'd pay you well."

"I'm sure you would, but if an innocent man goes to the chair, I don't think I could live with that."

"Are you really sure he's innocent?"

"Yes," I said. "I'm sure."

"Then I'll hire the best lawyer for him. Innocent people with great lawyers never get convicted. Have you ever heard of Larry Joe McCoy?'

I smiled. "The name seems familiar. Is he a western artist?"

She laughed and squeezed my elbow. "You're cute. Keep my offer in mind. It's a good one. Scruples are fine to have. But they're much more useful if you can back them up with money."

Nothing I could've responded would be helpful, so I said nothing. It usually works for Carl. I don't know if it worked for me or not, but a few minutes later, April and I were in her car.

"Did you get the recorder?" I asked.

"Of course, and I planted one." She reached into her purse and handed me two recorders. "We'll have to come back to retrieve it in a couple of days."

"I take it you've been shopping again. How sure are you that he won't find it?"

"Pretty sure, but if he does, he does. There's nothing to connect it to us. Besides, unless they killed Mrs. Woodbury, we're on the same side. I think Isaac's more likely to be impressed than mad if he does find it."

"I think you're right." I told her.

"I can't wait to tell your godfather you think he might be a western artist."

"You've seen his office. He'll take it as a compliment."

Before she could reply, my cell phone vibrated. I looked at the caller I.D. and answered, "Hey Carl, I trust you have good news for us."

"Always the optimist, aren't you? I wish I could say your optimism was justified."

Part 2 – Virginia Commonwealth

"But on other moonlight nights
When all love is out of sight
I sense the silent sadness bring
A cloud of doubt through everything.

But different thoughts somehow release
A wondrous sorrowful sense of peace
Illuminating truth, grief, fear, and light
Where love thrives in the mysterious night."

Guy Merrill New
"Music Therapy"

17 Lover's State

"Use your wisdom," Freak joined me for the conclusion, "Guided by your experience." It seemed like good advice when Nero Wolfe used to say it to Archie Goodwin, so I'd gotten used to saying it to my young partner. In my case, it usually meant I had no idea what he should do next.

This time I knew exactly what he should do. He and his new wife, April should spend the weekend acting like newlyweds. I knew the two of them well enough to know they would figure that out. I also knew what Emily and I should do. As I walked to the parking garage, I called her.

She answered with a question, "Well, darling, was I right?"

"Of course you were. As we speak, April and Freak are back in the office trying to find a murderer before Monday morning to save me from having to get on the plane."

"Think they'll make it?"

"Of course, they will. But just in case, we better make it a date weekend since I might not be here for Tuesday date night."

"I knew you were going to say that. Got anything planned?"

"Sure, I plan to drive home, and count on you to plan the rest."

"What time's your flight on Monday?"

I answered, "1:15, why?"

"I just wondered. See you when you get here."

Her voice had that mischief in it that she always gets when she's planning something surprising. I looked forward to the surprise. As I approached the garage, I saw my old friend Gus, smiling as usual. "Want me to bring it up for you?"

"No, thanks, I'll get it myself."

"Suit yourself," Gus said with his ever present smile. "I get paid the same, either way."

I've been parking at the Republic Garage's underground lot for years. For most of those years, Gus refused to let me pay him for the space. When I replaced my twenty year old Econoline Van with a Ford Escape, he finally agreed to let me pay for the space.

I don't know if he relented because my new SUV convinced him I could actually afford the space, or because he decided he'd repaid the debt he owed me. I suspect it's the former, since he never really owed me anything in the first place. As I pulled out, I put Lucinda Williams' 'Car Wheels on a Gravel Road' into the CD player. As the title suggests, it's a great road CD. On the drive home, my thoughts alternated between our case and Emily's surprise. The closer I got to home, the less I was thinking about the case. By the time I pulled into our driveway, I was only thinking about her surprise.

I pulled into the driveway as Lucinda sang the line 'There's no good there's no bad in this dirty little joint" from 'Too Cool to be Forgotten." I wondered briefly if that thought might apply to the case. I certainly hadn't encountered anybody particularly good, and the one person who was definitely bad had been shot dead.

"Your plan worked," Emily said as I entered our house.

"Don't they always?"

"No, but this one did. Jade and Blake are on the way over. Tonight we're going to play a new game called 'Scene It?'"

I smiled as if I'd hoped her plan would include company. It wasn't as challenging as it could have been. Blake Harrison's been my best friend since before I met Emily, and almost every evening Emily and I have spent with the Harrisons has been a fun night. We always end up playing a game, and Emily and I usually win. The few times we get together that aren't fun are usually caused by some case he's working in his job with the Dallas County Sheriff's department or some case of the agency that has me bothered.

Emily frowned, "You don't seem excited. Did you have a better plan?"

"No, I'm excited. How do we play this game? The way you were grinning I guess you're sure we can win." The main reason Emily and I often win is that she's very competitive and thrives on winning. When Blake and I compete one on one, it's usually a draw, but Emily's desire to win gives us the edge when we compete with Jade and Blake.

"I don't really know. I've never played, but the object of the game is to correctly identify the actors or characters from movies. Unless Blake brings Freak as his partner instead of Jade, I like our chances."

I liked our chances, too. Our mutual love of movies, old and new, is one of the things that brought us together in the first place. We'd once concluded that together we were the foremost experts on movie trivia after several months of playing NTN trivia in various bars. We only realized we didn't really hold that title, when Freak was hospitalized for several months and we started spending time there to comfort him.

Some people are impressed that I know Cybil Shepherd and Randy Quaid both made their film debuts in 1971's The Last Picture Show. Even though he wasn't born when that movie was released, Freak knows the entire cast, the director, producer and everything else about the second movie to be based on a Larry McMurtry novel.

He also knows everything about Hud, which was the first movie based on one of McMurtry's novels. The truth is that Freak knows more about almost every other movie ever filmed than I know about any single movie. Some people accuse him of spending too much time on the Internet Movie Database, but he actually spends more time correcting errors on that site than he does learning from it. I had to agree with Emily. As long as Freak wasn't playing, we were prohibitive favorites.

"So what do we get if we win?"

"I get the satisfaction of another victory, and you get to spend the next thirty-six hours being satisfied by a woman who is already elated."

"And if we lose?"

"Then you have to spend the next thirty-six hours trying to satisfy me."

I smiled. "So either way, I win."

"Either way, we win. Don't you love it when you let me make the plans?"

Blake and Jade rang the doorbell, and Emily went to let them in. We played the game for several hours. We also drank several Shiners and exchanged small talk. At eleven-twenty, I walked Blake and Jade to their car.

"I'm going to see if there's a ghetto version of this game with more James Earl Jones and Martin Lawrence, and less Nicolas Cage and Sean Penn."

"I'm sure there is. Do you think that will even the odds?"

Blake held his fist out for a fist bump. "Probably not, since except for skin color, you're blacker than I am. But it might keep Emily from knowing the answer to every question before either of us."

I smiled, "It might, but it might not. Feel free to give it a try."

After they drove off, I returned to the house. Emily had turned off all the downstairs lights, so I climbed the stairs with great expectations. By the time Emily and I left for the airport on Monday morning, all of those expectations had been exceeded.

After we kissed goodbye at DFW Airport, Emily said, "Do you think it's true that Virginia is for lovers?"

"I doubt it. If it were, you'd be coming with me."

She kissed me again. "Sweet dreams, darling. Try to sleep on the flight, so you'll be awake when it's time to go to work."

Some people can sleep on airplanes, some people can't. I've never slept on one, so I wasn't surprised to still be awake when flight 682 landed in Norfolk.

18 Baby Brother

At Norfolk International Airport, I rented a blue Ford Fusion from Enterprise. From there, I drove to the Holiday Inn on Military Highway. It always worries me when the directions include the phrase 'you can't miss it.' In this case, however, it proved accurate. By the time I got checked in and settled, it was 7:10 p.m. local time.

I had an address but not a phone number for Mrs. Woodbury's brother, John S. Lund. Blake can usually find even unlisted numbers for me, but he'd had no luck on this one. I took advantage of the hotel's free internet access and the laptop Emily bought me for Christmas last year to get directions from the hotel to Lund's address on Fremont Drive.

The house was in the Highland Park area only ten minutes from the hotel. Even before I found the house, I could tell the Highland Park near Hampton Roads Bay was far different than the ritzy Highland Park near Dallas. I didn't realize just how far removed it was until I actually turned off Virginia Beach Boulevard onto Church Street.

The houses reminded me of post Katrina footage of New Orleans. Each was on a zero lot line. Most were two stories, and none of them appeared to be more than a thousand square foot including both floors. Even the ones that looked lived in had at least one boarded up window.

Lund's house was just past O'Keefe, and it fit right in. Based on the way the porch cover leaned, I doubted that the second floor was safe. The grass hadn't been mowed recently, but most of it was dirt, so that didn't matter much. The entire yard consisted of two strips that we'd call a parkway in Texas. The only sign of occupancy was a green city issued trash container just outside what was left of a chain length fence.

Out of curiosity, I opened the container as I passed it and looked in. Not surprisingly, most of the contents appeared to be empty bottles of beer and wine. The beer bottles were mostly forties of either Miller Lite or Magnum. The wine bottles were Thunderbird and Mad Dog. I drank forties regularly back when I was playing Junior College basketball.

These days I don't drink fast enough to get one down while it's still cold. Only one thing in the trash can seemed out of place; a recent copy of the Dallas Morning News. Sadly, that meant I had found Trudy's brother. As much as I disliked her, I'd been hoping I had the wrong address since I turned onto Church Street.

"What the fuck are you doing in there?" The voice came from the one window on the second floor that wasn't boarded up. I still didn't believe the second floor was safe, but apparently John Lund believed it was.

"Sorry" I yelled back to him. "Sometimes I get a little curious. I'd like to talk to you about your sister."

He asked, "You a lawyer or a reporter?"

I thought about lying, but nobody likes lawyers and pretending to be a reporter seldom works out for me, so I said, "Neither, why?"

He didn't answer, instead he asked another question. "Is that your car?"

"It's a rental. But yes, it's mine."

"Wait there, I'll be down in a minute."

I waited for more than five minutes, but he did eventually come down. I'm glad I was waiting by my car instead of at the door. If I'd been close to him when I first saw his Joe Dirt mullet, he'd have noticed me laughing. I knew Lund was twenty-nine, which means he was a teen when Billy Ray Cyrus popularized the mullet.

Apparently, he didn't get the memo that the fad only lasted a couple of years. I tried to quit smiling by the time he got to the car and leaned on the hood. I think I succeeded, at least on the outside.

"What brings you all the way from Dallas Freaking Texas to my castle?"

"What makes you think I'm from Texas?"

"Your accent gives you away. But even without it, there ain't a soul in the state of Virginia that gives enough of a damn about her to come here to ask me about her. If you ain't a reporter or a lawyer, what're you here for? Are you a cop?"

"I'm a private eye. I'm investigating her murder." A light rain was starting to fall. I glanced at the house, then back at him. "We can talk in the house, if you'd prefer."

He laughed, "So the big city detective ain't too proud to enter my house to get out of the rain, huh? Ain't that mighty white of you? Maybe I didn't invite you in, because I don't want you messing the place up. Did you think of that?"

"You give me too much credit. I was just thinking how much I hate standing in the rain. Would you rather sit in the car?"

He smiled, "Now you're talking, while we're in there, you can drive me to the store."

His voice made it a statement, but his eyes made it a question. He wanted booze, and he hoped I'd take him there so he wouldn't have to walk through the rain. I saw no reason not to oblige him.

"Sure, hop in. You'll have to give me directions, though."

As he told me to get on 264, I noticed a liquor store on the right. "What's wrong with that one?"

"I don't like that one. My store's just a mile or two further."

True to his word, the store he wanted was only a little farther. He asked me to wait and got out of the car. I was worried that he might be planning something, so I parked the rental so I could leave quickly if he came out with buddies or leave even faster if he came out wearing a mask and carrying a pistol. I needed info on the deceased, but not bad enough to drive a getaway car after a hold-up.

Instead, he came out empty handed and approached the driver's side window. I put the car in drive and rolled down the window hesitantly.

"Can I borrow a couple of bucks? I'm over my credit limit. The owner says he'll sell me a forty if I have cash, but nothing else on credit until I pay him back."

The attitude he'd had as he yelled at me at his house was gone. I was looking at a drunk who suddenly didn't know where his next drink was coming from. It's a sight I've seen before. I killed the ignition, and opened the car door. He stepped back optimistically as I got out of the car.

"How much do you owe?"

"He says it's a hundred, but he's lying. A hundred is the cut off. He just cut me off cause he's a prick."

I didn't say anything. I just walked in the store. He followed behind me. As we entered, the owner nodded at me. Then he said to Lund, "You got cash now?"

I approached the counter, "How much does he owe on his tab?"

He pretended to think about it, "One hundred and seven dollars and change. I'll waive the seven and change."

"No need to waive it. Just show me the receipts and I'll pay the whole amount."

"You will? What do you mean receipts?"

I smiled, "The tickets, whatever Mr. Lund signed when he purchased one hundred and seven dollars and change worth of merchandise in this fine establishment. I'm happy to settle the account. I came all the way from Texas to do so, but I can't pay any bills without seeing them. I have a fiduciary responsibility to my client to spend her money wisely."

He blushed, and I knew Lund hadn't been lying to me about the amount. The store owner punched the touch screen on the point of sale terminal. A few seconds later he looked up at me, "Sixty-eight dollars and thirty seven cents. I can pull the tickets, but it's a pain in the ass. If you'll let that slide, I'll settle for sixty even."

I turned to Lund, "Does that sound right?"

Lund smiled broadly. When he smiled he reminded me even more of David Spade in Joe Dirt. I managed to suppress my laughter as he answered. "Damn straight it does."

I always keep one check in my wallet for emergencies. I pulled it out and started writing. Who do I make this out to?"

"Brother's Liquor, Inc."

I made out the check for one hundred dollars and handed it to him. Lund had two Miller Lite forties and a bottle of Mad Dog 20/20 in his hands. I nodded toward him. "You can comp him those three in exchange for our kindness in not reporting your duplicity to the authorities. The rest of that hundred goes to his account. Agreed?"

He eagerly agreed and Lund and I walked out to the rental car. Lund was whooping it up all the way back to the car. "Hot damn, you're something. I'll pay you back the hundred when I can. It was worth it just to see that son of a bitch all humbled like that."

"No need to pay me back, I'll bill it back to my client. That's how it works in my business." I knew I probably wouldn't bill Lisha for it, but he didn't need to know that.

He gave me directions back to his house. When we got there, he invited me in. "You're okay, Mister. I don't know if I can tell you anything about Gertie that will help, but I'll sure as Hell try."

I tried to prepare myself for whatever I might find when I entered his house. I definitely didn't want to ruin the friendship one hundred dollars had bought by being too disgusted by the inside of his house. No amount of preparation could have kept me from being shocked by what I saw when I entered his house.

19 Childhood Memories

Exquisite is probably too fancy a word to describe a house that's worth at most fifty thousand dollars. However, John Lund's living area was nothing short of exquisite. The front door opened into a small den with hardwood flooring. The one wall with no windows was mirrored to make the room look bigger. It worked a little, and the sparse, but elegant furniture added to the affect.

There were six framed prints on the walls. I recognized Chase's 'Landscape' and Monet's 'Garden.' The others were similar, full of leaves and trees. The peaceful art décor fit in perfectly in this living room, but didn't match the neighborhood at all. As I sat in the chair he pointed me to, I could see that the kitchen was also immaculate.

"Welcome to Castle Lund. What do you think?"

"Very nice, I'll try not to mess up the place."

"I was just fucking with you about that. I know you won't mess it up. This was my mom's house. When she died, I inherited it. I've been fixing it up ever since she died five years ago. The upstairs isn't quite done, but I'm getting there. At least I was getting there; I haven't had much money to buy materials lately. It's hard to make money as a contractor if nobody has money to build or remodel anything."

"Did you do the work here yourself?"

"Of course, why would I pay money to have somebody else do what I do?"

While I looked around, he handed me a business card. The card read JL Industries: Cabinets and Remodeling. The area code for the phone number wasn't for Norfolk. That explained why I hadn't been able to find a phone number for him. I decided not to ask about that.

Instead, I handed him my card and said, "You shouldn't. Maybe you could take pictures of the place to advertise. Somehow, even in this economy, there are some people with money. If you could just find a way to get them to see how good you are, you might get more work."

"Maybe, but if they liked the pictures, they'd want to see the actual work. When they see the house, they'll just drive off."

"You could fix up the outside too, couldn't you?"

"Hah! If I fixed up the outside, the gangs would break in and tear the place apart. Maybe you noticed, this ain't exactly a great neighborhood."

"I guess I did. You said this was your mom's house. Did you and Trudy grow up here?"

"I did. Gertie lived here until she was about eleven or twelve. I'm not sure."

Since I knew she testified in a murder trial here at seventeen; that surprised me. I asked, "Really? Where'd she go?"

"It's a long story, but I guess you got time for long stories." I nodded agreement and he walked to the kitchen. As he got to the refrigerator, he called out. "You want beer or wine?"

I called back. "Neither, I'm fine."

He walked back into the living room carrying the wine bottle and one of the Miller Lite forties. He handed me the beer. "You look like a beer man to me." He handed it to me and sat back down. "Did you ever meet my sister?"

The bottle was plastic; forties have changed some since my teammates and I used to drink them on the bus ride back from road games. I didn't comment on it. "I knew her a little. I knew her husband professionally. Our paths occasionally crossed."

"What'd you think of her?"

"I try to keep my personal feelings to myself when I'm investigating a case."

"You thought she was bitch, huh?"

"I didn't say that, but I'll admit we weren't exactly friends."

"You didn't say it, but you know it. My sister was a bitch. I don't know why, but she was. I used to think she was adopted, because Mama was too sweet to have a daughter like that, but she wasn't."

"Are you sure?"

"I'm sure. I asked Mama about it when I was twelve. She said sometimes children just grow up wrong. She took me to the park and showed me an elm tree that bent right at the trunk. She said that's how Gertie grew. She just got bent, she said. Nothing anybody could have done about it. Then she showed me some tall trees. She said I could grow up tall and straight if I wanted."

I waved my arm around the living area, "Looks like she was right."

He took a drink from his bottle and held it up. "Did I?"

I took a drink from the forty, "Hard to say, from only knowing you an hour or so, but I think so. Let's assume we both grew tall and straight and talk about how your sister grew the way she did."

"She's two years older than me, so she was always bigger. I don't ever remember not being afraid of her."

"Did she ever hurt you?"

"Not really, not any more than most big siblings hurt little siblings. Of course, when you're little you don't really see the big picture. I just knew she could hurt me, and I was scared of her." He hesitated, took a pull on the Mad Dog and just looked at the bottle.

"Of course you were scared of her. She was bigger than you. Anybody would have been."

He laughed. "Oh Hell, I ain't ashamed of it. I had every right to be scared. The neighbors had two sons who were both older than her. They were both bigger than her, and they were more scared of her than I was. I remember one time when I was about eight: we were all out in the yard just sitting around."

"Did you live here then?"

"We did, but we never hung out in this yard." He didn't need to explain why. "They lived three houses down." He pointed east and I made a mental note to get that address when I left. "Their yard was actually an empty lot beside the house. It's not empty now; somebody built a house there about ten years ago."

"So there's one house on this block that looks like it doesn't belong?"

"Not really, it's been empty for several years so the gangs have had plenty of time to make sure it fits right in."

"Tell me about the day y'all were hanging out."

"Gertie kept calling Jesse, 'Jessica.' She often did that, but it's the first time I remember her doing it around Jethro. Jethro was two years older than Jesse, but he was much bigger. Jethro started laughing. Jesse told him to stop laughing and Jethro told him to make her quit calling him a girl."

"Jesse looked at Gertie and stood up. At first, I thought he was actually going to challenge her. Instead, he just charged his brother and bowled him over. He started whaling on Jethro. Gertie stood up and took me by my hand. She said, 'Come on, John, these girls need some privacy.' I wanted to see how the fight ended, but I just followed her home."

"So you don't know who won the fight?"

He took a long pull from the wine. "Like always, Gertie won. She continued to call Jesse 'Jessica.' Neither Jethro nor Jesse ever tried to stop her. But Jethro never laughed about it again. I guess Jesse won, too."

It suddenly occurred to me that in my first day in Virginia, I'd found three plausible suspects in the murder of Trudy Woodbury. "Do you know Jesse and Jethro's last name, or what became of them?"

"I don't know if it will help much. It's Jones."

"It's a common name, but that helps. Do you know what they're up to now?"

"I don't know much about Jethro, but I can tell you about Jesse. You are not going to believe this, dude."

20 Sad Reunion

"I don't believe you." He told me I wasn't going to believe him, and I didn't. "Are you seriously trying to convince me that your sister bullied the boy so much that he decided he wanted to be girl?"

"I ain't saying that. All I know is he's not a dude anymore."

"Do you know it, or did you just hear gossip about it?"

"First, it was just gossip. He left town when he graduated high school and nobody I know even knew where he went. We weren't really friends, but we were neighbors and we got along okay. A couple years after he left, we started hearing rumors that he was living as a girl."

"And you believed it?" I asked.

"I guess I did. He was always a little girly. As we grew up, and Jethro and I would play football down at the park with some other guys, Jesse never came with us. At the time, I just assumed it was because he was smaller than the rest of us. He'd either just stay home, or hang out with some of the girls. But, it's not a rumor now. He came back to town for my mama's funeral and he wasn't a guy anymore."

"I guess that was a surprise?"

"Just the change was a surprise; Mama was kind of a surrogate mom for Jethro and Jesse. We figured they'd both attend and they did. Jethro came in from North Carolina, and Jesse came down from Baltimore. Apparently, I was the only one shocked. Gertie and Jethro already knew, and nobody else even recognized that she used to be Jesse."

"Did you talk to her?"

"A little; mostly she hung out with Gertie. They comforted each other like long lost sisters. I guess in a way they were long lost sisters. The three of them stayed here at the house while they were in town."

"Did Jesse keep the same name? I guess it's pretty unisex."

He laughed, "No, she changed it to Jennifer Courtney."

"I guess he was a big fan of 'Friends.' Is Courtney her middle name or last name?"

"He was. Courtney is her last name, if there's a middle name I don't know it. Gertie told her she should have gone with Jennifer Cox, but I think that would have been a bad idea, all things considered."

"Probably," I agreed. "Does she look anything like either actress?"

"Not really, but I have to admit, she looked okay. He was always small and feminine, and the hormones and surgery made it more so. I'm not saying I'd hit it, but if I didn't know the truth, I can't really say I wouldn't either."

I didn't really want to know more about whether John would sleep with his boyhood friend or not. It didn't strike me as immediately relevant to proving that Woodbury didn't kill John's sister, so I changed the subject. "Did Jesse hang out with your sister much when you were kids?"

"Not so much when I was little, but eventually they started hanging out regularly. Jethro and I didn't pay much attention to it because we were happy that Gertie wasn't picking on us. Gertie and Jesse might have been as close as Jethro and I were, but honestly, I don't know. Any time Gertie wasn't around, I was happy about it."

"So the four of you drifted apart, after hanging out together as little kids?"

"Not really, we were still a group, we just formed two sub-groups. Jethro and I would hang out together shooting hoops or playing football, and Gertie and Jesse would hang out doing whatever they did. Neither Jethro or I ever went to the court without the other."

I asked, "Why not?"

"Two white kids at that court is better than one white kid. I ain't saying either of us was scared, but neither of us was stupid."

"Were yours the only white families in the neighborhood?"

He laughed, "No but the other ones who had kids never let them go to the park. Jethro and I were accepted at the court, partially because we were neighborhood kids, and partially because Jethro was really good. He played Varsity as a sophomore and he always made sure I was accepted."

"Did Jesse or Gertie ever go to the park with you?"

"Gertie did sometimes. Jesse would have been eaten alive there. Even before he turned into her, we all knew she wasn't man enough to hang in that crowd. Gertie could because she was meaner than most of the guys and everybody knew it."

I took a sip from the beer and then lied to the new friend I'd bought for a hundred dollars. "I guess Jesse Jones' transition to Jennifer Courtney is interesting, but I doubt if it has anything to do with your sister's murder. You said Trudy only lived here until she was eleven. Why'd she leave and where'd she go?"

"Mama gave up on her, and sent her to Colorado to live with Aunt Sheila. She told me mountain air might calm Gertie down like it settled Sheila down. If it did, it only worked while she was there. Sheila and Gertie would visit several times a year, and if anything she was even wilder."

I asked, "How so?"

He took another pull from his bottle as he thought about it. He thought about it for six minutes. While he did, I took a few more sips from the forty. Plastic apparently keeps beer cold pretty well. He was clearly thinking, and it apparently wasn't coming easy to him. I wondered if he was trying to find a lie or trying to find an answer.

"I guess she seemed more confident about it. Where before, she used to bully people because she could, when she came back, she acted like it was what she was supposed to do. It's hard to explain. Did you ever get bullied in school?"

Getting bullied in school had never been an issue with me, but I'd seen it happen. I didn't want to admit that my size had kept me from being bullied much, but I didn't want to lie again, either. "People made fun of me some. I suspect it's the same."

"Probably not, but it doesn't matter. I think before Mama sent her away, she bullied people when she could, like the way a fourth grader might bully a second grader, but stay away from the fifth graders. When she'd come back, she was like a teacher who assumed she had a right to bully everybody."

I smiled, "I had a few teachers like that in my day. Did anybody ever fight back?"

"I only saw it happen once. She was picking on a nig… a black kid named Tyrone over at the basketball court when Tyrone's older sister came up behind her and shoved her down."

I didn't want to know, but I had to ask, "Was she picking on Tyrone about his race?"

"No, I never heard Gertie say anything racist. She was definitely an equal opportunity bully. Tyrone's sister, T-Money, realized she had the upper hand after the first shove, so she jumped on Gertie and pummeled her."

"How'd the fight end?" I asked.

"T-Money had Gertie pinned with her knee on Gertie's throat. She looked down at Gertie and told her to apologize to Tyrone."

"Did she?"

"No, she looked up at T-Money and said. 'You're dead, bitch! If you walk away now, Tyrone might live. It's your call.' T-Money hit her two times in the face, then got up and walked off with Tyrone right behind her."

"Did she carry through on her threat?"

He took a long drag from the wine bottle and gave me a hard look. "I don't know man, I honestly don't know."

21 Upsetting Verdict

"Tasheika 'T-Money' Monroe was shot in the back of the head in broad daylight on January eighth, 1999. She died instantly. Three witnesses identified James 'Seven' Seaton as the shooter. I prosecuted the case and the jury returned a verdict of not guilty. Other than ruining my fucking day, is there a reason why you're asking me about this case?"

I looked across the desk at a woman about my age with brown curly hair, pale skin and cute freckles. The name plate on her desk told me she was Samantha Martin, General Prosecutor.

"Sorry if I messed up your day," I answered. "In my line of work, I do that sometimes. I also have my share of bad days, too. I presume that happens in your line of work, also."

I didn't know what to expect when I phoned the Office of Norfolk Commonwealth's Attorney and asked to speak to the prosecutor who handled the Tasheika Monroe murder trial. What I got was an invitation to spend the afternoon at her office on the sixth floor of 800 E. City Hall to discuss the reason for my interest.

Samantha sighed, "Yes it does. But, I've never had a worse day than that day. Seven killed that girl, and everybody knows it. I don't win every case, but I don't lose many like that."

I knew a little about why she lost that one from reading the case file and from what John Lund had told me about his sister's involvement in the case, but I wanted the prosecutor's perspective. I waited for her to continue, eventually she did.

"You didn't answer my question."

"I guess I didn't. I'm asking about it because one of the witnesses was murdered recently. I wonder if it might be related to Ms. Monroe's murder."

"Call her T-Money; everybody called her T-Money. She was my daughter Erica's friend. That's one reason it pissed me off so bad that her killer walked. If that son of a bitch hadn't shot her, Norfolk High would have won the state championship in girl's basketball and Erica might have gotten a scholarship to Old Dominion University."

"Was it a good idea to have you prosecute the case, given that your daughter was a friend of the victim?"

"We had about thirty attorneys at the time. T-Money was friends with somebody we all knew. She was a star basketball player, class president and homecoming queen. Nobody in Norfolk could have prosecuted the case if only people who didn't know and like her were choices."

"So why did Seaton kill her, if he did?"

She shook her head, "I don't know. That's one of the things that hurt us at the trial. We never established a motive. That shouldn't have mattered, but it did. Two eyewitnesses who knew Seven personally identified him as the shooter, but without a motive it wasn't enough."

"Two?" I asked. I thought you said three eyewitnesses saw the shooting?"

She frowned, "I did, but one refused to testify. This was soon enough after the OJ trial; he was afraid his background would be checked and he'd be asked about every time he used the the n-word. Since he'd married a black girl, he didn't want to take the risk. There were probably more witnesses, but lots of people fear Seven. He's been a thug and a badass since he turned fourteen."

"Is he still around town? I'd like to talk with him."

"No, you wouldn't. But it doesn't matter, he left town right after the trial. He hasn't been arrested since he left, so I don't know where he went. Some of his old gang might know, but they aren't likely to tell you."

"No, I guess they won't, but it won't hurt to ask. Can you give me some names?"

"Actually, it might really hurt, but it's your funeral." She picked up a folder off her desk and handed it to me. "Here's everything we know about Seven's gang. Who's the witness who got murdered?"

"Trudy Woodbury, nee' Gertrude Lund was murdered in Dallas, Texas. Her husband has been charged with the murder, but my agency doesn't believe he killed her."

"Of course, it doesn't. Who's paying you to believe he didn't kill her?"

I made a motion with my thumb and forefinger simulating the buttoning of my lip. "Client confidentiality is very important in my business."

"So, Gertie got herself murdered, and you flew up to Virginia trying to prove her hubby didn't do it. She lied under oath and allowed a guilty man to go free. If I knew who killed her, I'd be more likely to canonize him than execute him. Tell me again, why should I help you?"

"I don't know if she lied or not, but I believe she might have. I knew Ms. Lund before she died, and I don't blame you for not mourning her passing. Wouldn't it be a shame though if we let the State of Texas execute an innocent man and let a killer walk?"

For the first time, she smiled. "From what I hear, that's the status quo down there."

"It used to be, I'm trying to lessen the frequency."

"Having any luck?"

I don't like to brag, but this occasion seemed to warrant it. "More than you might expect. Do I need to send you my press clippings to get your help?"

"No, I made some calls on you. I'll tell you what I can. But, I need you to promise me that if you find anything that proves Seven killed T-Money, you'll share it with me."

I thought about her request. It didn't seem unreasonable. "Okay, I promise to share any proof I find that Mr. Seaton killed Ms. Monroe. Will it do any good? You can't try him again, can you?"

"Not for murder, but he testified that he was with Gertie at the time of the murder. If I can prove he killed her, I can try him for perjury. We don't execute for that, but at least he'd spend some time in jail. Their testimony that they were together at a movie theater in Virginia Beach is the main thing we never overcame. I know Gertie was lying, but I couldn't prove it. I couldn't even offer up a reason for her to lie."

I also knew the testimony was backed up by two ticket stubs and three theater employees who remembered seeing them together. I chose not to mention either. Instead, I asked, "What about the threat?"

"What threat? Who made a threat? There was no mention of any threat in any of the police reports."

I'd been in Virginia two days, and I'd already learned a key detail in a murder that the prosecutor didn't know when the case was tried. Maybe I could bill the Commonwealth for the hundred I'd spent on John Lund's liquor store account. If they'd bribed him thirteen years ago, they might have got a conviction.

I said to Ms. Martin. "I don't have any proof or evidence. But I heard that Gertie had threatened to kill T-Money a few months before she was murdered. They'd had a fight and Gertie lost. Apparently, in addition to her other faults, she wasn't a gracious loser."

"You might want to double-check your sources. I can easily believe Gertie would threaten somebody, but T-Money would never have gotten into a physical fight. I can't even begin to explain what a sweet and gentle soul she had. She was always breaking up fights, and getting kids to become friends afterwards."

A high school kid breaking up fights reminded me of Freak's high school days. Of course, he always broke them up by joining in and winning, but it sounded similar. Emily had called it Superman syndrome. With T-Money, I doubted if it was the same motivation.

I asked, "Even to protect Tyrone?"

She hesitated before answering, "Maybe, who told you about it?"

I did the gesture with the buttoning of the lip again. This time I kept it buttoned. Ms. Martin stared at me hatefully for a long time. The stare reminded me of thirty-five to forty hateful stares I've received from Dallas County Prosecutor Dougie Kenth over the years. The only difference is that Ms. Martin is an attractive woman while Dougie Kenth is a little toad of a man with the most pathetic comb-over in the history of the pathetic comb-over.

Eventually, the hatred lessened and she asked, "You're really not going to tell me, are you?"

"Not today, I'm not. I might eventually if it turns out to be relevant to either murder."

"Dammit, of course it's relevant. If it really happened, how the hell did none of the cops investigating the murder find out about it?"

Ms. Martin kept cursing and rephrasing the question as if repeating it would give her the answer. I don't often have answers for rhetorical questions, but this time I did.

As soon as she quit ranting, I answered her, "Because Seven wasn't the most feared person around these parts."

22 Unexpected Help

I knew Samantha Martin would be asking the questions I wanted asked in Norfolk, Virginia. I wanted to know more about Jennifer Courtney's relationship with Gertie Lund. John had suggested that they comforted each other like long lost sisters after Gertie's mom died. It was the most humanizing thing I'd ever heard about Trudy Woodbury.

I woke up Wednesday morning expecting to spend an hour or two on the internet finding Ms. Courtney's address and phone number in Baltimore. Instead, I spent four and half hours finding nothing. Then, I spent another two hours making phone calls, and asking for favors from old friends, trying to find the elusive Ms. Jennifer Courtney.

My first call was to Blake. "I take it you started working as soon as you got to Virginia. I thought you might have started with some sight-seeing."

"Ha, the only sight I want to see is the runway lights at DFW International Airport."

"I know what you mean. By the way, you've apparently ruffled somebody's feathers already."

"Really, how do you know?"

"Several of my friends at City Hall told me they got calls from a prosecutor and a sheriff asking about you. Who'd you piss off this time?"

"Actually, I didn't irritate anybody. I'm cooperating with Commonwealth Prosecutor Samantha Martin on a cold case of hers. She just had to check my references before committing."

"I'll pretend I believe that. I guess she didn't call Kenth if y'all are cooperating."

"Or if she did, she immediately recognized him for the tool that he is. Thanks for letting me know. Can I trouble you for one other small favor?"

"I'm not sure you know the difference between a big favor and a little one, and it doesn't seem to matter if you're giving or receiving. What can I do for you?"

"I'm trying to locate a lady called Jennifer Courtney who may have moved to Baltimore, Maryland from Norfolk. Her birth name was Jessie Jones; she apparently changed it after she moved."

"Did you forget how to use the internet? Or has it not reached Virginia, yet?"

"No it's here, but I guess I forgot how to use it. I'm drawing a complete blank."

"Okay, I'll make some calls when I have time."

I thanked him and continued making phone calls to everybody I thought might be willing and able to help. Most called back quickly telling me they couldn't find anything. By the time Blake called at three-thirty on Thursday afternoon to tell me he'd drawn a complete blank, I was almost out of people to call. I made two more calls; then went back online to try that again.

Friday morning at eleven-fifteen my efforts, my patience and many years of being nice to the wrong people was rewarded. My cell phone rang, and I answered on the first ring without even looking at caller id.

"Carl, I've never heard you answer a phone call more impatiently. This issue must be very important to you."

I recognized the voice, but I couldn't place it. As I tried to put a name and face to the voice, he continued, "Always with the quiet act, huh? It wears thin over long distance, especially when I'm the one doing you the favor this time."

I finally recognized the voice, but I couldn't believe it. Agent Maurice Letot of the Department of Homeland Security had paid a visit to the agency's office soon after I'd leased it. He'd been curious about the previous tenant who turned the place into a fortress. He eventually agreed that my occupancy was perfectly legal, but not before many long discussions.

Many of those chats occurred at Walt Garrison's Rodeo Bar and included him telling me more about his job than I wanted to know. I never knew for sure if he was more obsessed with the previous tenant or April who was bartending there at the time. Since April no longer tends bar and he keeps calling, my guess is it's the previous tenant.

"I like favors. What favor do you think I need?"

"You're searching for a young lady you keep calling Jennifer Courtney. We know where you can find her, and I've decided to share that information with you."

I never called him or his department to ask about her, and I really didn't want to know how he knew I was looking for her. I did, however, want to find her, so I ignored the fact that helping detectives find potential witnesses probably shouldn't be a high priority for his department.

"Am I allowed to write it down? If so, I have a pen and paper handy."

"Yes, you may write it down. Her current name is Courtney Remington. She and her husband Winchester live in a lovely home in one of the nicer areas of Baltimore. If you were worried about her well-being, she appears to be fine."

After he gave me the address and phone number, I asked, "Winchester Remington? You have to be pulling my leg?"

"Sadly, I'm not." I could hear the mirth in his voice. "Fortunately, for you, in spite of his unusual name, he does not appear to be a threat to our great nation. That makes it probably legal and somewhat ethical for me to let you know where he and his wife live. Of course, I trust you won't mention that you got the information from me."

"I won't, I promise. Have you found Sal Perlini?"

"No, but one of our other agencies appears to be making process. You do recall that you promised to let me know if he showed at your office again, right."

"I do and I will. Thank you."

"No problem, mutual cooperation with good citizens is part of how we do our job. By the way, you do know Mrs. Remington's big secret, don't you?"

With Letot, it's not a good idea to assume my idea of a secret is the same as his idea of a secret. "I know one, but I don't know if it's a big one."

Letot laughed. "I guess you don't, at that. For some people, a woman born as a guy would be a big deal. I should have known that given the variety of friends you and Mr. Scholes associate with, it wouldn't seem big to you. Good luck getting Mrs. Remington to tell you what you want to know. People with big secrets tend to be reticent on all subjects."

Since he was in such a jovial mood, and I already had the address and phone number I needed, I decided to push my luck. "I don't suppose you might have an address and phone number for James 'Seven' Seaton?"

Letot's jovial mood disappeared. "I might. You don't, and you won't get it from me. You stick to doing what you do well. I'll continue to help you when I can. Stay away from things that don't concern you. I can promise you that Seaton had nothing to do with the murder you're investigating. Call me when Perlini shows up. He will. I'm sure of it. That's one reason I keep being nice to you."

He hung up before I could ask why he was so sure Seven had nothing to with Mrs. Woodbury's murder. That's probably for the best. Maybe some private detectives get away with arguing with the Department of Homeland Security, but it was probably smarter if I didn't try it.

23 Difficult Transitions

"My husband plays golf on Saturdays; you may pay me a visit tomorrow morning if you wish. I will listen to your questions. I do not promise to answer any of them, however."

"Fair enough," I answered. "Is eleven in the morning convenient?"

"It is most certainly not convenient. It would have been convenient if you never found me. But since you did, I suppose that will be fine. I may have some questions for you as well."

"Of course, I'll listen to your questions. I do not promise to answer any of them, however."

I thought I heard Courtney Remington laugh as she hung up the phone, but I couldn't be sure. It didn't matter; she'd agreed to meet me. That was all I could hope for given the circumstances. I would have preferred to meet her in the late afternoon, but I couldn't expect it. Instead, I knew I'd be getting up at five-thirty Eastern Time for the four hour drive from Norfolk, Virginia to Baltimore, Maryland.

The four hour drive turned out to be four and a half hours. Mannasota Drive is on the north side of Baltimore, so coming in from the south I had to deal with more traffic than I'd expected. As I exited I-95 onto Moravia, I quickly got the sense that Letot's description of the house as lovely would prove to be an understatement. At ten fifty, I walked up the sidewalk of her house, and confirmed it. The home had three floors, and from the outside, each one appeared to be the size of a normal house.

Suddenly, I was less curious about how a boy named Jessie Jones became a girl named Courtney Remington than I was about how he moved from the slums of Norfolk, Virginia to a mansion in Baltimore, Maryland. I rang the bell wondering what to expect.

Almost immediately, the door was answered by a petite brunette wearing a loose fitting tan blouse and blue tapered slacks over high heels. She could have been anywhere from twenty-five to thirty-five. It's hard to tell sometimes. However old she was, she looked good. She smiled as she opened the door. "May I help you?"

"Yes, Mrs. Remington is expecting me. I'm Carl Jennings."

"Of course, you are. Come on in and make yourself comfortable. May I get you something to drink?" She pointed to a couch that almost certainly cost more money than I've earned some years. I hesitated to sit on it. "No, thanks; I don't wish to waste Mrs. Remington's time. I'd just like to ask her a few questions and let her get back to her day."

She smiled, "How thoughtful. You're much nicer than I expected. I'm Mrs. Remington, nice to meet you, Mister Jennings."

She held out her hand. As we shook, I said, "Nice to meet you, also. You can call me Carl."

She held my hand, and nonverbally directed me to sit on the couch. "You're also much taller than I expected. For now, you may call me Mrs. Remington." As she curled into a Lazy Boy recliner, I noticed the red soles on the bottom of her high heels. I'm not an expert on expensive things, but I am married to a wonderful woman who loves shoes, and my office is across the street from Neiman Marcus.

"Nice shoes, Mrs. Remington. Would it be impolite to ask how much it would cost to buy a pair like that for my wife?"

She smiled, "Probably, but it certainly isn't the first question I expected you to ask. You have heard the saying that if you have to ask, you can't afford it, right?"

I nodded and she continued. As she talked she changed the angle of the heel and toe as if she were modeling them for an advertising photo shoot. "These normally sell for seven hundred and ninety-nine. Winchester and I both love a bargain though, so we waited until they went out of season and got them for just over five hundred."

I had no idea how or why shoes go in or out of season, but I know it's never a bad idea to get somebody to talk about something they like before asking about something they won't want to talk about. Using everything Emily had ever taught me about shoes, I kept asking questions and getting answers.

Soon, I knew why shoes go out of season, once they've been worn to the right event by the right celebrity. I also knew how Yves Ste Laurent, Jimmy Choo and Christian Loboutin manage to charge five hundred to a thousand dollars for a pair even though Target will be selling an almost exact duplicate within the year. The only thing I didn't learn in my first hour talking to Mrs. Remington was how to transition the conversation to the murder I was investigating.

Fortunately, she did it for me. "Carl, you've proved you can be polite long enough. My husband may be home in a few hours. If you can ask about a subject you have no interest in for an hour, I suspect you can ask for hours about any subject you are interested in."

She uncurled from the recliner and stood. "I'm going to have a wine spritzer. Are you sure I can't get you something, perhaps a beer?"

I thought about how cooperative John Lund became once we became drinking buddies, and agreed. A few minutes later she returned and set an Amstel Light on the table beside me and curled back into the recliner with her wine. She gave me a hard stare, "I'm still not promising to answer your questions, so be careful."

"Of course, Mrs. Remington, I'm just a private citizen. You have every right to not answer any question I ask. When I ask one you don't wish to answer, just say 'next question' and I'll move on."

"You may call me Courtney, Carl. Fire away."

She took a sip from the wine, so I took a sip from the Amstel. It wasn't a Shiner Boch, but it wasn't bad.

"How did Jesse Jones get from the house I saw in Norfolk, Virginia to being Mrs. Courtney Remington in this house in Baltimore?"

She laughed, "Like the song says, 'I just shaved my legs; then I was a girl."

I smiled, 'I didn't mean that. I know it's not that easy to change genders, but I also know that's none of my business. If you want to tell me more about it, feel free. I'm just as interested in that as I am in your eight hundred dollar shoes. I'm more interested in the change in your financial situation.

She took another drink. "You think if you know how I got wealthy, you'll know who killed Gertie? I doubt it; I didn't kill her."

"Honestly, I've never once suspected you. I just ask questions to see where the answers lead me. So far, they've led me to a lovely home owned by a man and his wife. So far, the beautiful wife has been polite, answered all my questions, and given me an imported beer. By my standards, I'm already having a good day. I'm starting to hope that eventually, I'll hear something from somebody that helps me find out who killed Gertie Lund.

She'd finished her glass and stood to get another. "Would you like another, Carl?"

I looked at my bottle which was still full almost to the neck. "No, thank you."

I watched her walk away and then walk back. I thought about John Lund saying that if he didn't know she'd been born a guy, he might want her. He clearly lied about that. There's no way he wouldn't want her if he didn't know about her having been born a man.

She put her glass on the table and curled back into the recliner. "Carl, I've decided to save us both some time. Instead of you asking me questions, I think I'll tell you some stories. They may not help you solve her murder, but I promise that you'll find them more interesting than my shoes."

24 Prom Dates

"The Courtney Remington story begins in 1992. The opening credits roll past a shitty house in a shitty neighborhood in Norfolk, Virginia. A half a dozen or so latch key kids are playing in a yard which is mostly dirt and weeds. The main players are two brothers, thirteen year Jethro and eleven year old Jesse, and the younger neighbor kids, Gertrude and John. I presume you've met some of them?"

"All but Jethro, I may meet him later. Do you always tell stories like you're pitching a screenplay?"

She smiled, "Sometimes, it's something I learned in therapy. It helps keep the painful things distant. There are a lot of painful things to keep distant. I can try not to if it bothers you; I don't intend to get into the painful things today."

"No it's fine. I just wondered."

"Anyway, it was about dusk and several of us were trying to catch lighting bugs. Every few minutes Jethro and John would slam the gate hasp closed and laugh or high five. Finally, Gertie took my hand and we walked over to see what they were doing. A little background, even then I was very small for my age. Gertie and Jethro were always protective of me when others tried to pick on me."

"Did either of them ever pick on you?" I asked.

She smiled, "Yes, but never if anybody else other than John was around. When it was just any of the four of us, the rules were different. When we got to the gate, we saw what they were doing. Gertie laughed, but I was absolutely appalled. They were catching grasshoppers and executing them. John would hold one with its body through the hole where a padlock would go if padlocks did any good in that neighborhood and Jethro would slam the hasp down beheading the poor thing."

I silently mouthed the word, 'wow', but said nothing.

If Courtney noticed me, she didn't acknowledge it. "I asked Gertie why they were doing that. She pulled me close and put her hands on either side of my face and leaned in very close to me. 'Because that's what boys do. You should kill the next one. It's really pretty fun if you try it. Come on, I'll show you.' She took a grasshopper out of John's hand and put it through the hole. As she held it there, she put my hand on the hasp."

Courtney reached for her wine and held it silently for ten seconds before drinking. She'd told me she wasn't going into painful things, but I could tell she'd lied. I drank from the Amstel and remained quiet. I've been told it's my best skill. After taking a drink from the spritzer that differed from Lund's pull on the Mad Dog in taste and style, but not in quantity, she continued.

"I knocked the grasshopper out of her hand and told her if that's what boys do then I didn't want to be one. I started walking away, but she ran up behind me, and took me by the hand. She told me she had something in her room she wanted to show me."

When we got to her room, she sat me down on the bed. She told me she understood why I didn't want to be a mean boy, but that I couldn't go around saying things like that. She said I could talk to her about it, but nobody else. I asked her why and she said she couldn't always be around to protect me. After she said that, she sat and cried. I never saw her cry again until her mom's funeral."

Courtney reached for the wine again and I could tell she was holding back tears. I stood up. "Imported beer sure goes through you, doesn't it?"

She pointed toward a hall and I walked out. When I returned after an abnormally long time for a bathroom break, I saw another Amstel on the end table by the couch. As I sat down, I noticed a box of tissues beside her wine glass which was full once again.

"Thank you. I'm fine now." She smiled, "Are all the private cops in Texas as considerate as you are?"

"I don't know, but I can't wait for the second scene."

She smiled again. "The second scene takes place in 1995, in the same tiny bedroom. It's about ten on a Sunday morning. The lone occupant of the room stands in front of the cracked door mirror wearing a blue denim miniskirt and a cropped tee shirt that reads 'I know what boys want.' As the camera pans from feet to head, it becomes apparent the boy standing in Gertie's room wearing her favorite outfit is not Gertie."

"When the door opens, Jesse backpedals fast enough to avoid being hit, but falls backwards onto the bed. 'Gertie', he exclaims. 'Why aren't you still in church?' She closes the door and explains that she told her mom she was too worried about Jesse to attend, and she let her stay home. She also said she figured I'd begged off to dress up and that she'd waited to come in to give me a little time before confronting me."

I noticed she'd slipped out of therapy/screenplay mode and tried to steer her back to a comfort zone, "to give Jesse a little time, you mean."

Courtney smiled, and again, I noticed that she had a very nice smile. "Thanks, but this scene is a happy scene. She said there was no point in pretending any more and agreed to let me dress up any time we could be alone in her room. Like I said, this scene is a happy scene. For the next seven months Gertie taught me everything she could about being a girl."

She picked up the wine glass. There was no hint of tears in her eyes or sadness on her face as she sipped. "It was the first happy period in my life. When she told me her mom was shipping her off to live with her aunt in Colorado, I cried for days."

I asked, "Do you know why she was sent to Colorado?"

"Of course, her Mom couldn't handle her, and hoped her aunt could. I assume you already know Gertie was in trouble a lot. I might be her only friend, maybe you should ask her enemies for the dirt on her."

"I could, and I probably will, but I always like to hear both sides of the story and if you're her only friend, who better to give me her side."

She laughed, her laugh sounded slightly masculine. It wasn't so much that I'd have noticed if I didn't know her history, but I did notice it. "Who am I kidding? I can't tell you the other side of the story. There's not one. My friend Gertie, may God rest her soul, was completely unmanageable. Except for the rare occasions when she tried to protect me or some other weakling, every bit of trouble she got into was trouble she started."

I nodded and took a drink.

She continued, "I thought my chance to dress up was gone forever, but Gertie protected me again. She told her mom that she'd go without a fight and even try to get along with her aunt on one condition. She insisted that her room and its contents be entrusted only to me. Her mom agreed to put a lock on the door and gave each of us a key."

"Was there anything of value in the room?"

"Not to anybody but Gertie and me," she answered. "Her clothes and her collection of fashion magazines meant the world to me. Gertie had it all planned out. She told me every time I wanted to dress to just go the house and tell her mom that she'd called and asked me to look up something in one of the magazines for her. Then, I could dress up while pretending to look for the right article. I guess it sounds lame, but it worked."

"The best part was that Gertie came back four or five times a year. Each time she'd come back with a suitcase full of the latest cute styles and current magazines. Nobody ever noticed that she always left with just the clothes on her back. As I got older, she'd bring more mature styles. I was fourteen when she left town. By the time I was eighteen, I knew more about dressing like a girl than she did. I moved away as soon as I graduated, and she insisted I take everything I liked with me."

I asked, "Did you leave on good terms with your family? Did you stay in touch?"

"I left on decent terms. If anybody knew my secret, they never mentioned it. I didn't stay in touch with anybody but Gertie. Her senior year, she wired me money for a bus ticket to Colorado. She said she needed me to help her pick out a prom dress and help her with her makeup and stuff. By then, she knew that I knew more about it than she did. When I got her dressed, she looked fantastic." This time her laugh was more feminine, "If I do say so myself."

"Was her date impressed?"

"Yes, he was most impressed. His name was Jesse Jones, and I wore a damn tuxedo, and pretended I was a New York fashion designer. I was scared; I was actually worried I wouldn't be able to pass as a guy, even though I'd been born one. She talked me into it by promising to let me wear the prom dress when we got home. She kept that promise, but I only got to wear it for an hour or so before she told me to take it off. She said all cool girls get laid after the prom, and we were both cool girls."

25 Witness Protection

"How do you like my screenplay so far, Mr. De Mille?"

"It's fascinating, but I need some more details. How big was the mansion in Colorado, and how did Aunt Petunia react to Gertie inviting her childhood friend to prom and sleeping with him afterward."

"Does that matter?"

I learned a long time ago that having an honest answer isn't the same as having a good answer, so I kept the answer to myself. "I doubt it, but the screenplay isn't complete without it."

She hesitated, but eventually she started pitching the script again. "The 'mansion' in Colorado is a nice three bedroom house in the quiet suburb of Aurora. Gertie's aunt is certainly not Aunt Petunia. The character of Aunt Sheila Tobias can be played by any extra who looks a little like the woman who played Frazier's wife on Cheers. She has no lines in the film."

"Is Sheila Tobias her real name?"

"On my only visit, I got the distinct impression that she was hiding more secrets than I was, but I did notice that most of the mail was addressed to that name." She smiled, "Who am I to question what is and isn't a real name?"

I smiled, "It's your screenplay; you can question anything you want. I can't wait to hear scene three."

"Scene three takes place in June of 2003 in a crappy efficiency apartment on East Baltimore Street in what the locals call The Block. Since New York cleaned up Times Square, The Block is probably the most depraved red light district in America. The apartment is littered with empty prescription bottles and boxes of cheap wine. Amid the mess, two transsexuals are taking turns helping each other prepare to work the streets and arguing about who owes more of the rent."

She apparently noticed my concerned look because she stopped and smiled at me. "Don't worry. This is the scene where Richard Gere climbs the fire escape to rescue Julie Roberts. As they fix up each other's makeup, there's a knock on the door. Reluctantly, for fear it might be the super wanting another blow job to hold off an eviction notice, the shorter girl opens the door."

"As the door opens, Gertie exclaims, 'Oh my god, Jessica,' is that really you?' I admit that it is, and she hugs me close and tells me I look great. As we start rehashing old times, my roommate walks to the door. She tells me she's going to work and suggests that I should do the same if I don't want to spend the next month blowing the super."

91

"I yell at her as she walks out, 'At least the super never hits us. That's more than I can say for most of the tricks you bring home.' She turns back and yells at me from the door. 'At least I'm getting customers. You spend too much time role playing with those internet geeks who never pay you a dime to earn any money. We'd have been evicted already if the super didn't have a crush on you.' She slams the door without giving me a chance to answer."

Mrs. Remington looked at me as if she expected me to say something, so I did. "Is the knight in shining limo on the way, or is she already in the room?"

She clapped her hands, "You are a detective. Gertie took me away from all that. She told me I couldn't live like that. She said I was too good to be a whore. I asked her what the Hell she knew about whores. I can't even count the number of sleepless nights I've spent recalling the strange look on her face when I asked her that."

She took another sip of her wine before she continued, "Eventually, she said what she knew about whores didn't matter. What mattered was that I shouldn't be one. She offered to pay for me to get an education. I told her I didn't want an education; I wanted gender reassignment surgery. She said that wouldn't help me get a job after the surgery. We argued about it, but she finally agreed to pay for the surgery, if I'd use student loans to get an education."

"You argued about what she'd give you money for, but she never just said she wouldn't give you any money?"

She stood up. "I'm going to refresh my drink, would you like another beer?"

I nodded and she went to the kitchen and brought back another beer and a full glass. She sat the bottle beside me and curled back in her recliner. "There's a scene I never intended to be in the movie, because it isn't about me, but I think I can tell you about it. You might find it interesting. Will you promise me you won't share it with anybody?"

"Promises are important to me; I don't want to promise what I can't deliver. If you tell me something that might prove her husband didn't kill Gertie, how can I keep that to myself?"

"It won't. Will you promise to keep it to yourself if it doesn't?"

"I promise."

"When she was seventeen, Gertie committed a felony. I'm the only person who knew that until now. I never told a soul while she was alive, and I never would have. It's possible that she didn't know that and gave me money to keep me from talking."

I stared at her as she stared at me. I could tell she felt guilty. I couldn't tell if she felt bad for letting her friend get away with a felony or for accepting money for doing so. As I replayed her screenplay in my mind, I realized that she had no reason to feel guilty.

"No it's not, Courtney. She gave you money to protect you, like she always protected you. She hadn't committed a felony when she pulled you from the yard and warned you not to talk about wanting to be a girl. Whatever secret you had on her wasn't the reason she helped you. She helped you because you were her best friend."

"I guess I was; strange how I never thought of it that way. She was my best friend, too. At least, she was at one time, we drifted apart after that."

I glanced around her house. "How'd you end up here?"

"Gertie was right. I needed an education. I got a degree in computer sciences and started my own programming company, Jones and Courtney Consulting. All the messing around on the internet had me ready. I was able to work from home most of the time. Before the surgery, I met clients as Jesse Jones in a monkey suit with my hair in a pony tail."

I laughed, "The official uniform of the Silicon Valley."

"Exactly, later on I started meeting clients as Jennifer Courtney." She smiled, "We never lost a client, and many started giving us more business. Jennifer was very flirtatious and very popular."

"When did you change Courtney from your last name to your first name?"

"When I married, I knew I wanted to take his last name, but I didn't want to give up the name Courtney since it had been so good to me. He knew most of my history, so he was open to the change."

"What part of your history does he not know?"

"Next question," she stated in the same tone sports agents use when trying to shield their clients from embarrassing themselves.

I changed the subject. "Tell me about the felony Gertie committed."

She repeated, "Next question."

I smiled, "Fair enough, I won't ask again unless you tell me I can. I will mention that the statute of limitations on even the most serious felony has to expire after the person who commits the crime is murdered. Your one-time best friend was murdered. It's possible that the murder was related to her felony."

She smiled, "No, it isn't, but I'll tell you anyway. Do you know she testified as a witness in a murder trial?"

"Yes."

"She lied under oath. She testified that she and Seven were at a movie in Virginia Beach at the time of the murder. She wasn't. She was in her bedroom having sex with me the entire day."

I raised my eyebrows, "All day?"

She blushed, "Maybe not the kind of sex you're thinking of; I may not have had the surgery yet, but I was already a girl."

"I understand her testimony was corroborated by two ticket stubs from the theater and several employees who saw them at the theater."

"How do you know that?"

"The prosecutor thinks a guilty man walked, she shared the trial transcripts with me."

"The employees of the theater were Seven's home boys. They'd have testified that he walked on the ceiling if he said they should. He and Gertie weren't at the theater together. They weren't even friends."

"Then why did she commit perjury for him? Did he pay her money?"

"I don't know, but I doubt if it was money. After she got sent to Colorado, she always seemed to have money to burn. Seven was a tough guy, but he wasn't a master criminal. I can't see him having enough money to influence Gertie."

"Do you know where Seven is now?"

I knew what was coming, so I lip-synched the words with her, "Next question."

I took the last sip of the Amstel Light and stood. "I'm out of questions that you'll answer. Thank you for your hospitality and your cooperation."

She walked me to the door. "I have a question for you," she said as she opened the door. "I've been told by people who were paid well to know what they're doing that all my connections to Jesse Jones have been severed. How did you find me?"

"Next question," I answered as she lip-synched the words with me.

I made several phone calls on the drive back to Norfolk. The last one was to Freak, who answered after the second ring, "Hey Carl, I trust you have good news for us."

"Always the optimist, aren't you? I wish I could say your optimism was justified."

Part 3 – Hollywood Talent

"The stars shine on the sidewalk
The stars shine for the sky
The stars sift through the silver screen
The gold is left behind

Will the cameras roll to capture your surprise?
When you feel this constitution
When you realize the mask was no disguise
When you find this revolution is won between the I's?"

The American Tarot
'Will the Cameras Roll'

26 Movie Night

"I take it he hasn't found anything that will solve the murder. When will he be back in town?" April had heard only my end of the conversation with Carl, but she heard enough to know that we weren't exactly closing in on the real killer.

"Not soon, he's heading to Colorado now. Apparently, she wasn't lying at the DMA about growing up in Colorado."

"How did we not know that?"

"Apparently, she was home-schooled after she went to Colorado, but they never told anybody she wasn't being home schooled in Virginia. That's Carl problem. We've got plenty of work to do here."

"That we do, we've got seven more appointments with rich people who don't miss our murder victim, probably didn't kill her, and will never be convicted if they did."

"Aren't you the Chief Morale Officer for this firm? You sound more depressed than Carl did, and he's the one who has to go to Colorado."

"I guess I just hoped we might have not really known her. I mean I've always known that some people have more haters than others, but it never occurred to me that anybody could be hated by everybody she knew. It's depressing. I don't want Woodbury to rot in jail since he didn't kill her, but I'm not sure I want whoever did kill her to pay for it either."

I smiled, "If it's any consolation, Carl did say he talked to one person who liked the dearly departed."

"Is that right? Maybe he's already found the killer. Anybody who can pretend to like her is capable of anything."

"I don't think she's pretending about that." By the time I finished relaying what Carl had told me about Courtney Remington and the rest of the people he talked to in Norfolk, we were physically back at the office and figuratively back to square one on the case.

Neither of us looked forward to spending two more days asking rich people about the late Trudy Woodbury, but it had to be done. As April sat at her desk transcribing all the recordings from the day's interviews, I sat in my office adding what we learned today to the file Carl had already started. None of it seemed important, but I've learned that it's better to include everything than try to decide what's important.

When I finished, I said to April, "First interview is at nine, probably not a good idea to spend the night closing down bars in Deep Ellum."

April nodded her head to let me know she'd heard me and continued transcribing for about ten more minutes before answering, "How about pizza and a movie at home? Isn't that what married couples do after the honeymoon's over?"

I agreed, and she called in the pizza order while I secured the office. The office has so many security features it took me longer to lock up than it took her to order the pizza. On the five minute drive home, we discussed what movie to watch. More accurately, April said we should watch Titanic again, and I chose not to argue about it.

Carl once told me that as soon as a man accepts that the highest grossing movie of all time is universally hated by every man in the world, he should know everything he needs to know about making relationships work. Carl's always right about stuff like that. Knowing it and putting it into practice are two different things, but I'm learning.

Once we got home, we settled in for the longest and worst movie I've ever sat through more than one time. As bad as the movie is, watching it with April in my arms is still a great way to spend three hours. By the time Kate Winslet posed for Leo Decaprio's nude painting, my mind was on April and the movie instead of Woodbury's problems.

April sat up quickly and reached for the remote, "Naked, why naked?"

By the time I realized what she had said, she had paused the movie and was looking at me like she expected me to have an answer. "I don't know, probably just to give a little eye candy to the millions of men who are going to have to sit through this movie over and over."

April smiled the way she used to smile at big tippers who said stupid things when she was tending bar, "Not Rose, Trudy. Why was her body found naked, even though there was no sign of sexual assault?"

"I don't know. I haven't thought about it. Do you think it's important?"

April frowned, "Maybe not. If you and Carl don't think it matters, I guess it doesn't."

I took April's hand and pulled her to me. "Carl is working on Gertie Lund's background. We're supposed to be working on the events leading up to Trudy Woodbury's naked body being found. I didn't say it wasn't important. I said I hadn't thought of it. That's not the same thing."

"You're just being nice."

"No, I'm not. How many times have you heard Carl say the most important thing is asking the right question? That may be the right question. If we can figure out why the killer took her clothes, maybe we'll know more about her murder."

"So if it is the right question, who do we ask?"

I thought about it for awhile and couldn't think of anybody. "I don't know."

"Maybe we should just ask everybody. Somebody has to know, and maybe they'll accidentally answer."

"Good point, and if even they don't, maybe we'll learn something from the way they don't answer."

"Plus, it gives us the 'one more question' we needed to come up with to go get the recorder from the Lawlers."

I reached for the remote. "Wow, we have a plan. Let's get through the rest of the movie, so we can get to bed in time to be well rested in the morning to execute it."

April folded her arms and smirked. "You just want another look at Kate Winslet's naked breast. I've got a better idea. I'll be in the bedroom naked. If you decide you'd rather paint me than watch Leo paint her, come on up."

As she climbed the staircase looking better than Kate Winslet could ever dream of looking, I turned off the television and tidied up a little bit. Then, I went upstairs to join my beautiful bride.

She was naked as advertised, but I'm not that much of a painter. We found other things to do that didn't involve Celine Dion singing in the background. Neither of us was well-rested in the morning, but we did execute the plan.

27 Mixed Drinks

"How the hell should I know why she was naked?' Evander Preston smoked a cigar I presumed was expensive as he spoke. He sat with his back to the window of a luxurious dining room at Stonebriar Country Club and waited for April or me to answer. I stared past him watching golfers tee off on the golf course below us.

Mr. Preston slammed his hand on the table. "I asked you a question, damn it. I have better things to do than sit here and stare at your lady while you watch people play golf. Why would I know anything about that bitch's dead body?"

Technically, I had better things to do than watch people play golf while Preston stared at April, but I chose not to mention it. We'd driven forty-five minutes to the club because he refused to meet us at his house in Highland Park or at our office. We then spent another twenty minutes waiting for him to show up.

That preceded thirty minutes of asking the same questions we'd spent the previous day asking and learning nothing useful. We did learn that some expensive cigars smell worse than cheap cigars and that Preston had little regard for cops and even less regard for private cops.

April broke the silence gently, "Of course, we know you don't know why she was naked. It's just that we've been trying to figure it out since we took the case, and we still don't know. You're obviously intelligent; would you mind thinking about it and sharing any ideas you come up with?"

Preston took another puff. His pudgy, ruddy face got even redder as he smiled broadly. "You're good, young lady. You're full of shit, but you're good. If you ever decide to get a real job, call me. You'd be great in media relations."

"She's also great in private investigations." I said calmly. "So what do you think? Why might the body have been naked?"

Preston took a puff off his cigar and yelled at a passing waitress. "Hey, Danielle, how about a tequila sunrise over here?"

Preston had missed sunrise by only a few hours, but I chose not to say anything about him ordering tequila at ten-fifteen on a Sunday morning. Nobody said anything until Danielle brought the drink.

She asked, "Can I get you anything else?"

Preston waved her away dismissively and took a drink. He savored it like it was a fine wine before sitting the glass back down on the table. "I do my best thinking when I have a little drink in front of me. Let's see now. Obviously, she might have been naked when she was shot. That seems like an obvious possibility."

I smiled, "So obvious, in fact, that even I thought of it."

"I'm sure you did, young man. That's why I suggested it first. Why did you reject that theory?"

"We haven't rejected it completely. We just haven't accepted it either. If we had a good reason for someone to decide to kill her at the same time she was naked and facing the other direction, maybe it would be more acceptable. Can you suggest one?"

Preston continued to look at April as he spoke to me. "You knew the woman, Mr. Scholes; wouldn't you say that somebody probably wanted to kill her at every conceivable moment?"

"I'll accept it as a working theory. If that's the case, though, why wait until she's naked to kill her. She didn't strike me as the type to spend much time naked."

"Well if it was the husband, wouldn't she be most likely to be naked at the house?"

April answered, "Maybe, but it doesn't matter. The police have confirmed that she wasn't shot in the house."

Preston looked at me this time as he addressed April, "Have they, indeed, dear? I didn't know that. You must be more than just eye candy if you already know what the police know. Perhaps, she was naked in the arms of another man and the husband snuck up behind her."

He looked at both us for a change, "Have you considered that?"

I answered, "I have, but I don't like it."

"Please tell me why you don't like it." Preston reached for his glass as he waited for me to answer.

"First, I don't think her husband killed her. More importantly, I can't believe there's another man dumb enough to take her in his arms."

Preston dropped his glass as he laughed out loud and slapped the table. A busboy rushed to the table to clean up the mess. By the time the table was clean, Danielle had replaced the tequila sunrise for him. He watched her closely as she walked away. She was a cute girl, but she was far too young for him to be watching that way.

When she was out of sight, he said, "I don't know if you're right, but let's hope so. That leaves you with trying to figure out why her clothes were removed after her murder. My guess is that it was to hide evidence of some sort. Maybe they fought and the killer left fingerprints on her clothes. Is that possible?"

April smiled, "It is. I knew we were right to ask you to help us."

Preston smiled back. April's smile can be dangerous, especially to a dirty old man on his second tequila sunrise of the morning. "Hey, do you kids want a couple of drinks? I'm buying."

I never drink alcohol, and I've never seen April drink during the day, but we were clearly in April's area of expertise, so I deferred to her.

She smiled, "My husband doesn't drink for medical reasons, but I'd love an acapulco gold if it's no trouble."

Preston called Danielle back and ordered another tequila sunrise and the acapulco gold for the lady. I asked for a Dr. Pepper when she looked at me.

"Medical reasons, huh?" He asked. "Is that the new euphemism for former alcoholics?"

I smiled, "Well, you know it's a day by day thing. You never really become a former alcoholic."

He took a drink and watched April drink hers for a little bit. He was paying for the drink, and we had a couple of hours before our next appointment, so I just let him. If it bothered April, she could stop it without my interfering. She didn't seem to mind, so we drank in silence for a while.

April finished her drink and put it in the middle of the table. Preston downed his and immediately ordered another round.

"Make mine a double." She glanced at Preston, "If you don't mind, that is."

"Hell, I don't mind. It's only money. Make mine a double, too. In fact, bring us both two."

The waitress smiled at April exactly the way April smiles at me when some scheme we're pulling goes exactly according to plan. I wasn't in on this plan, but I didn't care. April knew what she was doing. I didn't know everything, but I knew that.

Two more rounds and about an hour later, her plan came to fruition. Preston was slurring his words a little and April still seemed completely sober. We'd been on a first name basis since he finished the first double. We'd also spent very little time talking about the case. He was bragging to April about how exclusive this club was, when he stopped in mid-sentence to take another drink.

When he set it down, he looked at me. "Franz, old buddy, let's get back to the damn murder. I bet I know why she was naked. Did you know she had a big secret?"

"Really," I said casually. "What was her big secret?"

He leaned forward, and motioned us to lean in with him. We did. Fortunately, I'm not really a recovering alcoholic or his breath might have knocked me right off the wagon. His head was swaying a little bit, but he finally whispered, "I don't know, but I know she had one."

April leaned in closer as if she didn't mind. "How do you know?" she whispered.

"I saw her suitcase once." Evander leaned back and was speaking in a normal voice. "I didn't mean to see it. I didn't even believe it existed until I saw it."

I asked, "Her suitcase? That doesn't sound like that big a secret. Tell me about it."

"There's not much to tell. It's black leather, well crafted and used to be part of the legend that was Trudy Woodbury. The rumors I used to hear about it were so absurd that I never believed it even existed."

I was at a loss for words, but April said, "But now you believe it. How'd you happen to see it?"

He blushed. Through his ruddy complexion augmented by about a dozen drinks, it wasn't that noticeable, but it was noticeable. "I had one too many drinks at a bar near the arts district. It was one those artsie-fartsie bars with pictures on the bathroom doors instead of the words 'men' and 'women'. I went in the wrong one."

He smiled. "It's not the first time I've done that, but it's the first time I saw anything I've never seen before."

He didn't immediately continue, so I asked, "What did you see?"

"You're not going to believe me."

April took another drink and Evander followed suit. April sat her glass down and leaned in conspiratorially. "Try us."

"There was a naked blonde girl on the floor of the lounge." He glanced at me. "You do know they have lounges in those high class ladies' bathrooms, right?"

I nodded affirmatively and he continued. "Anyway, the girl was on her knees reaching into a leather case. Two ladies were sitting on the divan in expensive clothes. I recognized one of the ladies in expensive clothes as Mrs. Woodbury and got the door closed behind me before she saw me."

"How do you know it was her case?"

He took another drink. "I don't know that it was, but it looked like the one I'd heard rumors about. Plus, I saw her walk out of the bar with it about forty-five minutes later."

Evander's head nodded as he finished his glass and reached for another. When his hand stopped short of the glass and he started snoring, April and I decided we'd learned all we were going to learn from Evander Preston today.

As we stood up, the waitress walked over smiling at April. "That was fun."

April reached in her purse and handed her two twenties and a ten. "When he wakes up tell him we covered the bill. Don't let him see the tab."

"Of course, so perhaps, you'll be back with Mr. Preston again?"

"It's possible." April admitted.

The waitress handed the ten and one of the twenties back. "I hope so. I haven't had this much fun since I started working here. I'll take care of it."

In the parking lot, I turned to April, "I guess you drank him under the table. Are you sure you're okay to drive."

She kissed me quickly, "Acapulco gold has no alcohol. We used to comp them to drunks to help sober them up."

As she started up the car, she asked me, "Did we get any useful answers?"

"I don't know, but we definitely learned another useful question."

28 Another Question

We spent the rest of the afternoon talking to other couples about the late Mrs. Woodbury. Even with our new questions, we'd learned absolutely nothing we didn't already know. I'd grown tired of confirming that nobody liked Trudy Woodbury before the day started.

As we headed back to Southlake, I popped in the CD Charlie Ray had given me recently. As the third song segued from verse one to the hook, April asked, "Is that Rick Taylor playing guitar?'

I tried not to do a double take, but I was extremely surprised. "It is him. When did you become an expert on Texas country music?"

"I'm not an expert, but I did spend about five hours listening to him playing guitar shortly before he died. That sort of memory can stay with a girl. What is this?"

"This, my darling, is the current number three album on the Americana charts: the first and final release from The Rick Taylor Trio."

"But how?"

"Charlie Ray decided that Rick would have eventually done the right thing with the stolen song if he hadn't got killed too soon. He got Rick's dad to give him access to Rick's recordings. Charlie Ray told me he spent a few months rewriting some songs; a few months in the studio cross dubbing and voila, Rick has the individual success, he always craved."

"But it's too late for him to enjoy it."

"Maybe so, but Charlie Ray says the main reason he wanted it, was to validate himself to his father. His father is thrilled. Plus, the money is going into a trust fund for Rick's son to collect when he turns twenty-one."

April smiled. "That's nice. Is Charlie Ray going to quit feeling guilty now?"

"I don't know about that, but at least he knows he's atoned for any guilt he may have felt. How about you?"

"I quit feeling guilty about all of it when I realized that my help was a big part of bringing the killer to justice. I'm just glad my parents raised me to be a good girl. Imagine how many people might have died if I'd been a Kardashian."

I laughed to be polite, but my heart wasn't in it. Lisha's case was starting to drain my enthusiasm and talking about Rick Taylor's death wasn't doing anything to refuel it. I thought listening to Charlie Ray's successful album might cheer me up, but it didn't. If anything, it had depressed me even more.

April noticed my mood, "Cheer up, baby. In a few hours, you'll be at Fogo de Chao eating too much meat and enjoying the company of good friends."

"Trudat," I admitted. "Of course, Woodbury will still be in jail and a murderer will still be running around loose."

April exited 114 and pulled into a parking lot. She stopped the car and turned to me. "You're right. So do you want to give up and drive to Vegas? If I were still tending bar and you were still performing, Mrs. Woodbury would be just as dead; Woodbury would still be in jail, and nobody would be doing a damn thing about it."

I tried to object, "Carl…"

"Lisha hired Pegasus because of you, not Carl. This case is no fun, I'll grant you that, but it's what we do. We both left perfectly fun professions to become detectives. That means we should be detectives even when it's not fun."

"You're right. Let's do it." I smiled, "I'll talk to Carl to see if I can get you promoted to Director of Morale."

April started the car and winked at me. "Besides, I can't wait to see if our plan to get my recorder out of Isaac's command center works."

Melissa Lawler actually let us ring the doorbell before answering this time, but she answered so quickly that I knew she'd followed our approach on their security system. "Come right in," she said. "It's nice to see you again so soon."

We replied politely, and she ushered us into the room they call the East Den. We sat in the same luxurious chairs we had used the day before. Isaac Lawler entered the room carrying a tray of drinks and passed them around. As before, each of the ladies got a glass of wine, and he handed me a Dr. Pepper. Today, he was drinking Newcastle Brown Ale instead of Blue Moon.

He sat beside his wife and looked at us, "To what do we owe the pleasure of this return visit?"

"The pleasure is all ours, I assure you. April and I have been gushing over your security system ever since we saw it, and we're hoping to get a more in-depth tour."

As we'd hoped, Isaac positively beamed when he heard that.

Melissa looked quizzically at April, "I thought you said you had some further questions about Mrs. Woodbury."

April blushed on queue and adopted her sheepish pose. It really is a pleasure working with a talented co-star. I answered for her, "Of course, we weren't comfortable imposing on you so soon just to admire your system again, so we came up with some more questions related to the case.

If you'll humor us, we'll start with those and then beg to see your command center later."

"Of course, that's fine. You needn't have bothered, though. Isaac is always happy to show off his toy. Most of our friends are tired of hearing about it. He probably loves having new friends to impress with it." She looked at her husband, "Don't you, dear?"

"I suppose I do. Let's get those questions out of the way, so I can show off again."

"Okay," I said. "How much do you know about the murder?"

Isaac laughed, "Is this the scene where you trick one of us into admitting we know something only the killer could know? I thought that only worked on television."

I laughed to be polite. "Actually, it's not. I just wondered how much y'all read about it."

"I don't know about Melissa, but I know enough about it to know I don't like your chances of proving Woodbury didn't do it. If I recall correctly, her body was found naked in their backyard a few yards from his woodchipper. She was shot in the back of the head. He's a cop who apparently is prone to violence and was known to be having an affair. Did I leave out anything important?"

I smiled, "Nothing that's known to anybody other than the killer." I turned to April, "See I told you he didn't kill her."

"He's only proven he isn't going to confess, yet. He hasn't proven he didn't kill her." She smiled and winked at Isaac, "Can you boys quit playing games and cut to the chase now? I really want to check out that command center again."

Isaac's attention was fully on April. "Sure, let's cut to the chase."

We'd agreed to see how things developed before deciding who would bring up the question of the victim's nudity. Isaac was clearly comfortable enough with our friendship to accept April flirting with him as he sat beside his wife, so I stayed silent.

April continued, "The thing we're confused about is the body being naked. There was no evidence of sexual assault or even recent intercourse, so we can't explain why she'd have been naked."

Melissa asked, "Is that usually important?"

April glanced at me, so I answered, "Usually not, but we think it might be in this case. We know she wasn't killed in her home, but her body was found in her backyard. That suggests that the body was planted there in an attempt to frame Woodbury."

Isaac interrupted, "Not to the police, it doesn't. They obviously think it suggests that Woodbury killed her."

I answered him, "Exactly, but we don't think that makes sense. If Woodbury killed her, why leave her naked body a few yards from the woodchipper? Why not just put her clothed body in the woodchipper and let it eliminate all the evidence?"

As Isaac reached for his beer, Melissa answered, "I've watched enough episodes of CSI to know the woodchipper doesn't eliminate all evidence."

Isaac sat his beer down without taking a drink, "Damn, but on CSI, they're looking for evidence. If Woodbury had put her in that woodchipper, nobody would have ever looked. How long might it have been before anybody missed her?" He turned to me, "Okay, you've convinced me that he didn't kill her. How are you going to figure out who did?"

"I don't have a clue." I answered honestly, "But I'm hoping somebody will suggest a reason why her body was naked that helps."

"And you think that's important?"

April smiled her megawatt smile. "We think it may be crucial. That's why we're asking everybody who might be smart enough to figure it out to help us think of a reason."

Melissa and Isaac took turns offering suggestions that were either repeats of ones we'd thought of already or too absurd to even consider. My personal favorite in the latter category was Isaac's suggestion that she'd secretly been a member of a nudist colony and had been shot there. Shortly after that suggestion, April put our plan to retrieve her recorder in motion.

"Why don't you show us the command center again? Maybe, all that cool technology will inspire our thinking."

He agreed quickly and soon the four of us were in the command center letting Isaac show off his toys. The plan actually involved only three of us being in the command center, but I couldn't think of a way to make that happen.

Fortunately, April did. She took her half-full wine glass and held it in the air. "I propose a toast. To new friends brought together by random events."

We all reached for our drinks, and I noticed Melissa's glass was empty.

"Wait," I said. "It's not a real toast with one glass empty."

Melissa agreed and hustled to refill her drink. A few seconds later, April distracted Isaac as only she can, and I had the recorder tucked away in my pocket. I thought about telling Melissa that they might need a separate room set up to monitor what took place in the command center, but decided against it.

Melissa came back, and we completed the toast. We also let Isaac show off for about an hour before mentioning that we had plans and needed to leave.

As the Lawlers walked us to the door, Melissa said, "I may have thought of a reason the body was naked."

"Do tell," April said. Only April can say something like 'do tell' and not sound ridiculous.

"Well, it may be stupid, but I was thinking maybe the clothes she was wearing might have been evidence themselves and the killer didn't have any other clothes."

Isaac asked, "How could the clothes themselves be evidence?"

Melissa hesitated, "I don't know, maybe it's a stupid thought."

"No, it isn't stupid." I said, "Please go on."

Melissa didn't continue immediately, but after a few minutes she said, "They don't know where she was killed, right?"

April and I were on the porch now. We answered at the same time, "Right!"

"Maybe her clothes would have given it away. Like maybe, she secretly had a job where you have to wear a uniform and she was killed there."

"Why on earth would that woman be working?" Isaac asked dismissively as he started to close the door.

Melissa didn't reply. I thought of several possibilities, but I kept them to myself. Soon, we were back in April's car on the way to Fogo de Chao to meet Rachel and Osalumense.

As she started the car, April said, "Melissa's right, isn't she?"

"Probably, but I have no idea how to learn what uniform she was wearing when she was killed."

April smiled as she put the car in gear, "I do. We just need to ask the right person the right question. It'll be easier now that we know the question."

29 Stage Costumes

"Really, it's even better than I'd hoped. It's like being back with the revue, only with a different cast for every show."

Rachel had been gushing about her new job as a dominatrix since we sat down at the restaurant. April and Sam were pretending to concentrate on their food, so the conversation was pretty much Rachel and me at the moment.

If she'd managed to shock any eavesdroppers at other tables, they'd been too polite to show it. Even our discussion of the pros and cons of riding crops and cat-o-nine whips hadn't caused anybody to run from the restaurant screaming in fear.

I finally replied, "So instead of whipping me two shows a day, you get to whip complete strangers all day long."

Rachel continued, "Oh, it's not just that it's complete strangers. The cool thing is that every new client is a new script."

"How many different ways are there to write 'boy meets girl; girl whips boy; boy pays girl for the privilege?"

"You'd be amazed. For one thing, it's not just boys. Three of my clients this week were girls and six others were almost girls. I think the almost girls are my favorites. They come in to be forcibly feminized. It's so easy and so fun, four of them came in for their 'forced feminization' session wearing sexy lingerie with their nails already painted."

April looked up from her salad. "They pay to be 'forced' to do what they obviously want or need to do, anyway. Doesn't sound that different from what most people want out of life."

I looked at April, "Since when did you become the patron saint of deviant lifestyles?"

April didn't sound mad, but her voice was a little louder than normal, "Since I married a man whose idea of a great date with his new bride is to kill himself eating red meat while he and his ex-girlfriend chat about the proper technique for causing pain with a cat-o-nine whip."

Where Rachel had failed to shock anybody, April succeeded. The tables around us slowly went back to their meals while I tried to decide if April was really mad or not. When April saw that nobody at the other tables was watching us, she reached over and grabbed a steak from Sam's plate. She took a bite before putting it on her salad plate, and then looked at Rachel.

In a very soft voice she said to Rachel, "You have to project your voice when you play to a large crowd. Now that we have their attention, why don't you tell us all about the life of a Dominatrix?"

Rachel proceeded to do just that, raising her voice at all the right moments to make sure she shocked as many customers as possible. If any of them thought to suggest that the ladies show more restraint in their conversation, they declined to do so. Sam the Man is used to being left alone, since he's a seven foot tall Nigerian. I'm sure Rachel's used to it now also, since they've been dating for almost a year.

Eventually, Rachel tired of talking about her clients and her sessions. "Seriously though, the cool thing is the costumes. I get a new costume with almost every client."

April glanced up from her salad, "New costumes with each client? Maybe I should consider a career change."

Rachel and I both laughed. I always liked the way Rachel laughed. She used to laugh all the time when we toured together in the Absolutely Incredible Freak Show Revue and Burlesque. We all laughed a lot back then. We didn't make much money, but we definitely had fun.

For a long time after I closed the revue, I didn't hear her laugh much. I thought she was happy working at the costume shop, but I realize now that she wasn't. For about the millionth time, I wondered if I'd been selfish in shutting down the show when I did. Thinking about that always gets me thinking about Katherine, so I decided not to think about it.

I asked Rachel, "Are the costumes better than the ones you wore with the revue? The crowds always seemed to like those."

"I wouldn't say they're any better, but there's more to choose from. We did the show for three years, and I only ever had five costumes. I've only been at The Castle a week, and I've worn ten different ones." Rachel bit her lip, "Actually eleven if you count the one we wear when we're not with a client."

April asked, "You have a specific outfit for when you're not with a client? I hope it's cute."

"I wouldn't call it 'cute,' but it's impressive. It's a red leather catsuit with black embroidery at the left breast that reads, 'The Castle.' Underneath that, it says, 'Mistress Virginia'."

I asked, "Mistress Virginia?"

"Mistress Virginia moved to California. Mistress Caroline suggested I wear it until I decide on my own Dominatrix name."

Sam quit pretending not to be listening long enough to ask, "What's wrong with Mistress Rachel?"

"She says it's better to have a stage name." She laughed and looked at me, "Apparently, not everybody who's willing to pay a girl to whip them is as sane and stable as my ex-lover and co-star, Freak Show."

April sat down her wine glass and forced a smile. "Just make sure you don't forget the 'ex' part. If Freak decides to get back into show business, I'll be the one on stage with him."

For the first time, I realized that while Sam and I had been eating too much delicious meat and drinking iced tea, the ladies had been nibbling on salad and drinking too much wine. I leaned over to April to give her a kiss to remind her that Rachel is my ex-lover.

April and I were still kissing, when I heard one of the gaucho's clearing his throat. As we ended the kiss, I saw that the gaucho was actually trying to get Rachel's attention to suggest that she get off Sam's lap and return to her seat. Reluctantly, she did so. After a moment of awkward silence, a different gaucho came to our table and placed more meat on our plates.

Once she was back in her own chair, Rachel said softly, "Enough about me and the fun we used to have. How are you guys coming on the case?"

Sam and I continued trying to kill ourselves with red meat while April shared the progress, and lack of progress, we'd made on the case. Sam listened intently while pretending not to listen at all. Rachel asked a few questions as April talked about our interviews with various rich people. Most of her questions were about the houses, not the conversations. They both kept their voices low enough not to be overheard.

When April finished, Rachel looked at me. "So you're pretty sure the big question is why was the body discovered naked, huh?"

"We think it's important. Obviously, the real question is who killed her. If we knew more about that, we'll definitely know more about the killer."

"And you don't like any of the theories you've come up with so far?"

I laughed, "I actually love several of them, especially the nudist colony theory. The only one I believe is that she might have been wearing a uniform of some kind that would lead us to the killer."

Two more gauchos put meat down for Sam and me. April and Rachel took that opportunity to go to the salad bar. While the ladies filled their plates with relatively healthy food, I asked Sam, "Any thoughts on any of this? You know I know that big man of few words act is just an act."

He smiled, "I'm going to propose to Rachel. What's the best way to do it?"

My fork clanged against an empty spot on the plate after I dropped it, and it bounced to the floor. Seconds later, the restaurant staff had handed me a new fork and removed the fallen one. The girls were laughing when they returned to the table.

"We leave you two alone for a few minutes and you start throwing silverware? Tell me again why I married you."

Sam surprised me by answering, "We just thought a food fight would be the perfect way to cap off a romantic evening. Is that so wrong?"

Rachel put her arm around his waist, "Let's not. The last time you did that we got banned from a perfectly good restaurant. Besides, I know a better way to cap this off. I'm going to solve their case for them."

April answered, "You are?"

"Maybe, I think I know what uniform she was wearing when she was killed."

Rachel smiled smugly; then returned to her salad. After a long delay, Sam finally asked her, "Aren't you going to tell them?"

Rachel paused for effect before answering, "Sure, she was probably wearing a red leather catsuit with 'The Castle' embroidered on it in black." She was laughing so hard, she barely finished the sentence.

I still like Rachel's laugh, but not as much when the joke she's laughing at isn't funny. I especially hate when it sounds more like a psychic vision than a joke.

30 Hired Help

"Seriously?" You really plan to spend Lisha's money on a bodyguard for your ex-girlfriend?"

April was sitting in our client chair while I sat at her desk getting ready to call Secure Investigations. "Maybe this would be easier for you if we refer to Rachel as Sam's fiancée instead of my ex-girlfriend. After all, she and I only dated for a few months, and it was a long time ago."

"It would be easier for me if you could explain why you think a drunken joke by Rachel justifies that kind of expense. I'm not jealous of her; I just don't get it. Besides, she's not his fiancée. You told me yourself that Sam's not the marrying type."

"I might have been wrong about that. I might be wrong about Rachel's theory too, but I don't want to find out the hard way. I know what's it's like to have the girl you plan to marry murdered, and I'm not going to risk putting Osalumense through that."

April didn't say anything, so I continued. "If you don't think we should bill our client for it, I understand. I'm in favor of professional ethics, but I'm not letting her go unwatched until I have a chance to look into The Castle a little bit and see if it relates to our case."

"Okay, I get it." April smiled. "You're seriously worried about her. If you are, then I am, too. Do what you need to do. You should probably let Sam the Man know that you're doing it. He's likely to notice, and I'd hate to see somebody at Secure get hurt on our nickel."

April was right, of course. I don't know why I didn't think about that. I nodded and sent Osalumense a text, "r u alone?"

As always, he replied quickly, "Can be BRB."

I sent back, "call me."

As I waited for him to get to a private place and call me, I smiled at April. "This will actually save us money. She'll be safe when she's with him. We'll just need Pat's guys to keep an eye on her when she's not."

April smiled, "Which makes it a part time job, since they're pretty much attached at the hip." Her smile faded, "Unless he's the one who's going to kill her."

"You're kidding, right?"

"Am I? You have to admit that he's been pretty accepting of his girlfriend quitting a respectable job at a costume shop to enter the sex trade. Isn't it possible that he has an ulterior motive?"

My cell phone saved me from having to answer her. I answered it and Osalumense immediately asked, "Have you thought of a great way for me to propose?"

"Not yet, but I will. I promise. There's another little matter I need your help on first."

"Sure, Freak. You know I'll do anything for you."

He's said that about two hundred times since we've met and I've called him on it at least thirty. He's always lived up to it. This was only the third time I ever had to talk him into anything. Eventually, though, he agreed to let me know whenever he was going to let Rachel out of his sight, so the hired bodyguards could pick up her tail before he did.

When our conversation ended, April said, "I take it he thinks you're as crazy as I do."

"Actually, he's knows I'm as crazy as you think I am, but he's going along with the plan. He loves her too much to risk losing her."

"Of course, he does. How do you to plan to find out if this Castle has anything to do with the murder?"

"First, I'll talk to some old friends. Then, I'll probably go in undercover, probably as a client. I don't think they're looking for a male dominatrix."

"Probably not," April agreed. "I could apply. Two more dinners with Rachel, and I'll know everything I need to know. You better call Pat if we're going to make it to Frisco for our appointment."

"Actually, I was hoping you'd handle the next three interviews without me. I should really go see what Dr. Faulk wants, and I'd like to try again to get Larry Joe on board."

"I see. Why the big hurry?"

I hesitated slightly, "Mostly because I really want to find out about The Castle. The way I see it, the sooner we know, the less money we'll spend on bodyguards."

"If you say so, baby. Are you sure you don't just miss being whipped and you're looking forward to it?"

I reached for the phone instead of answering her.

Surprisingly, my friend Jeff answered instead of a receptionist. "Secure Investigations, Dallas's premiere investigators, how may we serve you?"

I hadn't planned it, but I suddenly felt the urge to disguise my voice. "Dallas premiere?" I asked in a high, haughty voice. "My people told me Pegasus Investigations is Dallas' finest agency. They suggested I call Secure Investigations because Pegasus would almost certainly be too busy to take my little case."

Jeff's voice was strained, "Ma'am, Pegasus is a nice, little agency. Secure Investigations and Pegasus have shared resources on many cases. But, I assure you that Secure Investigations is as fine an agency as you'll find in the Metroplex. We also have enough agents on staff that we're never too busy for a client. What can we do for you?"

I returned to my normal voice, and we shared a few laughs over my little prank. Finally, I said, "I need to hire the agency; do I talk to you or Pat?"

"Well, Pat's the boss and he's here, so I'll let you talk to him. Whatever you need, could you ask for me specifically?"

"Of course, we always do. We know you're the best, and so does Pat."

"Thanks, I'll transfer you, now."

Pat came on the line quickly, "Hey, Freak, how can we help you?"

"Is Jeff available to follow somebody for us for a few days?"

"We're always happy to take your money, Freak. Do we bill you or Pegasus?"

I told him to bill the agency and told him what I needed. I didn't tell him about Rachel's new line of work, but I did tell him I was suspicious of her new employer. He tried to talk me into letting him send a different agent, but I told him I really wanted Jeff for this one. He didn't waste time asking for my reasons since he knew I wouldn't answer.

When we had all the logistics arranged, he asked, "Is this related to the Woodbury case?"

"I don't know, Pat." I answered honestly, "But if it is, this is likely to get very ugly."

He laughed, "And you wouldn't have it any other way. I shouldn't say this, but we're not exactly in the weeds over here. If you need more help than your client wants to pay for, don't hesitate to call."

I assured him I wouldn't hesitate without mentioning that we still hadn't decided whether to bill the client at all.

April had her purse by the time I ended the call. "Happy hunting," she said as she came over to kiss me goodbye.

"Likewise, text me if you learn anything interesting."

"Of course, but don't count on it. I suspect I'm going to hear five more rich people tell me that Trudy Woodbury was a bitch."

I kissed April as she went to talk to some rich people. I followed her out and went to talk to two rich people myself. Like her, I doubted she was going to hear anything helpful or good from her rich people. What I didn't know at the time was that I was going to hear something very bad from one of mine.

31 Mixed News

Cynthia's administrative assistant, Tara, has long blond hair and wears more makeup than she needs. Today, she also had pink highlights in her hair. Cynthia's patients tend to be younger and more open-minded than the patients of some doctors. Tara looked up as I approached the desk and smiled.

"Hey Freak, Dr. Faulk told me to expect you; follow me."

I followed her to an examination room wondering if any of the patients in the waiting room had noticed and minded. When we got to the room, she said, "Have a seat. Dr. Faulk will be right with you."

I doubted it, but I didn't debate her on it. I smiled at her as she left the room and waited. She didn't give me a hospital gown, so I stayed dressed and sat in one of the two normal chairs instead of on the exam table.

About five minutes later, Dr. Faulk came in carrying one of the folders she uses to carry x-rays.

"Hey, Doc," I said. "Can you start with the headline before you get into the slideshow?"

She laid the folder on a counter and sat in the other chair. "Sure, in fact, I'd prefer it. 'Freak Show needs a kidney transplant.' How's that for a headline?"

"That should get attention. Make sure they spell my name right, will you?"

"Damn it, this isn't funny. Freak, you need a kidney, and you need it soon."

I'd asked her to give me the headline first and she had. For the next half hour she gave me the slideshow and the rest of the details. Basically, my kidneys were shot, and dialysis would only provide short-term results. I needed a new kidney soon and the chances of getting a donor from the donor list were slim and none. My only hope was to find a living donor.

"So, I just need to put an ad on Craig's List seeking a slightly used kidney, right?"

"They're not allowed to do that, but we both know you have friends who would donate. Unfortunately, it's not that simple. With living donors, it's important to find a true match. Do you have any living family members you can ask?"

"If I have any living family, I don't know about it. Even if I did, I don't know if I'd ask. You know as well as I do what kind of lifespan I can expect. Why waste a perfectly good kidney on somebody who's going to die soon anyway?"

Cynthia shook her head, "Only you would ask that question about yourself. That's one reason it wouldn't be a waste even if you only lived a year. I'll count on April to ask your friends, if you won't. But it would be much better if you had a family member to do it."

I thought about it for a few minutes. She'd already explained how small the risk to living donors is. "Okay, as soon as we solve this case, I'll try to find any living relatives and see if any have been thinking they have too many kidneys. How long do I have?"

"There's no way to know, but the sooner we do this, the better. As long as you don't die before you find one, you have a chance. But if your body rejects one, it would be nice to have time to try again."

She handed me several pamphlets and printouts with information on kidney transplants. I promised to read them. I glanced at them on the bus ride back to the office, but I didn't learn much she hadn't already told me. When I got to the office, I locked all of them in my desk drawer. I knew what I needed to be worried about now, but I didn't want April to worry about it, yet.

As I walked over to Thanksgiving Tower to try again to talk Larry Joe McCoy into representing Woodbury, I tried to decide if I should tell him about my kidney problem. I still hadn't made a decision as I stepped off the elevator and walked into his lobby.

When Adriana looked up from her computer, I put on my best poker face and asked, "Is the old man in?"

She smiled, "He is, but he has a potential client in his office. I'll let him know you're here."

She looked at me intently as she picked up her phone and dialed. "Mr. McCoy, you're godson is here, and he looks like a traffic cone that's been run over about four times today. I don't know what he wants, but it isn't good."

Apparently, I needed to work on my poker face. At least Adriana had made my decision for me. I pulled out my cell phone and started FaceBooking while I waited for Larry Joe to finish with his potential client. I laughed as I considered posting 'Anybody got an extra kidney?' to my wall.

Adriana looked up, "A laugh. Maybe, you're doing better than I thought when you first came in."

"Or maybe I'm laughing to keep from crying."

"I hadn't thought of that. If you need to talk, I can listen even better than he does."

"I know you can, but he's the one who might know the answers."

She laughed, "Which is why he makes the big bucks."

She went back to her computer, and I went back to my phone. A few minutes later, Larry Joe escorted a gray haired woman through the lobby. He was reassuring her that everything would be okay, but she didn't look reassured.

When she was gone, I said, "Maybe, if you'd lose that hillbilly accent, your reassurances will be more reassuring."

"Hell, boy, I reckon so. But if'n I lose it, they'll also be horse feathers. This here accent is part of my stock in trade."

I followed him into his office, and he closed the door behind me. "Sit on down, son. I figgered Adriana was just carryin' on like womenfolk do, but that sure ain't the case. You look like you done tried to sleep under a cattle stampede. If this is about me not lawyering fer that varmint Woodbury, I'll take his damn case. Don't reckon y'all found anything that'll help me win it, have ya?"

I was tempted to just accept his offer and wait for another day to mention the kidney, but I didn't. "It's not that. I may hold you to your offer, but it's something else. Do you know if I have any living relatives?"

Larry Joe exclaimed, "Damn. That explains it."

I'd never noticed that he sometimes loses his hillbilly accent when he was nervous until Carl pointed it out. Now, I always notice.

The accent was completely gone as he continued, "I presume Doctor Faulk is the reason you're asking. Are you looking for suitable heirs or potential donors?"

"My wife is my heir. Cynthia says I need a kidney soon, or April will be inheriting sooner rather than later."

"Did the good doctor tell you what your chances are of you finding a suitable donor?"

"Actually, she was too busy trying to talk me into looking for a family member I'd be willing to ask to donate to get into a discussion about the odds of surviving a transplant. I read in one of the pamphlets she gave me that with the right kidney, it usually works out. Do you know anything about it?"

"I reckon I know a little about it. Why don't you get back to finding out who killed Mrs. Woodbury, while I rustle you up a kidney you can use?"

It didn't take long for the accent to return, "You sound pretty confident. Should I be reassured?"

"If'n you trust me, I reckon you should. If'n you don't, feel free to keep a' worrying."

"I trust you." I told him honestly, "But I never said I was worried."

He laughed, "Your face did, Son. I ain't claiming I can read every face, but I guaran-dam-tee you, I can read yours."

He pushed the intercom button and Adriana answered, "Yes, sir?"

"Please make an appointment for me with Dr. Cynthia Faulk at her earliest opportunity. If needed, any appointments of mine can be rescheduled."

"Yes, Sir. I'll take care of it."

He looked at me, "Have you told April, yet?" He continued after I shook my head. "This should make it easier. It never hurts to chase bad news with good news."

"What's the good news?"

He smiled, "You ain't about to die, son. At least not on account of a kidney, I promise."

32 Organ Donor

"How can he promise you won't die? He's a lawyer, not a doctor. If Dr. Faulk is worried, we should be worried."

Obviously, April didn't trust Larry Joe as much as I did. "Honey, if he says it's going to be okay, it's going to be okay. He wouldn't lie to me."

"Are you sure? He is a professional liar, you know?"

"It's pronounced 'lawyer,' darling," I joked. "Seriously, he's known me since I was born and he's never lied to me before. Why would he start now?"

"Maybe so you won't worry yourself to death. Or maybe so you won't use your kidney problem to guilt him into taking Woodbury's case. Did you even ask him again to take the case? That is what you went there to do, right?"

"It was. I guess I got sidetracked."

"Of course, you did. Who wouldn't have? Let's go talk to him tomorrow. I want him to take the case, and I want to hear him say why he's so sure you're going to be fine."

I didn't bother trying to talk her out of it, since I wanted the same things. I also knew I couldn't talk her out of it, so I changed the subject. "Okay, we will. Did any of today's rich people tell you anything interesting?"

"If they did, I missed it. You're welcome to review the recordings if you want."

"No thanks. I think I've heard enough rich people today. Let's call it a day."

She agreed. Since it was only seven thirty, way too early for Deep Ellum to be happening, we walked to Uptown and got a table at the McKinney Avenue Tavern. After we ate, April beat me four straight games of Silver Strike Bowling, then we walked home. It had not been the best Monday of my entire life.

Tuesday morning at ten, Adriana escorted us into Larry Joe's office. April got to the point immediately. "What do you mean by saying you're 'going to rustle up a kidney'? You know it's not that easy. People sometimes wait years for a matching kidney. And we all know Freak isn't the ideal candidate for a transplant."

Larry Joe spoke softly, "Easy, little missy. Calm yourself down and have a seat." He pushed the intercom and said, "Adriana, hold all calls."

He looked at me. "I need to tell you something about your medical history that I hoped to never tell you. Do you want to talk about it with your wife here or would you rather do it in private?"

I looked at April and took her hand, "I think we became one before God last week. Besides, you're not tough enough to make her leave, and I'm not stupid enough to try."

April looked at him, "You don't have to be tough. Freak trusts you, so I trust you, too, just maybe not as much. If you need to say something I shouldn't hear, I'll leave."

Larry Joe thought about it for a long time before answering. Finally, he said, "No, it's nothing you don't need to hear. It's just not something I wanted to talk about. In fact, it might be easier for me to tell it to you instead of Freak."

April smiled, "Go ahead."

"Okay, here goes. Freak's condition is called Congenital Analgesia and both his parents had it. People who have it are advised not to have children because of the short lifespan and the high odds of passing it on. That's especially true for couples who both have the condition like his parents."

I said, "We both knew that. Maybe you could fast-forward to the part of my medical history that is currently relevant."

Larry Joe laughed. "I did that yesterday when I told you I'd get you a kidney. Your lovely wife apparently has more patience for the full story than you. If you'd prefer to go chat with Adriana while I tell April what she came here to learn, feel free. She won't mind the company."

April squeezed my hand. I told Larry Joe, "No I'll stay. I guess I'm just more of a headline reader. Go on."

"Freak's mom and dad knew the odds, but she desperately wanted to have a child. He tried to talk her into adopting, but she wouldn't hear of it. She wanted it more than she'd ever wanted anything in her life. He told her she was crazy, showed her all the genealogy reports and tried to talk her out of it."

Larry Joe didn't go on. He just looked down at his desk as if he was consulting his notes. Finally April said, "Thankfully she insisted, and this wonderful man beside me was born to come into my life and save it."

I saw a tear welling up when he looked up from his desk. I'd seen him cry before, but not often. He made no effort to conceal it or wipe his eye. "Yes, she insisted. But he absolutely refused. He told her he could not condemn any child to living the cursed life he'd been given."

He looked straight at me, "His father died when he was only eight. The truth is your father hadn't yet forgiven his father for dying so early or even for having two children."

121

My parents had never mentioned an aunt or uncle, "Two children?"

"Your father had an older sister who died when he was about five. The more he learned about his condition, the angrier he became at his father. In college, I talked him into trying therapy. He went a few times, but it didn't help. After his last session, he told me he didn't need therapy, he just needed a father who wasn't so selfish."

April asked, "Did he ever come to terms with it? It sounds like a terrible way to go through life."

"I think he finally did. Freak's mother helped a lot with that. It also helped that both of them lived long enough to be there for most of his childhood." Larry Joe was past the point of welling up by now, and he finally reached for a tissue to wipe his eyes. When he finished, he looked at me. "It also helped that you turned out to be such a vibrant, wonderful and happy kid. You made him realize that the condition can be as much a blessing as a curse."

I was ready to hear the headline, even though I had already figured out what Larry Joe was beating around the bush trying to avoid having to tell me. "So, if mom wanted a kid, and her husband wouldn't give her one, how did I get here?"

April shrieked, "A surrogate. Freak has a surrogate father. That's it, isn't it? He's got a biological father who can donate a kidney, and you know how to find him! That's great."

"Yes, he has a surrogate father, and I know where to find him."

April jumped up to hug him, quickly realized he hadn't stood up and turned to me. I stood up so she could hug me. When we were both seated again, Larry Joe had composed himself.

"Wait, how do you know his father will donate?"

Larry Joe stared at her. "He'll donate. I promise you, he'll donate. If he only had one kidney left, he'd donate it to keep your husband alive a little longer. That's what fathers do."

I smiled. "So, Daddy-O, is this a good time to ask you again about taking Woodbury's case? Isn't that also what fathers do?"

"I'll take the case, but only if you promise that you will never again call me Daddy-O."

"You got it, Pops. I'll never call you Daddy-O again."

He winced and asked, "Have you found anything helpful during your investigation?"

That's my Pops, always with the right question. I wished I had the right answer.

Part 4 – Colorado Bulldog

"It's no consequence of the circumstance.
It's more the affect of cause and effect.
If you should conceive a plan to deceive,
You might not get what you expect.

Hell hath no fury, so say the stories
Like that of a woman who's been scorned
But sometimes a man who has his own plan
Will create a more furious storm."

The Rick Taylor Trio
'Consequence'

33 Drinking Buddies

As Freak and I discussed the case, I made my way from Baltimore back to the hotel in Virginia. When we finished talking I was convinced that together we'd learned absolutely nothing that was going to help us solve the case. I was also convinced that everything related to Trudy's background was going to be a waste of time.

Even so, I knew I needed to go to Colorado and talk to her aunt and anybody else I could find. I also wanted to talk to Samantha Martin again, but I didn't want it badly enough to spend the rest of the weekend in Norfolk, Virginia. I decided to fly to Denver on the first flight out Sunday, and then decide if I needed to return to Norfolk or if I could handle it by phone.

As I pulled into the hotel parking lot, I realized my decision was mostly going to be based on whether I hated being away from Texas and Emily more than I hated conducting business over the phone. Once I was in my room, I went online to book a flight to Denver. It took me thirty minutes to realize that I wasn't going to be able to fly non-stop.

After I realized that, it took me about five minutes to book a flight to Denver with a stop at DFW. I called Emily to let her know I'd be passing through and she suggested a Sunday date. I liked the idea, so I changed my connecting flight from 10:05 a.m. to 6:00 p.m. I felt confident that Emily would plan a date that justified the layover. That left me with a Saturday night to kill in a city where I had no friends.

Knowing that the Rangers were playing, I went online to find a sports bar that would have the game on the television. I found a place called AJ Gators and got directions from the hotel. As I turned onto Virginia Beach Boulevard, I remembered that I did have a friend in Norfolk, and decided to visit him instead of watching the Rangers' game by myself in a sports bar. It might not be as fun, but at least it would seem a little less pathetic.

I stopped by the liquor store on 264 and picked up a couple of forties and a bottle of Mad Dog 20/20. If you have to buy your friends, it's good to have friends that come cheap. At 7:27 local time, I knocked on John Lund's door. He opened it almost immediately.

He saw the booze I carried and invited me into the house. I believe he'd have invited me in even without it. As he put the booze in the refrigerator, he said. "I figured I'd be seeing you again."

I asked, "Really, why?"

"The cops came around asking about the fight between Gertie and T-Money. I figured you had something to do with that. Did you?"

"I'm sure I did, sorry about that. I talked to the lady who prosecuted the case. I told her about the fight, but I promise I didn't mention your name."

"Hell! Don't apologize. You did me a favor. The cop who came out wants me to do some remodeling at his house. We spent like ten minutes talking about T-Money kicking Gertie's ass and another hour talking about all the things his wife wants redone at their house. Maybe, I'll be able to pay you back the hundred sooner than I thought."

"Well, I'm leaving town tomorrow and I probably won't be back to collect. When you get an extra hundred, put it towards finishing the upstairs. I suspect your mom would like that."

He smiled, "She would. I'm going to get it fixed up. It would already be done if the economy hadn't gone in the tank, but I'm going to get it done. I bet I'm heading for better times, now. All cops have money. When I do a good job on this guy's house, his other cop buddies will see it and hire me to do their houses."

"That's great." I said, feeding off the optimism in his voice. I hadn't heard any when we talked before, and I sure wasn't going to say anything to dampen it.

His smile faded a little, "Hey, it's probably not right for me to be excited if the only reason I'm going to get back on my feet is because somebody died."

I thought to myself that it definitely wasn't right if he'd killed somebody, but I kept that thought to myself. Instead, I said, "Nothing wrong with appreciating the silver lining after the cloud of a tragedy."

He stood up quickly, "Speaking of which, I should at least offer you a beer since you bought them." He walked to the kitchen and came back with one of the forties I had brought and a store brand can of soda.

I asked, "On the wagon?"

"Not really, but I'm staying sober this weekend to make sure I'm at my best Monday when I go look at the job the cop wants me to do for him."

It's never a good idea for a drunk trying to stay sober to be around somebody who's drinking. I handed him back the forty. "I'll pass. You can put this one back in with the others to celebrate when you get the bid next week."

He took the beer, opened it and handed it back to me. As he put the lid in his pocket, he said, "I insist. Somebody has had a drink in this house every weekend since at least 1988. If you'll have this one, I can stay sober and not break the streak."

"And if I don't…"

"Then, I'll drink it. If I do, I'll probably cap it off with a couple more. Why don't you ask me what you came here to ask me?"

I couldn't very well tell him I'd come by to keep from drinking alone in a strange city. "What can you tell me about T-Money?"

"You mean other than the fact that she's the only person in the world who ever stood up to my sister?"

"You already told me that. What else can you tell me?"

"Let me think." He paused for about half a minute. He took two sips from his soda before continuing. "She was also the most popular kid in Norfolk. If she had an enemy, I never heard about it. The fight with Gertie was the only time I ever saw her make anybody mad."

"So, she only had one enemy."

"I don't know. I mean it may be just me not wanting to think my sister killed her, but after the fight I never heard her threaten T-Money or talk bad about her. Seven was a bad-ass nig…uh… thug. He might have killed her for some reason of his own."

"If so, why did Gertie testify that she was with him?"

"I don't know. Maybe he threatened her. You have heard that he's one bad dude, right?"

I looked at John Lund closely as he took another sip from the soda. I could tell he was trying to sell himself on the idea that Gertie had nothing to do with T-Money's murder at least as much as he was trying to convince me. I wasn't buying it, but I also wasn't interested in selling him on the idea that she did.

I took a couple of drinks from the forty. "It's been mentioned several times. Why don't you tell me what you know about Seven?"

He laughed loudly. "I guess because I don't want to commit suicide now, right when it looks like things might be turning around for me."

"Is he still dangerous? I thought he left town."

He shook his head. "I thought you were the big city crime fighter. I don't know if he left town or not, but he's still dangerous. If he killed T-Money and just walked away, why shouldn't I think he could kill me and walk away? Or have somebody do it for him."

"If he could kill you here or have you killed, couldn't he have done the same to your sister in Dallas?"

I took a few more pulls on the beer as he thought about it.

Finally he answered, "I suppose he could have. Is he a suspect?"

"He might be. Maybe I'd know for sure if you told me more about him."

He stared at me for two full minutes as I drank more of the beer.

"I don't miss her that much. Can you do me a favor and throw the bottle in the trash can out front on your way out?"

I easily agreed, and made sure to pour out any remaining beer before I tossed it. As I started the car, it occurred to me that if I'd been right when I suggested that Seven was only the second most feared teenager in Norfolk in 1996, I'd never really seen how scary Gertrude Lund Woodbury could be. I didn't sleep well knowing I was trying to clear a man who married her because he once thought they were kindred spirits.

34 Sunday Dreaming

In the wee hours of Sunday morning, I checked out of the hotel, drove to the airport and dropped off the rental. To paraphrase the old commercial, I'd done more this morning before 6:00 a.m. than I sometimes do in a day. I boarded flight 1273 and settled in hoping to catch up on my sleep on the flight. .

At 9:32 Dallas time, I kissed Emily for the first time in almost a week. We kissed several more times as we waited for the next shuttle bus to arrive. If she was as disappointed by its arrival as I was, she didn't show it. The shuttle dropped us off only a few yards from her SUV, so neither of us broke a sweat on the walk, which is no small miracle even in the morning in Texas.

As the first blast from the air conditioner in her SUV hit me, I asked Emily, "What do you have planned for our mid-day date? A little afternoon delight, perhaps?"

She smiled, "You hate quickies even more than I do. Let's just have fun today and get you on that plane. When you get back, we'll have time for all the delight a gentleman of your advanced age can handle."

I laughed like I always do at a joke we've been enjoying since before I was old enough for even Freak to call my age advanced. "So, are the bingo parlors open yet, or are we going to the park to feed the pigeons?"

She grinned, "None of the above, Escamillo. First, you're going to treat me to brunch. Then, I have a treat for you this afternoon."

We exited DFW south onto 183 and headed west. As we passed 360, I remembered that after talking to John Lund last night, I had forgotten all about the Ranger game and still didn't know who won. I thought about asking Emily, but decided against it.

"Okay, Silent Bob," Emily said using one of the many nicknames she sometimes calls me, "tell me what you've learned so far."

I told her almost everything I'd learned as we drove to Fort Worth. She was far more interested in Courtney Remington's Christian Loboutin shoes than she was that Courtney had been born a boy named Jesse. We were pulling onto Forest Park when I had her completely up to date.

"If this James 'Seven' Seaton guy really killed the girl, couldn't he have killed Mrs. Woodbury?"

"He could have, but I don't think he did."

She asked, "Why not?"

I hadn't mentioned the call from Maurice Letot, and I didn't plan to mention it. "This murder seemed too well planned. Whoever killed her, also framed Woodbury. I don't think that's the way Seven operates."

She thought about that briefly. "Maybe, he's changed his style as he's gotten more experienced."

I didn't answer as we pulled into the parking lot of Sapristi. As we walked to the entrance, Emily said, "And maybe, there's something you haven't told me?"

"Maybe," I admitted.

"And you don't plan to tell me?"

I nodded as I opened the door for her.

"Okay, the detective is officially off duty until I drop him off at the airport. Let's talk about fun things like shopping, movies and how delicious this brunch is going to be."

I agreed, and we did. The brunch was indeed excellent. Between bites of Sapristi's delectable apple pancakes, I said to Emily, "If this is the part of the date that's your treat, I can't wait to see what you have planned for my treat."

She smiled, "Well, the food won't be as good and the atmosphere will be a little less high-tone, but I think you'll like it."

"So where are we going next?"

"It's a secret."

I took several guesses, and she laughed at most of them. She also made fun of my reluctance to eat some of what Sapristi's had to offer. Every time she managed to get me to try something new, it turned out to be delicious and we laughed about that, too. At 12:58, we left Sapristi's stuffed to the gills and giggling like schoolgirls. As we crossed the parking lot, I asked again. "So where are we headed now?"

"It's a secret," she repeated.

Twenty minutes later, she took the Nolan Ryan Expressway exit off of I-30, and it wasn't a secret any more. "If you're going where I think you're going, it's going to be hot."

"It will; we won't." She said as she handed me our tickets which were in a suite.

I grinned, "Watching baseball from a suite, the next best thing to being there."

She playfully hit my arm, "If you'd rather watch the game with the fanatics in the heat, I'm sure somebody in the bleachers will trade with you and join me in the air conditioning."

"My love, I'd rather watch the grass grow with you from a suite than watch the Rangers win the World Series from the dugout."

"I love you too, Escamillo."

We were silent as Emily negotiated though the parking lot. As we rode up the elevator, I said, "We're going to need this to be a pitcher's duel, if we're going to see all nine innings before leaving for the airport."

Emily corrected me, 'Eight and a half, you mean?"

"Of course, I meant eight and a half." Even as a long-suffering Ranger fan, Emily's confidence rubs off on me.

Emily smiled and held my hand as we got off the elevator, "That's better. Last night only took two and half hours, I like our chances."

Emily loves going to the games to watch people, but she never watches on television except with me. "You came to the game last night?" I asked.

"No, I figured you'd be watching the game in a bar like you did when you went to Vegas. I decided to watch it with you. That way we'd at least be doing something together even if we were a million miles apart."

I squeezed her hand a little tighter and tried not to feel guilty because I'd almost watched the game just as she predicted without even thinking of doing something she'd be doing. I thought about saying I watched American Idol for the same reason, but the occasion didn't call for my brand of humor.

Instead, I told her the truth, 'Well. That didn't work out. I was working and missed the whole thing."

We settled down to watch the game. Okay, I settled down to watch the game. She spent more time talking to her co-workers and their relatives who shared the suite with us than watching the game. Since her co-workers were present, we managed to keep our public displays of affection to a professionally acceptable level.

We didn't see the whole game before we had to leave, but we saw enough of the Rangers' win to leave happy. The Rangers didn't really look like a contender, but at least they appeared to, as their manager would put it, 'know the way baseball go' these days. For long suffering Rangers fans, that in itself, is an encouraging sign.

By five-fifteen, we were at the airport. Airports are a more suitable venue for passionate public displays of affection than suites at ballparks. Emily and I took advantage. Nobody told us to get a room, so I don't think we went overboard.

Once past security into the boarding area, the detective was officially back on duty. As such, I immediately started making plans for Denver. Anyway, I would have, if I had any idea what to plan. Asking questions and hoping the answers lead some place is the way I do my job. I've never felt less confident that I knew what questions to ask.

As I boarded the plane, I tried without success to think of the right question to ask Trudy Woodbury's aunt. As the plane took off, I tried to think of any questions I could ask anybody in Colorado that might be helpful. Since I didn't know who else I might talk to in Colorado, I couldn't think of what to ask.

We landed at Denver International Airport at 7:16. By 9:27, I had located my luggage which had ended up on the wrong flight to the right city. I rented another blue Ford Fusion while the airline looked for my luggage, so I was ready to go when they finally did. At 10:41, I arrived at a Holiday Inn in Aurora, Colorado.

I dropped my bags on the floor and lay down on the bed, hoping to dream of watching the Rangers win the World Series with Emily in my arms. Instead, I dreamed of escorting Trudy Woodbury to a prom. It was not a pleasant dream, but I woke up knowing at least one right question.

35 Tequila Sunrise

"Why on earth would I want to talk with a private detective from Dallas about my niece?"

That was the very question I expected from Sheila Tobias which is why I decided not to call to arrange an appointment. It was now six-thirty on a Monday evening, and I'd taken turns watching her house and ringing her doorbell since nine-thirty in the morning.

"Do you want her killer to get away with her murder?"

The look she gave me made it clear she would have hung up the phone or slammed the door in my face if either option existed. Fortunately, since I'd watched her pull her black Lexus GX in her driveway, I had time to meet her at the door while she fished her house key out of her purse.

She stopped fishing and stared at me. "The man who killed her is in jail awaiting justice. You have every right to pretend that's not the case. I assume he's paying you well for pretending. However, I have every right to tell you to leave me alone."

"Police officers in two states have told me this week they aren't sure her husband killed her. As soon as they are sure he didn't kill her, they'll want to talk to many people. You won't have the right to tell them to leave you alone. You'll be absolutely amazed how few rights you actually have."

She laughed, "Are you trying to threaten me? Young man, real cops with real badges have tried to threaten me many times, and it's never worked. You're wasting your time."

I stared at her for a minute. She was much younger and more attractive than I expected. Her straight jet black hair hung just below her shoulders. Her eyes were dark and piercing. Her body looked like a model's body generally looks ten or fifteen years after she quits modeling.

"I suppose I am." I told her, "But as you pointed out I'm getting paid to waste my time."

I turned and walked back toward my car. I called over my shoulder, "See you, later."

She yelled back, "Not if I see you first."

I didn't bother to tell her that if she saw me first, I was in the wrong line of work. The idea when you run surveillance on somebody is not to be seen at all, let alone be seen first. I was suddenly very interested in why Sheila Tobias had been threatened many times by real cops.

While waiting to board the plane in Dallas, I'd called Blake to see if he had friends on the Aurora police department. He didn't, but he promised to check with his friends to see if he could find one. I hadn't checked back on that, so I called his cell phone as I drove back to my hotel.

"Hey Carl, how's the Rocky Mountain State treating you?" Caller I.D. has cut at least thirty seconds off of every phone call. If I ever get the chance, I'd like to shake the hand of whoever invented it.

"Better, since it is spring instead of winter. Did you find anybody who has any friends on the Aurora Police Department?"

He laughed, "Not exactly, but I came close. Teresa Randall was in the Air Force with a cop who now works for the Denver Cold Case Unit."

"How does that help?"

"Do you get so lost when you cross the Red River that you don't even realize that Aurora is a suburb of Denver."

I laughed, "No. I figured that out when I made the flight arrangements. Doesn't Detective Randall hate me?"

"No, like most honest cops, Teresa hates Larry Joe McCoy. She likes you. Let me call her and get the digits. I'll call you back with them."

I thought about calling Emily, but I reluctantly decided against it. Long distance is not the next best thing to being there, especially when you're driving and waiting for other calls. I had just decided for the third time in twenty minutes not to call Emily, when the phone rang. I didn't recognize the number, so I answered professionally, "Pegasus Investigations."

A familiar woman's voice asked, "Is this Carl Jennings?"

"It is," I admitted.

"This is Detective Teresa Randall. Blake says you need some help on a case in Colorado."

Actually, I needed help in Colorado on a case in Dallas, but I didn't correct her. "I do. He says you know somebody here who might be willing to help."

"She will help you. I'll call her and give her your number. Her name is Annette Paul."

"Why are you so sure she'll be willing to help me?"

She laughed, "Because I'm going to ask her to help. That's the wrong question. What you meant to ask is why I am going to ask her."

"True," I admitted. "Why are you?"

She hesitated slightly before answering, "Because, I like you and your partner. A few years ago, I was wrong and you were right. Since then, neither of you has ever ragged me about it nor told anybody else about it. Most men would have rubbed my face in it a hundred times since then."

I thought I heard her voice crack a little as she spoke, but I wasn't sure. "All cops make mistakes, Randall. It wasn't that big a deal."

"That's true, but when a young female cop makes a mistake on a high-profile case, she usually makes the rest of her mistakes from behind a desk. Thanks to you, I'm not behind a desk."

"I think the Chief has more to do with that than I do. It was his decision."

"You still don't get it, Carl. If it wasn't for what I'd learned from you guys, I'd have kept making the same mistakes. Annette will call you, soon. If she can't help you, call me. I'll see what else I can do."

Detective Paul didn't call until 9:15 the following morning. I'm not a morning person and barely answered before it went to voicemail, "Pegasus Investigations."

"Mr. Jennings?"

"Yes."

She started with the standard disclaimer. "I'm Detective Annette Paul. I told Detective Randall I'd help you and I'll try. You must understand that there are rules that govern what a police detective can tell a private citizen, even a licensed private detective with a stellar reputation."

I guessed that the detective had done her own background check on me before calling. I didn't mind, my reputation being stellar and all. "Of course, I would never ask you or anybody else to act unprofessionally on my behalf. I wouldn't have a stellar reputation, if I did, would I?"

"I guess not. This is just the first time I've been asked to do a favor for a male regarding police work. As female cops, we tend to stick together, but the guys don't usually need our help."

"I'm sure that's not true; I bet some just aren't willing to admit it when they do."

Detective Paul's laugh was throaty and deep. "Probably, I may understand more why Teresa asked me to help you. What can I do for you?"

"I'm investigating the murder in Dallas, Texas of Trudy Woodbury, nee Gertrude Lund. The victim apparently lived in Aurora with her aunt for much of her formative years. I'd like to learn more about her time here, but the aunt isn't talking."

"How do you think I can help?"

"I don't know, but I get the impression the aunt has had occasion to be noticed by law enforcement."

"If she has, that's easy enough to check. It's probably even ethical for me to do it. What's her name?"

"Sheila Tobias."

"No Shit!" She screamed, "Miss Tequila Sheila! How fast can you get here?"

36 Frustrated Cops

"I guess that depends on where you mean by 'here.' I'm at the Holiday Inn on Abilene Street in Aurora."

"I'm on the third floor of the Denver City and County Government Building on Cherokee. It shouldn't take you more than thirty minutes. Will you meet me here at eleven?"

I assured her I would, and she gave me the address and directions. Ten minutes later, I had showered, dressed and was on my way to Denver. I went through the drive-thru of a McDonalds on Mississippi and grabbed two Egg McMuffins to eat on the way. It didn't compare to the breakfast I'd shared with Emily the day before, but delicious breakfasts aren't often part of life on the road for a detective.

I got to the police building by ten-thirty. If there was an admin station, I didn't see it. That's probably because I went in the wrong door. Without talking to anybody, it took me four minutes to find Detective Paul's office. The door was closed, so I couldn't tell if she was in there or not. I decided to wait until exactly eleven to knock.

Several people walked past. Nobody offered to help me, but nobody asked me to leave, either. I considered that to be breaking even. At ten minutes until eleven, her door opened, and I saw a black man in a well-tailored suit at the door.

He turned back. "After you talk to him, bring him down if you want. I think you're grasping at straws, but I'll talk to him if you think I should."

He turned and saw me standing in the hall. He was at least a foot shorter than my six foot nine, but he carried himself with a presence that made him seem taller. He spoke in a calm, firm tone, "This floor is off limits to unescorted visitors. Can I help you?"

I had a feeling I was going to need his cooperation. "Sorry, I guess I didn't realize that. I have an eleven o'clock appointment with Detective Paul. Would you mind if I poke my head in and see if she'll be my escort?"

He laughed, "Oh, I'm sure she'd love to be your escort." He took two backward steps to the door and leaned in, "Annette, your detective is here. Apparently, he's already comfortable enough to think he can come and go as he pleases here."

Detective Paul was already around from her desk. She smiled at me, "Thanks, Lamont. I'm sure it was an innocent mistake. You know as well as I do that security around here is a joke. We'll be down to see you later if it's warranted."

Lamont didn't say anything, but he walked away with a casual arrogance that made it look like he'd just won a major battle. I looked at Detective Paul. She was about three inches taller than Lamont, and probably weighed about what I do. She wasn't fat, but she was extremely muscular. She wore blue jeans and a long sleeved plaid shirt.

I nodded at the departing Lamont, "Is he overly formal, or are you too casual?"

She smiled, "Probably both, but if you're going to get any help here, it's probably going to come from him. You'll want to get along with him."

As she spoke, she moved around and sat behind her desk. I sat opposite her. "I'm willing; any suggestions on how to do that?"

"Well, it would help if you were about a foot shorter, but I don't suppose you're that willing. Let's discuss Miss Tequila Sheila and see if we even need to bother."

"Interesting nickname; does Tila know she's using it."

"Actually, it has nothing to do with Tila, and Sheila doesn't use it. That's just a name vice squad came up with for her. She threw an unopened bottle of Jose Cuervo at an officer a few years ago. She's been Tequila Sheila ever since."

"In Dallas, we call that assaulting a peace officer."

"That's what we call it in Denver, also. In Aurora, it apparently falls under the category of charitable donations. Mr. Jennings, what do you know about Sheila Tobias?"

"You can call me Carl. I know almost nothing. I know her address. I know she has no interest in discussing her late niece with a private detective from Dallas."

"That's it? You're not much of a detective are you? You should at least know that she once threw a bottle of Tequila at an officer."

There was a smile in her voice as she said it, so I smiled back. "Actually, Detective Paul, that's still hearsay to me. I haven't had an opportunity to confirm it, yet."

The smile in her voice spread to her face. It appeared a little out of place as if she didn't smile often. "You can call me Annette. Tell me what you can about her late niece. Was she a biological relative?"

That question bothered me, since it never occurred to me to ask while I was in Virginia. Everybody said Gertrude was sent to live with her aunt in Colorado, but nobody referred to her as a family member. I began to wonder if I hadn't asked the right question again.

Detective Paul interrupted my reflection, "Damn, Teresa told me about your famous silent act, but I didn't expect it on the first question."

"Sorry, I was just kicking myself a little. I spent five days on the east coast talking to people, and I never thought to ask that question. Does Tequila Sheila have many relatives who aren't biological relatives?"

"Maybe, tell me about the niece you know."

I don't make a habit of telling everything I know about anybody or anything, but I wanted her help, so I told her what I could. It only took five minutes, which either means I'm a fast talker, or I don't know very much about Trudy Woodbury. I suspect it's the latter.

When I finished, Annette asked, "Is that all you know or all you're telling?"

I smiled without comment.

After a minute, she said, "I get it. Teresa told me a little about you. I knew what to expect when I agreed to talk with you. She also told me I can trust you. Can I?"

She fixed me with the hard cop stare. It wasn't as penetrating as the stare Woodbury used to be famous for, but it was close. I've always suspected he practiced his in front of a mirror. Now, I wondered if she practiced, also. I don't like to answer even simple questions while getting the stare, so I waited until she relaxed before I answered, "Yes."

"That's it?" She shook her head, "No list of references, no list of reasons why I should trust you?"

"Would it help? Wouldn't I have reasons and a list of references even if you couldn't trust me?"

She stood up and walked around her desk to the door. She closed the door and locked it, and then walked back to her desk. "If I tell you some more hearsay about Sheila Tobias, will you let me know if you confirm it?"

"I presume it's about something criminal. I generally share information about criminal activity with the police, so sure."

"Generally?" she asked.

I smiled, "Sometimes I don't turn myself in for speeding."

"No, I guess not. Nobody does. Yes, it's something criminal." She looked down at a notepad on her desk. I think she was reading as she continued, "Do you promise to tell me everything you find out regarding criminal activity related to Sheila Tobias?"

Obviously, Detective Randall had told her I could be trusted, but that I could be trusted even more to keep my promises. I didn't see any reason not to agree.

"I promise. I'll let you know if I find out she's involved in anything serious. I assume you don't care that much if she speeds."

"I don't give a damn if she speeds off a freaking cliff. Will you also promise not to repeat anything I tell you to anybody?"

I think it was Ben Franklin who said, 'In for a penny, in for a pound.' I seemed to be throwing promises around like candy lately, "Sure, I promise not to repeat what you tell me unless you okay it."

"If I okay it, we'll be having a celebration here that rivals the parties when the Broncos won their Super Bowls."

She started to give me the hard stare again, but decided against it. "We think Tequila Sheila has been prostituting children for over twenty years. I want her in jail for it."

I tried not to look shocked, but I know I failed. "Jesus Christ! You think you need a promise from me to get me to cooperate on something like that. Detective Randall and I have had disagreements before, but I can't believe she thinks so poorly of me that she told you that."

"She doesn't. I never told her about it. I like her, but I don't trust her that much. The department's lawyers have banned us from even discussing the possibility that Ms. Tobias has been involved in prostitution. If you tell my boss about this conversation, I'll be fired."

"I won't."

"I know you won't. Let's go talk to Lamont."

I walked with her down the hall toward the elevator trying to figure out what the Hell we'd gotten ourselves into with this case. I now had cops in two states wanting me to help them solve cases and I still had no idea if either of them had anything to do with the case that the cops in Texas thought they'd already solved. I really needed to ask the right question soon.

37 Wayward Girls

"How much have you told him?" Lamont sat behind an ornate mahogany desk in a large corner office. The plaque on the outside of the door read 'Lamont Allen -Commander - Vice Squad.' Behind him, the two windows showed different views of the downtown Denver skyline.

Annette sat in a chair beside mine looking across the desk at him. Or maybe, she was looking at the skyline. I couldn't tell which. She said, "Not much. It's your case, I'll let you decide how much to tell him. He won't repeat anything unless we tell him he can."

Lamont looked at her. "I trust your judgment. You know that." He turned to me. "It's a long story. Don't take notes. She told you why, right?"

"She did. I won't. The last thing I want to do is get somebody in trouble after they try to help me."

He laughed. "Honestly, I'm hoping you'll help me."

"Maybe we can help each other," I said.

He nodded, "Maybe. In November of 1990, I'd been on the force for three months. I was twenty-two, but I looked barely seventeen. The Vice Squad Commander asked me if I'd be willing to go undercover at South Denver High. He'd heard rumors that some of the girls were turning tricks and he wanted somebody to check into it from inside the school."

"I presume you agreed."

"Of course, I didn't join the force hoping to retire as a beat cop. During the school year, we found five preppie girls that were hooking. We kept arresting them and turning them loose. The commander wanted the pimp, not the girls. We never got one to talk, and they always transferred to an out of state school within a month after we questioned them."

Annette cleared her throat like she was going to interrupt, but said nothing.

Lamont looked at her, "Hell, I might as well tell him. One girl didn't transfer. The last girl we arrested, Tammy Chang, committed suicide in her cell. After that, it seemed to stop. If there was any more prostitution among the students, we never found it."

Annette cleared her throat again. "I was a junior at South when Tammy died. It was pretty well known that she was one of the girls turning tricks. I never heard another rumor about it over the next two years."

"We kept an eye on all the high schools after that, but we never caught wind of any tricking from the high schools again. By 1994, I was working full time in Vice. By 1999, I was Vice Commander, and we were congratulating ourselves for eliminating the underage prostitution problem in Denver. Hell, I got this job at least in part because of that."

He paused, so I said, "But?"

"The 'but' is that we were completely wrong. You know how they say cops are always one step behind the criminals?"

"I've heard it said. But if it's true, I don't understand why so many people are in jail."

He smiled, "Maybe it's not always true. In this case, it was. While I was building my career, Tequila Sheila was making a fortune pimping out preppie underage girls who never attended any of the high schools we were monitoring."

I asked, "Dropouts?"

"No, the dropouts don't end up as preppie whores. They end up on the street. We've always had a decent handle on those. We've even had some success with our rehabilitation/career training program for them. The girls I'm talking about weren't dropouts. They were home schooled, and most were related to Sheila Tobias."

"Once we figured out that underage girls were still being pimped out, we started making arrests again. The girls weren't the target, but we never got the pimp. However, several times Sheila Tobias would post bail. When we questioned her, it was always a variation of the same story. 'My niece has always been a handful. I'll talk to her.' Or 'My cousin's daughter never listens to reason, I'll see what I can do.'"

"Hell, we thought she was a female Father Flaherty until it occurred to Annette that she might be the pimp. We looked into it, and the connection made more and more sense. We set up a sting and thought we were going to make the bust in 2001. The timing turned out to be horrible, and we never got a second chance."

"What was wrong with the timing?"

They both winced. Finally Lamont spoke softly, "The raid was set up for the afternoon of September 11th. By the time things were back to normal enough to consider another attempt, she had sold her place in Denver and moved to Aurora."

"Didn't she always have a place in Aurora?"

Lamont looked at Annette, "Did she?"

"I don't know. We never checked on it. Why do you think she did?

"Just something I heard. Is it important?"

Annette wasn't happy. "You tell me. You're the big city dick."

I was silent. Lamont looked at us carefully. His brow was furrowed, and for the first time he looked old enough to have been on the force for over twenty years.

Finally, he said. "We're working together here. Annette, why don't you tell us what you found out about Gertrude Lund, then we'll see if Mr. Jennings will tell us what all he's heard?"

Annette looked at Lamont, then back at me. "I didn't learn much. She definitely lived here for several years. She got a Driver's Education Permit in 1997. She got a speeding ticket in 2000. There's no record of her ever attending school or even being home schooled, and she was never charged with anything other than the one speeding ticket, which was dismissed, by the way."

Lamont looked at me. "Does that surprise you, or does it make sense?"

"Honestly, neither. Nothing on this case has made any sense to me, so I've lost the ability to be surprised."

"Since we're working together, are you going to tell us anything to add to what we know?"

"I can't add to what you know. I haven't had much luck confirming facts lately. But I will tell you what I've heard that I tend to believe. Gertrude Lund came to Colorado when she was eleven. That would have been 1993. Her brother and their friends were told she was being sent to live with her aunt."

Lamont asked, "Biological aunt?"

"I already asked him that. He doesn't know."

"I didn't, but I think I do now. I believe Sheila Tobias is Gertrude Lund's biological aunt."

"Why?" they both asked at once.

"I've had more time to think about it. If she wasn't, I'd have got some hint of that in Virginia. I don't always ask the right question, but I usually ask the obvious ones. I'd have asked if it were an issue. Besides, if Trudy was just one of her whores, would she have allowed her to fly a non-paying date in from Baltimore for her prom?"

Lamont answered, "Probably not, did she?"

"I trust my source on this. In 1999, Gertrude paid the airfare for a friend to come to Colorado and be her date for a prom. The house where they met was in Aurora."

Lamont asked, "Are you sure? High school girls and proms are a huge fetish for some guys. Are you sure your guy wasn't a high roller enjoying a fantasy he'd paid for."

I thought about Courtney Remington and how Gertrude had to promise to let her wear the prom dress that night to get her to wear the suit. I barely kept from laughing as I answered, "I'm sure."

"Okay, so Gertrude was probably a real niece who came here to be with her aunt. How can we use that information to get more information on Tequila Sheila?"

I admired Lamont's focus on what was important to him, but I still didn't care much about Tequila Sheila. My mission was to get Woodbury released from jail and find out who killed his wife. Annette and Lamont discussed possibilities while I listened and thought about the options.

At 12:29, Lamont slammed his hand on his desk and stood up. "Mr. Jennings, we've taken a chance and shared confidential information with you. Now, you just sit there like a mute. If you aren't going to offer suggestions on how we can get an investigation into Tequila Sheila restarted, maybe you should just go."

I resisted the urge to stand up. Even standing up, he didn't have much height leverage on me, so I said in my softest voice, "Maybe. But maybe, you're asking the wrong question."

He sat back down. "What do you mean the wrong question?"

"You're already the Commander. You don't want Tequila Sheila in order to get promoted. You want her because it gnaws at you that she got away with it, right?"

"I never thought about it that way, but yeah. We don't care who gets her. That's why we tried to get the Aurora police involved, but we could never get them interested."

"So I gathered, and now you aren't even allowed to pursue it."

Annette grunted, "Yeah, you know that. What's your point?"

"My point is that I am interested, and I can pursue it. I'll get the defendant's lawyer to subpoena all records related to the victim's aunt and the case will be wide open again."

Lamont smiled like a Cheshire cat, "I like it, once it's all back in the open, nobody will blame Annette or me for taking an interest."

Annette was less thrilled, "Except for the fact that I opened it up. He came to see me, remember. The chief isn't stupid. He'll make the connection."

"Will he?" I asked. "I didn't check in with anybody. Did you tell anybody I was coming?"

Annette laughed, "Just Lamont." She looked at Lamont, "You in?"

"I'm in. I want that bitch." He looked at me. "I don't even care if I can trust you. If there's a chance we can get that case reopened, I'm all for it. Try to get out of the building as unnoticed as you came in. Please tell me we won't hear from you again until the lawyer gets the subpoenas."

I stood and shook their hands. "You won't."

As I got to the door, Annette asked, "Promise?"

I left without answering.

38 Legal Maneuvers

Getting out of the Denver City and County Government Building without being noticed proved just as easy as getting in. As soon as I had the rental back on the road, I called Janice Reynolds' direct line. She answered on the third ring with a professional greeting.

I said, "Hi, it's Carl Jennings. I've found some interesting information about Trudy Woodbury's past that might help his defense. Is this a good time for you to discuss it?"

"Are you pulling my leg?"

"No, I think I've got something, but it's complicated."

She laughed. "Okay, I believe you. I guess you really didn't know. Larry Joe called me about an hour ago to tell me he was taking Woodbury's case. You should call him with your complicated information."

"Okay, thanks. I'm sorry to have bothered you."

"Don't worry about it. I'm so happy to be off that case that it's a pleasure to share the news. Besides, I'm happy to see that the County isn't the only place where the lines of communication get bollixed."

I called Larry Joe's office and Adriana told me he was in a meeting with a client. "Is it important? Should I interrupt him?"

"I hope it's important, but it's not worth interrupting him. Have him call me on my cell phone when he can."

She assured me he'd call within an hour. I doubted that, but it didn't matter. I had another plan, and I didn't need any help from anybody in Dallas to put it in motion. I drove the rest of the way to the airport to exchange the rental car. It took longer than it should have to get the clerk to understand that there was nothing wrong with the car, I'd just decided I wanted a different one.

Despite the difficulty, I eventually left the airport in a metallic gray Chevy Malibu with tinted windows. Sheila Tobias had already seen me driving the blue Fusion. It's possible to tail somebody who knows your car, but it's easier if they don't. Just in case she's really the criminal mastermind two Denver cops described her to be, I thought it wise to make it easier.

I was almost to her neighborhood when Larry Joe called. I pulled into a Wal-Mart parking lot to talk to him. In Texas, you can't park in June to talk on the phone unless you leave the car running for the air conditioning. In Aurora, Colorado, you can, so I did.

Larry Joe got right to the point. "Adriana tells me you might have rustled up something interesting."

"I think I might have. How much did Woodbury offer to get you involved?"

"We ain't exactly worked that part out, yet."

"So that's why you didn't bother to let me know you had. It was a tad embarrassing to have to hear from Mrs. Randall that she's off the case."

"I reckon it was, sorry about that. I figured Freak would tell you. I reckon he figured I'd tell you."

"No problem, it's not that big of a deal. Maybe, I'll give him a hard time about it when I talk to him. In the meantime, how hard is it to subpoena records related to a criminal case in which no charges were filed?"

"It ain't like fishin' a stock pond, but it can be done. Tell me about it."

I told him. I left out the names and positions of my two sources, but I did explain why I didn't want it known that they'd discussed Sheila Tobias with me. He told me he'd take care of it and call me back when he had. During the conversation, his Texas accent disappeared. That usually happens when he's nervous. I used to like it when he got that nervous, but I don't when we're working together.

At 4:11, I was parked near Sheila Tobias' house waiting for any sign of her. I was still waiting when Larry Joe called me at 5:08. "I need the names of some other people associated with Mrs. Woodbury's past so I can subpoena records on everybody. That's the best way to make sure your request in Denver doesn't come down on your sources."

I gave him three names from her time in Virginia. I mentioned her brother John Lund, Tasheika 'T-Money' Monroe and James 'Seven' Seaton. I left out her neighbors Jesse and Jethro Jones. I didn't want to risk any goodwill I'd built up with Letot checking on Courtney Remington. My curiosity regarding James Seaton outweighed my desire to stay in his good graces.

Larry Joe wasn't impressed. "You've chased her history across the country and you've only found four people that she knew. You may not be as good of a detective as you think you are."

I laughed, "Or maybe you don't always recognize when somebody's playing his cards close to his vest."

"Touche," he said. "I'll get a couple of local names from Freak and get started. It'll probably take a couple of days."

I went back to waiting for Sheila Tobias. At 6:41, she pulled her SUV into the driveway. I watched her walk to the door, unlock it and enter her house. If she noticed me, she showed no sign of it. Once she was in, I went back to watching the house. I moved the car every couple of hours to keep from drawing attention. Nobody went in or out.

At one in the morning, I gave up and went back to the hotel. I set my cell phone alarm to wake me up at 5:30, so I could get back to my post before she left the house. If I slept long enough to have dreams, I woke up too suddenly to remember any. I'm not a morning person, but I managed to get ready fast enough to be parked outside her house at 6:29 with a dozen donuts on the passenger seat and six bottles of water in a cooler in the back seat.

Her car was in the driveway, so I doubted if I'd missed anything. Her car was still in the driveway, and nobody had come in or out at 9:15 when I finished the first bottle of water and the fourth donut. By that time, I was extremely bored. Being bored on a stakeout is an occupational hazard.

Of course, it's one thing to be bored in your own city, knowing you can go home as soon as you get the answer you're looking for. It's an entirely different thing to be bored almost a thousand miles from home not knowing if there are any answers to be found.

I was happy when my phone rang giving me something to do until I saw on the caller I.D. that it was Maurice Letot. I thought about letting it go to voice mail, but I was too bored not to answer it. Boredom can be a dangerous thing.

39 Federal Case

"What the Hell are you trying to pull, Carl? I told you to stay away from James Seaton."

"Oh, I'm sorry. Is he in Colorado? I didn't realize that. You wouldn't tell me where he was, so I just went about investigating the people I could find. Are there any other states you don't want me to visit?"

Letot sighed. "You're not funny. Okay, maybe you're a little bit funny. But you know what I'm talking about. I don't know exactly how you talked D.A. Kenth into issuing a subpoena requiring the Commonwealth of Virginia to produce all documents related to investigations into James Seaton, However, I do know you're behind it, and I want an explanation."

"You give me too much credit. I didn't even know such a thing could be done."

"Are you claiming that you had nothing to do with it?"

"I'm not claiming anything. Did you learn about it from Virginia or Texas?"

"Why should I tell you that?"

Another question for which I didn't have a good answer; this was definitely becoming a trend, not a good trend. While I tried to think of an answer, Sheila Tobias came out of her house. The wisdom of driving while talking on the phone has been debated for years.

The stupidity of talking on the phone while trying to discreetly tail an arch-criminal is self-evident. I have no intention of learning if it's wise to hang up on the Department of Homeland Security, so I answered his question.

"You probably shouldn't, but I thought it might help. I know Woodbury hired Larry Joe McCoy as his attorney. That's probably what made Kenth interested in the details. Things seldom work out well for district attorneys who don't cooperate with McCoy."

Letot laughed, "That's an understatement, but I already know that. How did McCoy get Seaton's name?"

I phrased my answer to Letot carefully while I watched Ms. Tobias' Lexus turn out of sight. "You want to know how McCoy got the name, and I want to know which end you heard it from. If you'll answer my question, I promise I'll answer that one for you."

He hesitated. "Okay, I don't know why it's so important to you, but I'll tell you. I heard it from Dallas. As far as I know, it hasn't processed yet, so I doubt if anybody in Virginia even knows about it."

I breathed a silent sigh of relief. Samantha Martin had been very cooperative, and I still had a chance to let her know what was happening so she didn't get blindsided by it. I needed to finish with Letot, so I could make that call.

"McCoy learned about Seaton from me, but we're not investigating him. We're using his name as subterfuge to protect somebody who is helping us investigate another person."

"You expect me to believe that?"

"Not really; was it Kenth who let you know about the request?"

"You don't need to know that, and you'll never guess if I don't tell you. Who are you protecting?"

I smiled as I said, "You don't need to know that, and you'll never guess if I don't tell you."

"No, I guess I don't need to know that. Of course if you don't tell me, then there's no way I can help you protect them. I'd hate to say something to the Denver Chief of Police that might get somebody in trouble."

So much for the thought that he couldn't guess who I was protecting. I didn't give him the pleasure of telling him he was right. Instead, I bluffed, "Go for it. Nothing you say to the Denver police will cause my person any problems."

After a slight pause, Letot laughed, "Damn, at first I thought I knew who were protecting, but I guess I was wrong."

I long ago noted that Letot only believes me when I'm lying. Given his rank with the Department of Homeland Security, I seriously hope I'm the exception to the rule.

"Does it matter?" I asked. "I'm trying to find out who killed Trudy Woodbury. You don't want me around Seaton. If Seaton didn't kill her, we shouldn't have a problem."

"I guess not. Just make sure you don't get caught up in the moment and decide you can free Woodbury by turning the case into the James Seaton case. We know what Seaton has and hasn't done. When the time is right, he'll pay for what he's done. Don't screw us up by getting him accused of something he didn't do in Dallas."

I managed to end the phone call without making any more promises I might regret. I immediately placed a call to Norfolk County to talk to Samantha Martin. I held for seventeen minutes before she came on the line.

"Mr. Jennings, I'm sorry you had to hold so long. Is this about Seven? Have you found something?"

"It is about James Seaton, but I haven't found anything. I just wanted to let you know that Mr. Woodbury's attorney is trying to subpoena your records regarding Seaton."

"Interesting, what does he hope that will accomplish?"

"I couldn't really say. I just wanted you to know it was happening."

"I appreciate that, but it doesn't matter that much. I'd post the damn records on the internet if I thought it might help send the bastard to jail. When I get the subpoena, I'll make sure it gets handled quickly. I'm glad you called, though. I want to ask you a question."

"Go ahead; I'll try to answer if I can."

"It's an easy question. Does your agency serve papers or just investigate big-time criminals. The reason I'm asking is because I'm impressed by your integrity, and I might recommend you to my daughter if you do."

"Well, it's not our bread and butter these days, but we do it. Why would your daughter need papers served by a Dallas detective agency?"

"She's a real estate attorney down there. She says she sometimes has trouble finding anybody to serve eviction notices in certain neighborhoods."

"Sure, have her call us. What's her name?"

She answered, "Stephanie Briscoe."

"Not Martin?" I asked.

"No, she's married. That's how she ended up in Texas. She met David her senior year at Boston College. He was on the men's freshman team, and they used to scrimmage the women's team. I'll give her your name. Be sure to call me if you learn anything interesting about Seven."

I told her I would, and we said our goodbyes. I was still parked outside Sheila Tobias' house. Once again, I wondered about her occupation. I'd been unable to find any hint that she had a job, except the possibility that she might be a pimp. Even if she was, it seemed likely that she would have a cover story of some kind.

No matter how much trouble Gertie was as a child, there's no way her mother would have sent her here unless she thought her sister had a legitimate job. Of course, that theory presumed that they were actually sisters and I hadn't confirmed that either. I had many questions and few answers, and I'd sat here talking to Letot as the person with the answers drove away.

On the off chance that she might come home for lunch from wherever she was, I stayed there until two o'clock. She didn't, so I drove to the Five Guys Burgers off Parker Road. Fortified by a bacon cheeseburger and plenty of French fries, I drove back to her house. Not surprisingly, she pulled into her driveway at six-thirty. She may not have a regular job, but she seemed to keep a pretty regular schedule.

Again, she didn't notice me and again she didn't leave the house once she was in for the evening. By 1:30 in the morning, I was back in my hotel room dreaming about regular jobs. If I had a regular job, I'd probably be getting more than five hours of sleep a night. What I didn't consider is that some jobs that let you get home before seven still can't be called regular jobs, not even close.

40 Trouble Bound

Thursday morning at eight-thirty, I was again parked down the street from Sheila Tobias' house with a cooler full of bottled water and a box of donuts. Her Lexus SUV sat in her driveway. At nine-twenty, I finished the second donut and took a sip of water. Half an hour later, Sheila Tobias came out of her house, and my phone rang at the same time.

I wasn't going to spend the rest of my life in Colorado not tailing her, so I didn't even reach for my phone. Instead, I started the car and got in behind her as she made her way out of her neighborhood. By ten-fifteen, we were headed north on I-25. If I'd had any theories on where she might lead me, none of them included leaving Denver County heading north.

At eleven, we passed Fort Collins. I don't leave Dallas often, so I was wondering what might be north of Fort Collins, Colorado. My question was answered when we left Colorado and entered Wyoming at eleven-forty. Given the accusations the Denver police had made about Ms. Tobias, I immediately thought of the Mann Act.

It occurred to me that if Lamont Allen couldn't convince his boss to let them investigate, maybe I could get the FBI interested. As we exited I-25 toward US-85 in Cheyenne, it occurred to me that maybe the FBI was already interested. That might explain why the Denver police had backed off in the first place. It might also explain Letot's interest.

From US-85, we turned onto Greeley Highway. As we passed Jefferson Road, she pulled into a restaurant that looked like it might have been a Steak and Ale at one time. The parking lot was mostly empty, which isn't a good sign for a restaurant during lunch time. She parked in the handicap space and went in. I waited until she was inside before I drove past the entrance.

As I did so, I saw a large sign by the front door which said, 'Coming Soon - Trouble Bound.' That explained the empty parking lot, but it didn't explain why Sheila Tobias had driven almost two hours to get here. I found an inconspicuous place to park and pulled out my phone to record the location on my navigator.

I could probably find the place without it if I needed to, but since Freak keeps talking me into buying new toys, I might as well use them. As I did, I remembered the call I'd ignored earlier. I checked the history and saw that the call was from Freak's cell phone. He didn't leave a voicemail.

I called him back, but he didn't answer. I didn't leave a voicemail either, since I didn't have anything to tell him. I drank some water and ate a donut while I looked at the building that would soon be Trouble Bound. Based on the name, I guessed it was going to be a bar, not a family restaurant or steak house. I rolled down the window and listened to the sound of construction. When I did, I realized that the construction sound was coming from across the street where all the pickup trucks were parked.

The seven vehicles parked in the Trouble Bound lot were all cars or SUV's. I'm no expert on opening restaurants, but I know enough to know that it requires contractors. The only contractor I've ever known who didn't drive a pickup is John Lund. I wondered if all the work was done and the opening was imminent, or if the work wasn't being done and the opening wasn't coming soon.

At twelve-thirty a middle-aged man in a nice suit came out and walked to one of the two SUV's that wasn't Ms. Tobias' Lexus. As he backed out of his space, I saw that he had Colorado plates and two of those window stickers with a child's name and their sport on them. Apparently Casey played baseball for the Englewood Pirates and Cassidy played volleyball for WMS, which I presumed to be a middle school in the Englewood area whose mascot is a panther or a cougar. He drove away too fast for me to tell which.

At five after one, a blue sedan pulled into the parking lot. I noticed it also had Colorado plates. The driver sat in the car for ten minutes before exiting. He was about thirty with frosted brown hair. He wore cargo shorts and sandals. The back of his tee shirt was a picture of a man on a motorcycle and the phrase 'Only dead fish swim with the stream,' which, of course, isn't true at all.

His arms were tan, but his legs weren't. Apparently, he didn't wear shorts outside often. He hurried to the front door, not quite running, but definitely hurrying. He had to wait three minutes for someone to let him in, and he fidgeted like a schoolboy as he waited. He shifted his weight from foot to foot, and repetitively used the glass door as a mirror to brush his hair with his fingers.

Not much was happening that I could see from the parking lot of the future night club Trouble Bound. The restaurants in the area that were open seemed to be doing a good business including the Burger King which was calling to me like the Sirens called to Ulysses. I figuratively lashed myself to my spot by reminding myself that if I missed something, it could seriously delay my return to Texas and Emily.

At 2:14, the man in the cargo shorts came out. Again he hurried as he got in his car. From this angle, I noticed that the front of his tee shirt also had the motorcycle picture and phrase about the fish. Somebody must feel strongly about the concept to put it on both sides of a tee shirt, but I couldn't figure out why. I spent the next two hours watching nothing happen, and wondering who first suggested that live fish never swim with the stream.

At four-thirty, Ms. Tobias came out. She stopped to make sure the door had locked behind her, then walked to her Lexus. As I followed her back onto Greeley Highway, I noticed that the other cars in the Trouble Bound parking lot all had Colorado plates, also. I started looking at every plate I could without losing my quarry. There were a few Colorado plates, but except for the Trouble Bound lot, it was mostly Wyoming. I suspected that might mean something, but I had no clue what it might be.

I followed her back onto US-85 and southbound on I-25. By the time we got past Fort Collins, I had a good idea that she was heading home. Traffic was a little heavier this afternoon than it had been this morning, but not at all like a Dallas rush hour. At six-thirty, I watched her pull into her driveway. Instead of stopping, I drove past as she walked to her door and headed back to the hotel.

I'd decided on the drive back from Wyoming that if she was a criminal mastermind, she was going to need to be caught by the cops. The best I could hope to do is help get them interested and point them in the right direction. I hoped some time surfing the internet might help me learn if Trouble Bound in Cheyenne was the right direction. Even if didn't, Freak would be proud that his middle aged partner was embracing technology as a tool for detective work.

After two hours on the internet searching for information about Trouble Bound, I'd found a bad movie, some songs by the Blasters, Operation Ivy and Iris Dement; a photographer who specializes in bondage photography, several tattoo galleries and an anime series called serebii. About the only things I hadn't found was a nightclub in Cheyenne, Wyoming or any place else near Denver, Colorado.

After I gave up on learning anything helpful, I learned that Malcolm Muggeridge is the author of the quotation, 'Never forget that only dead fish swim with the stream.' I also learned that Mr. Muggeridge blames Thomas Jefferson for most of the 'ills and miseries of the modern world.' I was still reading about Muggeridge when the phone rang.

I answered the phone with a question, "Hi Freak, have you solved the case, yet?"

"Not even close," he answered. "Have you?"

"About the only thing I've learned is that Malcolm Muggeridge is an idiot."

"Did he kill Trudy?"

I was still surfing the web and I'd just gotten to Wikipedia. "No, he's been dead for almost twenty years."

Freak paused before replying, "I see. You're working on your eccentric act. You're getting better at it. This isn't the time for it, though. I need to tell you a couple of things, and they're not good. You're not driving are you?"

I wasn't driving, but I was sitting down. I decided to stand up before answering, so I could begin pacing immediately. Freak is one of the world's foremost optimists. When he says something isn't going to be good, it usually means it's going to be really bad. This didn't turn out to be an exception.

41 Medical Leave

"I'm going to have kidney transplant surgery tomorrow. You may need to solve this one without me."

As usual, Freak got right to the point. I didn't care much about the case once I heard the phrase kidney surgery. I'm not an expert on kidney surgery, but I know it's a risky thing. I also know it's even riskier if you don't have a family member willing to donate a matching kidney.

"I suddenly don't care who killed Trudy Woodbury. I'm coming home."

Freak sounded much calmer than I felt, "No reason. Everything's arranged here. I've got a living donor with a matching kidney. Doc says my odds are about ninety-eight percent of being up and around in a couple of weeks living a normal life right up until the day that something else kills me. But she also says if I go back to being a detective too soon that will be what kills me."

"How's April taking it?" She's a tough girl, but she's been through Hell in her short time on this planet. Having a husband needing serious surgery less than two weeks after the wedding couldn't be easy on her.

"She's fine, but she's insisting that she's not leaving my side before this is over, so she won't be doing any detective work for awhile."

"I don't blame her, and I wouldn't ask her to. I've solved cases by myself before, you know. I might be able to muddle through this one also."

"I'm sure you can, but you may not have to. Jeff's already on the case. I think it would be best if we kept him. Can we afford to pay Secure Investigations enough to keep him on full time without bankrupting Lisha?"

Jeff's been a top operative for several years. Before Freak joined the agency, Jeff was the one person I'd have liked to hire if I ever got busy enough to expand again.

"We'll figure out a way. I'll call Pat and see what we can work out."

"Good, I'll be happier knowing he's on it. I won't feel as much like I'm letting you down again."

"Freak, you've never let me down. You've saved my life and you've saved my agency. The only way you could ever let me down is if you let your Superman complex get you killed. Get the kidney surgery taken care of and do everything your doctor tells you to do and nothing she tells you not to do. That way we'll all get to celebrate when we solve the case."

Freak sounded relieved, "Okay!"

"Who's the donor?" I asked.

Freak laughed, "Lawrence Joseph McCutcheon, as you love to call him."

"He's giving you a kidney, and you know it matches? Just how close a relative is he?"

"You'll never guess."

I remembered the meeting when Larry Joe had referred to Freak as his son. I'd brushed it off at the time as Larry Joe getting caught up in the emotion of the moment. I should have remembered that Larry Joe doesn't get caught up in emotions. That's probably why he's the most famous lawyer in Dallas.

"Probably not, but I'll try. I'm guessing he's your father."

"Damn. I stand corrected. How you'd know?"

"I didn't know until just now, but Daniel Leeds suggested it to me a couple of years ago. How long have you known?"

"I just found out Monday, which is when he agreed to take Woodbury's case. We were dueling to the death with our light sabers, and Darth McCoy looked at me and said, 'Freak, I'm your father.'"

Freak can joke in any situation. That's one reason almost everybody loves him. It's also one reason I used to not like him. I asked, "Do I even want to know the back story on you and your biological father?"

"Probably; but we should talk about it with April and Emily at The Rodeo Bar. Let's save that for when I'm back on my feet, and the man who killed Trudy Woodbury is in jail."

I answered instinctively, "The man or the woman who killed her."

"Of course, although I now have a real good reason to believe the killer is a man. I should probably bring you up to date on things here before you call Pat."

I agreed that he should, and he did. When he finished, I also believed the killer was a man. I also believed that Freak's superpowers extend far beyond an easily explainable inability to feel physical pain.

Part 5 – Detroit Muscle

"We fill up the tanks in our SUVs,
And blame the price on the oil companies.
We buy Hondas, Nissans, and Toyotas,
While we blame the debt on General Motors.

Now we riot in the streets, pretend that we Occupy Wall Street
But we know the truth is that it won't help.
We're cursing at the president; burning down the government.
But if we face the truth, we'll blame ourselves."

Charlie Nothing and the Nothing Special Band
'Pre-Occupied'

42 Bodyguard Duty

"Secure Investigations, Dallas' premiere investigators, how may we serve you?" Pat requires us to answer the phone that way, so I do. It's a little arrogant, and probably isn't true, but I never mentioned that to him. I like my job too much.

The voice on the other end sounded like a well-heeled old lady, "My people told me Pegasus Investigations is Dallas' finest agency. They suggested I call Secure Investigations because Pegasus would almost certainly be too busy to take my little case."

I should have realized immediately that well-heeled old ladies seldom call detective agencies, but I didn't. After yanking my chain for a few more minutes, my friend Freak Show finally told me why he had called. "I need to hire the agency; do I talk to you or Pat?"

I put him through to Pat and went back to what I'd been doing, which was basically nothing. Our receptionist was on vacation, and Pat had chosen not to bring in a temp. I couldn't blame him for not paying a temp to do nothing, but I was getting bored fast. If business didn't pick up soon, I was going to start looking for another job or another line of work.

Pat walked out of his office and said, "Set the machine to handle the phone and come on back."

Pat's not a young man, he's sixty-one years old and he's been running this agency since operators had switchboards. I don't think he even realizes that the voice mail system handles unanswered calls without being turned on and off. If the receptionist hasn't bothered to explain it, I saw no reason to explain it. I simply followed him into his office.

"Freak wants us to tail a woman for a few days. It's a bodyguard thing. He requested you, but I explained that I don't like to waste your talents on that. I know I promised you I wouldn't ask you to do that kind of work, but he was pretty insistent. I told him I'd ask you."

"You've got four guys doing nothing but serving papers. I'll take a bodyguard job. Who does he need followed?"

"Her name's Rachel Davis. He says you know her. He says she's taken a new job, and he's got a bad feeling about it."

When Freak has a bad feeling, bad things usually happen. I don't believe in psychic powers, but I do believe that some people can process more things with their subconscious minds than the rest of us can with our conscious minds. Freak and his partner Carl are both like that. Things most people never notice suddenly occur to their subconscious, and they suddenly have answers to questions nobody else would think to ask.

"I know her. She's his ex-girlfriend. Did he give you all the details?"

"No, he said to have you call him."

"Okay, I'll call him; anything else?"

"Just be careful. Freak wouldn't be worried about her unless he has a good reason to be worried. Don't relax because he says it's just a bad feeling. He's probably holding something back."

"Probably not," I countered. "But I'll be careful anyway. You've only told me a thousand times that the best way to become an old detective is to be careful as a young detective. Trust me, I believe you."

"Good. Get out of here. You've got a body to guard, and I've got work to do."

I didn't hesitate, "Yes, Sir."

I stood and walked to the door. As I reached it, he called out. "If she's his ex, she's probably got a body worth guarding. Make sure I get a chance to review any surveillance pictures."

I laughed and repeated something he'd also said a thousand times. "And the best way to become a dirty old man is to be a dirty young man and get old."

If he replied, I was out of earshot when he did. I called Freak's cell phone as soon as I got back to my office. When he answered, I said, "Hey Freak, it's Jeff. Thanks for asking for me. Pat doesn't like to give me simple cases that will keep me away from the office for extended periods of time. He says it's cause he's training me to take over the place when he retires, but I sometimes think he's training me to be his receptionist."

Freak laughed, "Pegasus definitely wins the battle of who has the best office help if that comes to pass."

"True, unless April takes over as a primary investigator first. If you and I end up as receptionists, I might win that battle. Of course, that would make Pegasus the national champion in the 'who has the hottest investigator category. Tell me about Rachel and what you want me to do."

"I'm worried about Rachel. It's probably nothing, but I want her watched twenty-four seven until I know what's going on."

I hadn't expected that, "Twenty-four seven? Pat said you just wanted me to check on her at work."

Freak didn't answer right away. His partner's silent act might be contagious. I've heard silence can be a tool in a negotiation, but I've never really believed it. It didn't matter since this wasn't a negotiation.

I asked the obvious question, "Who'll be watching her when she's not at work."

He answered with three simple words, "Sam the Man."

My reaction to his answer wasn't simple, and it certainly can't be summed up in three words. Actually, maybe it can: 'I hate Osalumense.'

Freak sensed my reaction before I had a chance to voice it. "That was a long time ago, Jeff. You're both different people now. Rachel needs to be protected, and you're both good at it. Plus, I'm going to pay you to do it."

"You're going to pay Pat. He's going to pay me like he always does. I'll do it. Just don't expect me to act like Sam and I are friends. You and I are friends. You and he are friends. That's where it ends."

Freak sighed, "Fair enough. I wish you could let bygones be bygones, but I guess you can't."

"I can when I want to. I don't want to. What's your plan?"

"Sam will drop April off at the dungeon around noon each day. You just need to watch her until he picks her up after work, usually around six. He'll call your cell phone when they head there."

I'd heard rumors at Freak's wedding that Rachel had taken a job as a dominatrix, but I didn't really believe it. His social circle isn't above letting people believe their jokes.

"Do you want me to follow her inside or just watch from the outside?"

I could almost hear Freak smiling as he answered, "Use your wisdom guided by your experience."

"I'll take that to mean you don't know what I should do. Why don't you tell me what you're worried about and maybe we can figure out what I should do?"

"That's the problem, my good man. I have no idea what I'm worried about. I just know I'm worried. I don't want my paranoia to get her fired, but I don't want her to get hurt, either."

I've heard Freak tell more lies than I can count. He's really good at it. This wasn't one of his lies. He's not that good. I knew for certain he just had a bad feeling about Rachel's new job, and that he wasn't holding anything from us.

"Do I start today?"

"No, she works Tuesday through Saturday. Sam will call you tomorrow morning."

"Where's this dungeon?"

"It's called The Castle and it's in the old Steak and Ale at Abrams and L.B.J. You know where that is?"

"Yeah, I know where it is. Okay, I'll do what I can. If you figure out what's causing you to worry, let me know."

"I will. It's probably nothing, but I'll call you if something more concrete comes up."

When I hung up the phone, I walked into Pat's office. "The job doesn't start until tomorrow. I guess I'll stay on the phones, today."

"No, I've already got a temp on the way. She'll be here soon. You can go."

By noon, I was in my Mustang GT hardtop driving north on Central Expressway. It couldn't hurt to take a look at her dungeon before heading there tomorrow. It's always better to know than to not know.

43 Surveillance Photos

At one o'clock I pulled into the parking lot of a Pizza Inn at Abrams and 635. I decided to enjoy the buffet while I watched the activity next door. It was a great plan, which would have worked great if any of the windows in the Pizza Inn dining room had faced the old Steak and Ale building which they didn't.

Instead, I enjoyed the pizza buffet while watching daytime television and trying to decide on the best way to stake out the building next door. At one forty-five, the answer walked in the front door. He wore a blue and red Pizza Inn shirt and appeared to be in no hurry. As he strolled toward the counter, the manager behind the counter started yelling at him.

"I told you last time if you came in late again not to bother. You've been officially fired since eleven-thirty."

"Whatever, Dude! I'm here, now."

"Doesn't matter, Mitch; you're fired."

I noticed they were settling in for a long argument, so I gave my waitress a ten and walked outside. I saw two vehicles that hadn't been there when I arrived, a bright yellow four door Chevy Colorado pick-up and an old blue Dodge minivan with a white passenger door and a damaged bumper.

The back window of the Minivan had several stickers promoting the legalization of Marijuana. I kind of like the one that said, 'We lost the war on Drugs. Isn't it time to withdraw the troops?' I stood on the wall by the minivan. At two fifteen the kid in the Pizza Inn shirt walked out and walked toward the van. I'd guessed right.

"Hey, Dude!" I called out as he approached. "Did they really fire you?"

"Yeah, Man. Can you believe that? I was hardly late and the shit-head canned me anyway."

"That sucks. I guess you could use a little extra money right about now, couldn't you?"

He looked me eye to eye for the first time. "I could, what do you want me to do?"

"You don't have to do anything. I just want your Pizza Inn uniform and car topper for a few days."

His eyes showed disappointment as he thought about it, "No can do, Dude. Got to give that shit back or they can hold my final check."

"I won't need it for long; I'll give it back to you so you can return it. He already fired you. You can tell him to go screw for a little while; serves him right."

"Damn right it would." He paused before continuing. "Wait, how do I know you'll give it back? I need that check."

I pulled out my cell phone and my business card. I gave him the card and asked him for his phone number. He gave it to me and I punched it into my phone. While I saved it, I asked, 'How much do you expect that last check to be?"

"A hundred bucks, maybe one twenty. They don't pay worth shit, here."

I took five twenties from my wallet and showed them to him. "Give me the stuff and I'll give you this. You get the hundred now, and when I give you back your stuff you can go get your final check."

Three minutes later, I sat in my car with everything I would need to pretend to be a pizza delivery guy, and Mitch was driving home with one hundred dollars and no shirt. I started watching the activity next door. There didn't seem to be much. Occasionally a car would park near the front door, and a guy would get out and walk furtively to the front door.

Each time, he would ring the bell and wait nervously for something before entering. I guessed the wait was for somebody to buzz him in since nobody ever came to the door. At four-fifteen, having watched three guys go in and two of them leave, I decided to drive around the building one time to check things out.

The only interesting thing I saw was a baby blue T-Bird with the retro round rear window like the fifty-seven used in American Graffiti. When Freak first saw the new version, he told me it looked so much like the old one that he half-expected to see Suzanne Somers in the back seat every time he passed one. I'm not the movie expert Freak is, but I understood that joke.

I noticed the front windows were all the way down, which made sense in this heat. It didn't however make sense in this neighborhood. We weren't exactly in the hood, but this area of town dotted the police report pretty regularly regarding car-jackings and break-ins. I should know. I've had too much idle time lately to spend reading the Dallas crime statistics.

When I parked again between the Pizza Inn and The Castle, I saw a smoking hot blonde girl wearing spandex sweats and carrying a large bag get in to the yellow pickup I'd noticed earlier. I wondered briefly if she looked that sexy in sweats, how she might look in something more revealing. I also wondered why she was wearing sweats in ninety-eight degree weather.

Two more hours of sitting around allowed me to watch one more guy enter and three guys leave. At six fifteen, a tall redhead came out wearing jeans and a pink tee shirt that said 'I get frisky when I drink whisky.' If I didn't know she'd just come out of a house of domination, I'd be tempted to offer her a whisky to see just how frisky she might get.

At six-forty, a thirty-something woman in a grey pinstripe suit walked out. The skirt went just below her knees and her black, high-heeled boots disappeared beneath the dress. She was the first woman to exit the building who wasn't stunningly beautiful. For her age, though, she was still attractive. Tomorrow when I started taking surveillance photos, I expected to have several that Pat would want to see.

The woman in the suit walked to the T-Bird. Since it was the only car left in the lot, that didn't surprise me. It also didn't surprise me when she walked to the trunk to put her bag in it. What did surprise me was when a man wearing a chauffeur's outfit stepped out of the trunk, knelt before her and kissed both of her boots.

When he stood back up, she handed him the keys and he opened the passenger door for her. Once she was in the car, he walked around to the driver's side and let himself in. As soon as he started the car, he rolled the windows up. As he drove out of the parking lot onto 635, I thought about following them. I decided against it. My job was to protect Rachel, not investigate the lifestyles of the rich and deviant.

Actually, my job didn't start until tomorrow. I could have followed them without putting Rachel at risk. I decided not to, because I'd come to prepare for the job, and I wanted to be sure that I'd prepared myself adequately. I waited thirty minutes and then drove around the building one more time. There were no other cars in the parking lot, so I decided to take a closer look.

I parked again and got out of the car. I walked around the building looking for places to hide. I wasn't necessarily planning to hide, but I like to know I can if I have to. I also like to know where somebody else might hide. There weren't any great hiding places, but there were a few that would do in a pinch.

A couple of trees looked climbable, and what shrubbery existed didn't look too painful. I've climbed higher trees and hidden in thornier bushes over the years. As the man says, I knew the job was dangerous when I took it. I also hoped to sit in my car on this job thanks to my new uniform. A delivery guy sitting outside a pizza place isn't likely to draw much attention.

The other thing I noticed as I walked around is that all the windows were painted black. That didn't bode well for my chances of protecting her inside the building. I didn't like that one bit. The best I could probably hope for is that if something happened, it happened outside. Other than that I'd just have to look for suspicious behavior among the people entering the building.

Knowing what I know about the purpose of these visits, I had no clue what would qualify as suspicious. I decided not to panic until I saw somebody act normal.

44 Unwelcome Coincidence

Osalumense called at eleven on Tuesday morning. "We'll be leaving in five minutes. You'll need to be there by eleven-twenty."

I didn't bother telling him I'd been watching the place since seven-thirty. It wasn't any of his business how I went about mine. I like Rachel. I don't know what she sees in him, but I don't care. All I was hired to do was keep her alive.

"I'll be there. What are you driving?"

"A black Ford F-350."

The only entrance to the place is from the west bound service road of I-635, so I moved my Mustang to the parking lot of the convenience store behind the Pizza Inn. I wouldn't miss his F-350, but he wouldn't see me until I wanted him to see me. That is, if I wanted him to see me. If he parked in front, I wouldn't have to move to watch her.

At eleven-twenty-five, I watched him pull into the parking spot closest to the door. They kissed before she got out of the truck. She had to use both side steps to get to the ground from the height of the cab. She managed to do that gracefully, even in her red high heeled boots. The boots contrasted nicely with the black leather skirt she wore.

Her curly black hair was tied up in a bun. It definitely isn't her best look, but every look works for her on some level. I wasn't close enough to take a good picture for Pat, but I knew he'd have appreciated it. As I started the Mustang to get into a better position, my phone rang.

It was Osalumense, "I thought you were going to watch her. I just dropped her off."

"Yes, you did. I'm here to observe, not to be observed or to talk on the phone. By the way, I love those red boots she's wearing. Did you buy them for her? "

"Yes, sorry for bothering you."

He hung up before I could reply. I watched him drive away and moved to what looked like the best position to observe and protect. The spot I chose was close enough to the pizza place that my uniform should be believable, but not close enough to make them want me to move. I could also see most of the parking lot of The Castle and had a good view of the front door.

I backed into the spot like I always do. It's almost always more important to be able to get away quickly than it is to get in quickly. Plus, my surveillance camera is mounted on the dash. Pat hasn't yet sprung for the dashboard vid-cam, but this was the next best thing. I could take pictures with the remote from inside the car or from anywhere close to car. I could also set it to take pictures at intervals, if I had to leave the area.

The lady with the blue T-Bird arrived at nine-thirty. I took ten pictures her getting out of the car and walking into the building. I also took a picture of the car itself. I like nice cars. That's why I drive a 2006 Shelby Mustang GT, even though I can barely make the payments.

Pat occasionally mentions that it's a terrible car for tailing people, especially when I lose a tail. I always reply that it's black and therefore completely unnoticeable. I seldom lose a tail, so he generally lets it slide. He may also let it slide because he knows it's my pride and joy.

Nothing exciting occurred in the hour and a half that passed between the arrival of the lady in the T-Bird and the call from Osalamense. Boredom is part of my job. I settled in to day one of guarding Rachel's body. Pat was right; she definitely has a body worth guarding. That fact alone wasn't likely to keep this from being a boring job.

At twelve-thirty, the yellow pickup I'd seen yesterday pulled into the parking lot. The same girl whom I watched drive off in the truck yesterday got out of the truck. This time she wasn't wearing sweats. Today, she dressed to impress. More accurately, she dressed to impress perverts whose fantasies lean toward the Catholic school girl look right down to the pig tails.

Taking pictures is also part of my job, so I did. As I did, I noticed that the front door opened for her as soon as she got to it. She didn't ring a bell or use a key or a swipe card. It just opened as she approached it. After she entered, I took a couple of pictures of her truck. I like the Chevy Colorado, but yellow isn't a good color for a pickup.

At twelve-fifty, the first customer of the day arrived. He drove a dark gray Volkswagen Jetta. He parked near the door, but hesitated until almost one o'clock before getting out of the car. As he got out of the car, he looked around nervously. He appeared to be checking to see if anybody saw him. He didn't notice me, since I was parked in the other lot.

As he looked around, I took several good pictures of his face. He appeared to be about thirty-five years old. He also appeared to be a pretty normal guy. Guys looking like him serve on the PTA's of every suburb in America. I don't know how many go to places like The Castle to be dominated on an ordinary Tuesday afternoon, but I hope it's not very many.

At one-fifteen, I watched a guy in a blue Buick Century pull off the service road into the Pizza Inn parking lot. He slowed almost to a stop in front, then gradually made his way past me. If he noticed me, he showed no sign of it. He pulled forward and turned like he was going to park next to the VW.

At the last moment, he changed his mind and parked one space away. Apparently, he felt the need to follow public urinal etiquette rules when parking outside The Castle. I found that amusing. He stayed in the car for several minutes, before he got out. His furtive manner as he got of the car was becoming a trend. I liked the trend since it made it easy to get good pictures as he looked around.

Once he was inside, I had some time to reflect on the other trend I'd begun to notice. The employees of The Castle all seemed to drive cool vehicles, like T-Birds or tricked out pickups. The customers all drove boring sedans. I wondered what that said about the domination business.

By five-thirty the guys in the VW and the Buick had left, as had five other guys in five other equally boring cars. One client remained inside with his Hyundai Sonata parked right in front of the door. All the clients had left at least one space between cars and looked around nervously making it easy for me to take pictures. If anybody from The Castle or the Pizza Inn had noticed I was out here, I'd seen no sign of it.

I knew from Rachel's schedule and yesterday's observations that the place generally closed around six. I didn't expect to see any other activity except people leaving. At five-fifty, I saw activity. A red Saturn Sky pulled right in beside the Hyundai. The driver didn't hesitate as he got out and walked to the front door.

I suspected he was an owner or investor, not a client, but the door didn't open for him like it had for the other employees. In spite of that, he didn't look nervous at all as he waited. He also didn't look around so I only got pictures of his back. I also got pictures of his car, which definitely didn't qualify as boring.

The Sky isn't as fast or powerful as my Mustang, but it looks just as sporty. Honestly, it may look even sportier. That car would make it hard to keep a tail, especially since it was bright red. As I admired it, I took pictures of it. The license plate was a Massachusetts' cardboard dealer tag, but I took pictures of it anyway.

Two minutes later, I saw Osalumense's F-350 pull into the lot. Almost simultaneously, I saw the front door burst open. I refocused the camera on the front door, but before I could see who came out or start taking pictures, the F350 blocked my view. He was looking toward the building not toward me, but he was still right in my way.

I jumped out of the car and ran around the back of the truck. I got there just in time to see the Saturn back out quickly and peel out of the parking lot. Whoever it was, he wasn't pleased with how his two minutes inside The Castle had gone. Personally, I was less pleased with the twenty seconds that followed.

45 Job Opportunities

As Osalumense parked the F-350, I walked back to my car hoping I hadn't drawn any attention to myself with my fifteen yard dash around the truck. I'd accomplished nothing, except increasing my heart rate. It could be a coincidence that his truck had been in my way just as the only person I didn't have a good picture of left The Castle in a hurry.

I'm a detective, though. Detectives don't trust coincidences, and I don't trust Osalumense either. I looked toward his truck and saw him calmly talking on his cell phone. I hoped he was talking to Rachel who was about to come out the front door, but he could just as easily have been congratulating the guy in the Saturn for killing her.

I barely had time to try to dismiss that thought before Rachel walked out the door, smiling as if nothing had happened. I supposed that was because nothing had happened. Unless she was the one who ticked off the guy in the Saturn Sky, she probably didn't know a thing about it.

Freak and Osalumense had made it clear that I was not to let Rachel know we were watching over her unless it was needed to save her life. I wanted to know why he had parked his truck right in front of me, but this wasn't the time to find out. I sent him a text: 'call when you can talk.'

I didn't expect a reply, but I got one. 'I will…@9.'

Texting while driving isn't illegal, at least not yet. It isn't safe, but it isn't illegal and everybody does it. As I replied, 'ok', the lady who drives the T-Bird walked out the front door and walked directly toward my car. I'd expected this to happen sooner or later and I was prepared.

I had my Pizza Inn uniform and all the props I should need. As she approached, I lit a self-rolled tobacco and oregano cigarette and looked toward the Pizza Inn. She tapped sharply on my window. I stubbed out the cigarette before I turned to look at her. I rolled down the window and tried to look like I was trying not to look guilty.

She gave me a hard stare that would have humbled Woodbury even before he got humbled by being thrown in jail. It's a stare designed to instill fear. My plan required me to act scared, so that worked out well. It especially worked well, since I was just a little intimidated by the attitude she projected.

"Young man, please explain what you've been doing in the parking lot of my building the last two days."

My plan had been to stammer. Her imposing presence made it easy. "Er, I'm just waiting for, uh, my next delivery. They wo…. won't let me, uh, smoke inside."

She looked at me contemptuously. She looked from my eyes to my name tag. From there, her gaze went to the 'joint' I'd left visible in the ashtray. "You aren't allowed to smoke those out here either. Maybe, I should go tell your boss."

"Please don't." I said as pathetically as I could muster. "I really need this job."

She smiled. Surprisingly, it was a very pleasant smile. None of the practiced stare or hardness showed in this smile. It was soft and seemed sincere. "I bet you do. Your secret is safe with me. You're a cute boy, Mitch. My name's Caroline Smart. If they fire you; knock on my door. I might be able to find work for you."

She'd turned to point to the door I'd been watching all day as she talked. She followed her own turn and started walking away before I could thank her. The offer intrigued me. It gave me an excuse to barge in, or at least barge to the door and hope for admittance if I thought something bad was about to happen inside.

I liked that. Knowing as I do what went on in that building, I didn't like thinking about what work she might have to offer the character I'd played in the previous scene. Rachel had left safely, and I'd already decided not to follow anybody as they left today. I could have left, but I didn't. I drove my car around behind the convenience store to make it appear that I was actually on a delivery.

I made my way on foot back to the best of the hiding places I'd found. By best, I mean least likely to be caught, not most comfortable, appealing or with the best view. For some reason, I wanted to see Caroline leave in her blue T-Bird. Maybe, I just wanted to see if her chauffeur was in the trunk again.

Whatever the reason, I was standing by the Pizza Inn trash dumpster hidden behind the fence at seven-forty when I saw Caroline walking toward the Pizza Inn. That didn't bode well for my disguise, but I didn't know what to do about it. I knew that however cute she thought I was would be offset by how rank I smelled after hiding by a trash dump for over an hour.

Caroline came out of the Pizza Inn three minutes after she went in. She walked straight to her T-Bird and drove out onto I-635. I waited another ten minutes before making my way to my car. I was driving home when my cell phone rang. I was shocked to see on the caller ID that it was Mitch.

"Dude, I need my stuff back, now! Can you bring it to me, or can I meet you somewhere for it tonight."

I've known drug addicts that can go through a hundred dollars in a day, but Mitch didn't strike me as the type. "Do you need that last check already? Maybe, I can give you something to tide you over."

He laughed, "No dude. The boss came to his senses. He called and said I could have my job back if I showed up on time tomorrow. I need my stuff."

"That's great!" I lied. I had a feeling I knew what had caused the manager's change of heart, but I didn't see any reason to tell Mitch. "Can I just meet you tomorrow morning at the store?"

He hesitated, but finally he answered, "Okay. Hey, all I need is the car topper and my name tag. I've got extra shirts if you need one."

"That would be great." I told him honestly. The shirt was the only thing I couldn't do without, anyway. I'd seen every thing I'd been hiding by a trash dumpster to see, so I got back in my car and left. I needed a shower desperately, but I also needed to take care of some things at the office. Knowing if I went home first, I'd probably want to stay there, I headed for the office.

At eight-thirty, I let myself into the office. I don't know which surprised me most: that Pat was still in the office or that he was sitting at the front desk furiously typing away at the computer. Since I've seen him work late before, but I've never seen him touch a computer, I decided it was the latter.

46 Bad Economy

"What are you doing here?" We both said simultaneously. Neither one of us answered immediately.

Pat looked at me for a few seconds. "You smell like a trash dumpster."

"That's because I've been hiding in a trash dumpster for the last hour. You don't love the smell of rancid pepperoni and anchovies?"

He grinned, "Not on people."

"I suppose not. I'll only be a few minutes. I need to use the badge maker to do up a Pizza Inn badge and rig up something to work as a car topper."

"What's wrong with the badge you're wearing?"

I had forgotten I had it on. "It's not mine; I have to return it."

Pat held his nose between his thumb and forefinger. "Use the shower in my office. I'll see what I can rig up for you."

Pat's office has a private bathroom complete with a shower. He almost never mentions it, but I know he takes pride in having it. I'd never known him to invite anybody else to use it. I knew I smelled like a trash dumpster, so I didn't read much into this exception.

I spent just enough time in the shower to get the smell out. I stepped out of the shower and saw that Pat was way ahead of me. I put on the clothes he'd left me and walked to the lobby. He was still staring at the computer.

When he heard me, he said, "Sit down."

I didn't say anything as I sat down and looked at him. He looked older than I'd ever seen him look.

"I don't have to tell you that business isn't good, do I?"

I shook my head. "How bad is it?"

"It's bad; I let Bill and Russell go this afternoon. I recommended them both to Pete Lambert. He's going to interview them next week. I'm probably going to shut down by the end of the year."

He waited for me to say something, but I couldn't think of anything to say. He continued. "I could talk to Pete for you, too. He says he plans to hire two or three guys by the end of the year. Do you want me to recommend you?"

I had an answer to this one. "No thanks. It's not my kind of work."

"I thought you'd say that. You know they do more than process serving. I'm sure you'd have to start out doing that, but he'd realize soon enough that you're better used elsewhere."

172

I asked, "Soon enough for who?"

Pat sighed, "Probably nobody. I'm trying to do the best I can."

"I know. Look, I understand what you're going through. Take care of the guys the best you can. Don't worry about me. If you decide you have to shut it down, I'll be okay. Maybe I'll open my own agency."

"Jeff, you don't want to do that. It's a bad economy. This isn't the time. Maybe Lambert's agency isn't the right one for you, but we'll find something for you. I promise we'll find you something before I shut it down."

I could feel his pain as if it was my own. I didn't want to add to it, so I changed the subject. "Any luck on the Pizza Inn badge?"

He smiled and stood up, "I wouldn't exactly call it luck."

I followed him to the workroom and he showed me his handiwork. The name tag looked completely authentic, and he'd somehow fashioned a car topper out of some plastic that was passable, if not perfect.

"Wow, I should have come back here instead of spending money to rent the real thing."

"No, the real thing is always better if it's available. Besides, the money is an expense item. We can't bill for the stuff lying around in this workshop."

He pointed to a trash bag lying in the corner. "Is there anything you should tell me about the case before you go home to wash your clothes?"

"Not yet, but you are probably going to love the surveillance photos before this is over."

He laughed. His mood was much better than when I'd come in. "That's one thing I'll miss about this archaic and god-forsaken business."

I picked up the bag of clothes he'd pointed to earlier. I left without saying anything else. At nine-ten, I was back on Ross Avenue headed home. My desire to tear Sam The Man a new hole for blocking my view had waned some during my conversation with Pat, but I was still upset.

I was home long before he called at nine-fifty. "I thought you were going to call at nine."

"Sorry," He said sounding truly apologetic. If he'd sounded this sincere two years ago when he apologized for knocking me out with a right hook, I might have forgiven him.

Today, I didn't care about that. "Why in the Hell would you block my view of the front door? How can I protect Rachel if I can't even see her come out?"

He answered immediately, "I didn't mean to. I didn't even realize it happened until I saw you behind my truck. I didn't know what to do, so I just parked the truck as soon as I could. What should I have done? Should I have stayed to provide cover or just left?"

Either Freak had been teaching him to lie, or he was telling the truth. I decided to trust him. I also decided to quit thinking about my past issues with him. A wise man once told me that the only person you hurt when you don't forgive is yourself.

"I don't guess there was anything you could do at that point. Parking worked out. Did you see anything I might have missed?"

"All I saw was one guy storming out of there like he'd been bounced. He drove away in the little sports car. You saw that, right?"

"I saw him peel out, but I didn't see the guy at all. Can you describe him?"

"I only caught a glimpse; not real tall, pretty stocky. If I had to bounce him, I'd definitely expect a fight. Especially, if he looked as mad as he looked as he stormed out of there."

I'd seen the guy go in the place, so I knew he was a little less than six foot tall. Since Osalumense is about seven tall, he probably wasn't lying about the height. To him, even six foot wouldn't seem tall.

I asked what Pat always calls the check-digit question. "Did you see what color hair he had?"

He laughed, "Black. His hair was blacker than mine."

If Sam The Man ever had hair, I've never seen it. His skin is as black as night, so I knew what he meant. I'd already seen that the guy in the Saturn Sky had dark black hair, so all I'd learned was that I wasn't being played.

"Did you notice anything else?"

"Just that he looked mad. Do you think he's the threat Freak's worried about?"

I answered him honestly, "I don't know. I just don't know."

47 Best-laid Plans

Wednesday morning, I woke up with a clear plan for the day. I'd watch The Castle from the Pizza Inn parking lot until Mitch showed up; then I'd give him his uniform back and warn him about the possibility that he might get a delivery to somebody expecting him to be me.

That plan seemed like a good one right up until I finished brushing my teeth. As I was rinsing out my toothbrush, it occurred to me that I was guarding Rachel because Freak had a bad feeling about Rachel's place of employment. His intuition is legendary more for its accuracy than its attention to detail.

Caroline might be the kind overseer of a dungeon and protector of the ladies who work for her. She might also be a psychopathic killer looking to lure innocent pizza boys into her web of death. I'd paid Mitch a hundred dollars for his uniform, not to expose him to potential danger.

However, I was being paid to protect Rachel, not Mitch. I called Freak. He sounded nervous when he answered, "What's up? Is Rachel okay?"

"She's fine. I've got another concern though. If she's really in danger, I may have put somebody else in danger. Can you keep an eye on somebody for a couple of hours today while I watch Rachel?"

"Dude, I hired you so I could detect while you guard a body. I didn't expect you to add to the number of bodies who need guarded."

"I didn't either, my friend. But life often presents unexpected challenges. These challenges present the opportunities which allow us to strive for greatness."

"We're already great, Jeff. Unfortunately, my superpowers don't include being in two places at one time. Obviously yours don't either, or you wouldn't have called. I take it Secure doesn't have anybody available."

I didn't think this was the right time to mention how unavailable Secure Investigations staff was. "The thing is, it's probably nothing. I don't want to embarrass myself by having a coworker follow a pizza guy around for no reason."

Freak laughed, "You worry too much about what other people think, but I'll humor you. Let me make a couple of calls. I'll see if I can find a qualified operative."

Freak's always believed that I worry too much about other people's opinion. Since he's never worried about that at all, it's not surprising. Maybe if I'd been born with money and actual superpowers. I'd worry as little as he does.

The Leather Suit Case

At nine o'clock, I once again parked in the convenience store parking lot. If I didn't hear from Freak before I gave Mitch back his stuff, I'd have to find a way to warn him that he might be asked to deliver a pizza to a woman, who while being pretty hot for a woman her age, might be an insane serial killer.

At nine-fifty, Freak called. "I think I've got it worked out. Sam The Man will watch your guy, while you watch Rachel."

It took me just under two seconds to find several reasons to object to that plan and just over three seconds to dismiss them all. "Okay, I'll call him after he drops Rachel off and let him know the situation."

Freak replied, "Cool." I've known him for years. I don't know if this was the first one word sentence I'd ever heard him say, but I know it was the first time I'd ever heard him sound relieved as if he'd been worried about something. I realized he'd been worried that I might balk at his plan.

"Freak, it's cool. I took your advice, finally. What happened in the past is in the past."

"Great! What prompted this change of heart?"

I didn't have a good answer to that. "Wise counsel is wise counsel regardless of how long it takes to sink in."

After I hung up, I realized that Freak never quit sounding nervous during the conversation. That worried me a little. Actually, that worried me very much. I watched The Castle for another hour until I saw Mitch's van pull up. He parked in the same parking spot he had used yesterday.

He called out through an open window when he saw me walking toward his van, "Hey dude, thanks."

I answered as I handed him his stuff, "No problem. I should let you know I did talk to a few people yesterday while wearing it. If anybody says anything weird, that will be why."

He looked puzzled. I suspected he had that look often. "Weird, like what?" he asked.

"I don't know exactly. I guess if someone asks for Mitch thinking they're going to find me and sees you, they might say something."

"You didn't do anything illegal, did you?"

I laughed, "No, it's nothing like that."

"What is it like?"

He didn't sound puzzled at all. He sounded suspicious. I've found the truth is often the best way to deal with suspicion. "I'm a private detective. I'm working on a case. Sometimes it's best to have a disguise. I used your uniform as a disguise."

His suspicion turned quickly to awe, "No shit? That's too cool."

"Well, it's a job. I wish it offered more security, but it's a job."

"It beats my job."

I figured he was right about that, but I didn't say anything.

He looked at me, still impressed. "I'll tell you what. If anybody says anything, I'll just tell them I loaned my nametag to another driver. That shit happens all the time."

That would work. I wondered why I didn't think of it. Maybe, I'm the one that should look puzzled often. He went into the Pizza Inn, and I went back to watching The Castle. At eleven-thirty, Sam The Man pulled into to the parking lot. Once again, Rachel's dismount from the truck was gracefully executed in spite of the skyscraper pink heels she wore.

It was also once again preceded by several minutes of goodbye kisses in the truck. I took no pictures of the goodbye, but I took one or two of her getting out of the truck and going into the building. The plan was for me to call him after he dropped Rachel off, but he beat me to the punch.

When I answered, he said, "If you need pictures of my girlfriend's ass, there are lots of better ones on the internet. I can email you the links if you need them."

He sounded serious, but I glanced over at him sitting in his truck and he was grinning from ear to ear. In the years since I'd quit talking to him, I'd forgotten what a twisted sense of humor he has. "No that's okay; I think I got everything I need. You two were in clear violation of Dallas' Public Displays of Affection code."

He laughed, "Okay. Who am I supposed to be protecting and how much danger is he or she in?"

"See the van parked by the Pizza Inn?"

I have to give him credit. He glanced casually. If I hadn't known he was looking at it, I wouldn't have noticed it.

He asked, "The one with all the pot bumper stickers?"

"That's the one. The kid who drives it delivers pizzas. He loaned me his gear yesterday and I pretended to be him. If I irritated anybody, they might take it out on him."

"Did you irritate anybody?"

"I think that depends on whether Freak's intuition is right. I sat outside this building all day, and somebody noticed. If nothing's amiss, nobody should be in danger. If somebody associated with this place is a killer, then anything's possible."

"Okay, we'll have to assume anything's possible. I'm going to move my truck to the other side of the Pizza Inn. There's no reason to risk Rachel or anybody else seeing that I'm still out here. You let me know when he leaves, and I'll pick up the tail."

"That sounds like a good plan." I wasn't thrilled that the pizza delivery guy and the bouncer were doing most of the planning on the case. However, I was happy to have a plan.

48 Car Wreck

Sam moved his truck and I returned to watching The Castle. The blue Thunderbird showed at eleven-fifty. Mistress Caroline got out of the car. I saw no sign of the chauffeur in the trunk from earlier. It occurred to me that he had probably been a client engaging in his own personal fantasy and not an actual employee of hers.

I suppose people are entitled to their own kinks, but I can't imagine what could excite a guy about being locked in the trunk of a car, even a really cool car like her Thunderbird. Pat frequently reminds me not to pass judgment, but some things are hard not to judge. I put the kinks of the establishment's clientele out of my mind and focused on the task at hand.

At twelve-fifteen, the yellow Colorado pulled into the parking lot. The same blonde girl got out. She was wearing a business suit with an extremely short skirt today. She looked better in it than she did in the sweats or the school girl outfit. Pat was definitely going to love the surveillance pictures from this case.

At twelve-twenty I saw Mitch walking out to his van with several pizzas to deliver. I called Sam to let him know, and he assured me he was on it.

"I've got your pizza boy's back. Don't let anything happen to Rachel."

"I won't," I promised, hoping I could deliver.

I knew that since Caroline had seen me, I couldn't simply pretend to be a delivery guy and sit outside the pizza place all day. I needed to vary the routine a little. Lunch hour seemed like a good time for a delivery guy not to be parked outside doing nothing, so at twelve-thirty, I got out of the car and walked into the pizza place. I had my phone, my gun and a camera in the bag. I walked back out and moved my car to the other side of the Pizza Inn where it couldn't be seen from The Castle.

I climbed the fence behind the trash dumpster onto the roof and found a good spot to watch the front door. From the roof I had a slightly different angle than I'd had before, but what I saw was almost exactly the same: nervous guys in boring cars driving up to The Castle. As before, each one looked around nervously giving me a perfect chance to get a good picture.

I stayed on the roof for two and a half hours. Mitch came back and left seven times while I was up there. Three times I saw Sam's truck behind him and four times I didn't. It didn't matter; he sent me a text each time to let me know he had it under control.

At three o'clock, Caroline came out the front door and walked to her Thunderbird. She wore a conservative blue pantsuit, with low heels. If I didn't already know she ran a house of domination, I would have pegged her as an executive or an attorney. She walked with confidence, pausing only once to glance at the Pizza Inn parking lot. She did not look up toward the roof.

After she pulled away, I climbed down off the roof. I drove around to the front to continue my surveillance in air conditioned comfort. Right after she left, I saw something slightly different. A middle-aged woman in a white 2008 Cadillac Escalade Hybrid parked in front of the door. Unlike the other women I'd seen go inside, none of these pictures were going to interest Pat very much.

Also unlike the other girls, she looked nervous. She looked even more nervous than the guys I'd seen thus far. As they had, she gave me several good photo opportunities by looking around as she waited for the door to open. I briefly wondered if she was nervous because she had a gun in her small purse that she planned to use. I quickly dismissed the thought.

Nobody that nervous could hit anything with a gun anyway. I guess if men patronizing a dominatrix tend to be nervous, women might be even more so. That's probably too broad a generalization to draw based on watching one extremely nervous woman enter The Castle. However, I can only form an opinion based on what I see, and what I saw was one extremely nervous woman.

After she went in, I saw two more nervous men enter before she came out. The first drove a bright red 2009 Chevy Impala, which looks much sportier than the Impala my grandfather taught me how to drive when I was fourteen. The second man drove a late nineties Dodge Dakota pickup.

Other than the distinctly different vehicles, the two men who showed up between three-thirty and four o'clock acted exactly the same. They paused for the same number of great pictures and hesitated for exactly five seconds before knocking on the door. The excitement of surveillance work is much like the excitement of being a fireman.

At four-fifteen, my phone rang as the lady in the Escalade came out the front door. She looked a little less nervous now, and very much more in a hurry. She walked briskly to the hybrid as I answered the phone.

"Jeff, we may have a problem!" It was Sam The Man and he sounded as nervous as the people I'd been watching visit The Castle for the last two days.

"What's up?" I tried to sound calm. Since I felt pretty calm, that wasn't very hard to do.

"I don't know, but your pizza boy just carried a pizza into a real nice house in Lake Highlands. Aren't they supposed to wait outside for safety?"

"I guess so, but maybe they get bigger tips if they go in. I'm not an expert in the field. Why are you so worried?"

"He parked his car right behind a car I recognized. How many people do you know who drive blue retro Thunderbirds complete with the round window in the back?"

I wasn't calm, now, "Just one. Get in there and get him."

He snorted, "Yeah, right. What do I say?"

I had the first inspiration I had since I'd decided to rent Mitch's stuff. "Say you're Pizza Inn security and entering a home is a clear violation of company safety procedures. Tell Mitch to report back to Jeff immediately. He'll know that means you're with me. If there's a threat, he'll head here; if there's not, let him explain what is going on."

"Okay. I can do that."

"Try to get him out of there if possible. I don't like the coincidence."

I heard him shutting the car door as he said, "Me either. Keep watching Rachel. I'll handle this."

I no longer cared much about discretion. I moved my Eclipse directly across from The Castle and backed into the closest parking place to the door. I shut off the engine and spent twenty minutes nervously and helplessly waiting for any word from Sam or any sign of Rachel coming out of The Castle.

At four-fifty, Sam The Man called. He didn't laugh, but his voice did, "You were right. Mitch was in serious danger of contracting a potentially fatal sexually transmitted disease. Fortunately, I arrived in the nick of time to prevent anything from happening."

"She wanted laid? She runs a damn whorehouse for submissive men, and she has to seduce pizza boys to get laid. That doesn't make any sense."

I regretted the comment before Sam The Man had time to respond, but I couldn't think of anything to say that would make it better.

He sighed deeply before speaking slowly and softly, "You know you shouldn't have said that, right?"

"I know."

"And I know I shouldn't have kicked your ass at Club Clearview when I did. Instead of taking turns apologizing for the rest of our lives, can we just agree to drop it?"

"I can if you can. What about Rachel?"

He laughed, "I didn't mention my first reaction to her new career. I don't see any reason to tell her what you said."

"Thanks, man."

"No problem, I won't make it there in time to pick her up. I'm going to call her and tell her I'm working on something with Freak, and let her know you're picking her up."

Two minutes later, he called back to say she'd be right out. When I hung up the phone, I started up the Mustang to get the air conditioning going. Seasoned private eyes like me are used to the heat, but I try to protect damsels in distress without subjecting them to undue discomfort.

As Rachel walked out the front door, I saw the red Saturn Sky speeding across the parking lot past the Pizza Inn. It screeched to a stop in front of The Castle. I could barely see the driver because of the tinted windows, but I saw that he was looking out his passenger window. That meant he was looking at Rachel. I saw him raise one arm to shoulder height, but I didn't see a gun.

Even though I didn't see it, I knew it was in his hand. There was no way I could shoot him without risking hitting Rachel. I had no time to decide what to do. If I had, I don't know what might have happened. I put my pride and joy in gear and floored it. The 4.6 liter, 281-cubic-inch, 319 hp engine did its job. I went from zero to the side of a red Saturn Sky in almost no time at all.

As my left front bumper hit the Saturn's rear bumper we both started spinning. I came to rest with my hands shaking and my engine smoking. I jumped out of the car with my gun in my hand, and looked for Rachel. I saw her hiding behind a tree and turned toward the Saturn.

It spun for another second or so before finally stopping. I pointed my gun at the driver's side door which faced me. I still couldn't make out the driver, but his hands were below window level. He put the car in gear without looking my way and took off in the direction he was pointing. He had a flat tire, but I doubt if that's what caused him to run over the curb as he passed the Pizza Inn and got onto the service road.

If my baby could still run, I might be able to catch him, but I was here to protect Rachel, not chase a shooter in my wrecked car. Besides, I doubted very much that my car was operable. Ford designed and built the Mustang for speed and comfort, not confrontation. Even if Carroll Shelby himself had built this one, it wasn't likely to run after what I just did to it.

As Rachel ran to my side, it occurred to me that the driver of the Saturn might soon learn the hard way that God designed and built Sam The Man for confrontation, not speed or comfort. I wanted to be there when he did.

49 New Job

Pat was at the front desk when I got to the office at ten-thirty Thursday morning. He looked up when I walked in, "Long night?"

The night hadn't been that long, but the morning spent trying to get my car towed had been a pain. I doubted that Pat really cared about that, so I just said. "Do I look that bad?"

"No, you look fine. I heard you had some excitement."

I shouldn't have been surprised. Even though Pat does almost no field work, he hears everything that happens that might concern him. Obviously, an attempted homicide being thwarted by one of his employees qualifies as something that might concern him.

It hadn't occurred to me to call him during the three hour crime scene investigation or my ensuing discussions with various members of the Dallas Police Department. I'm not sure why not. I didn't bother asking who'd told him about it. For one thing, he wouldn't answer. Also, it didn't matter.

"It might have been more exciting if I hadn't been there. When Freak has a bad feeling, something bad usually happens. I'm glad he hired us. Should I have called you?"

"I don't see why. From what I hear, by the time it got exciting, it was over. Unless you needed a proverbial pat on the back, there's not much I could have done."

"I didn't. Do you want me to tell you about it, or type up the report?"

He waved me away and buried his head in some paperwork as he answered. "Type the report, of course. Have you talked to the client?"

I answered, "Not directly, Sam picked up Rachel after the shooting. He said he'd let Freak know what happened. Should I call Freak?"

"No, you type up the report. I'll call the client. I should try to contribute something to my own agency."

It was ten minutes after noon when I finished typing up the report and uploading surveillance pictures. Pat had been standing silently at my doorway for fifteen minutes. I hit the print button and looked up at him.

"It's done."

"Good. Why don't you go get something to eat while I read it? We'll talk about it when you get back."

"What about Rachel?"

"She's fine. She's with Sam and Freak at the Pegasus office. She couldn't be safer."

I knew that to be true, so I headed out. I went to one of the fifteen Subways within walking distance of our office and had a meatball sub. Our office is only a ten minute walk from Pegasus, and I considered dropping by, but decided against it. Sam and I agreed to let bygones be bygones, but that didn't mean we were best of friends who should just drop in on each other uninvited.

As I walked though Deep Ellum back toward our office on Canton Street, I noticed the number of 'For Lease' signs more than usual. For the first time, it really hit me that the same signs would soon be up where the 'Secure Investigations' sign currently hung. I felt bad for Pat, who'd been running the place since before I was born. It occurred to me that I should feel bad for me, but I couldn't do it.

I felt bad for the once vibrant historical district that now had little left but a few bars, a few art galleries, and a boatload of empty buildings. I felt bad for all the people who used to think they were going to make money with one of the businesses in the area. Even when it thrived, Deep Ellum was busier, and more dangerous, at night. But now it wasn't that busy even at night.

As I passed the building that housed 'Coyote Ugly' for a few months before it closed down, I tried to think about myself instead of the area. I should have been worried about my career more than a stupid bar that opened up because of a stupid movie and failed quickly and predictably. Instead, I just felt glad that Rachel was still alive. Either I was just living in the moment, or I was naively ignoring the fact that my boss had recently told me my job would be eliminated by the end of the year.

At twelve-forty-five, I walked back into the office. Pat wasn't at the front desk so I walked back to his office. He wasn't there either, so I walked to my office. He was sitting at my desk.

He looked up from my monitor as I walked in, "Nice pictures. You might make more money taking pictures than what I pay you."

"I could probably make more money standing out in front of the library with a cardboard sign, but it's not what I want to do. Other than the pictures of hot girls, did you see anything interesting in the report?"

He smiled, "A man my age deserves more respect than that. I only studied the pictures to better understand the report."

"Did they help?"

"They did. Obviously, the one picture you most wanted to take isn't there. Do you think its bad luck or by design?"

I knew he was talking about the lack of a clear picture of the guy who fired at Rachel. I'd been thinking about that question almost constantly since I'd run my Mustang into his Saturn Sky. I still hadn't decided.

"I don't know." I answered. "What do you think?"

"From the pictures and your report, it looks like bad luck. He doesn't seem to know you're even there during his first visit. He just happens not to turn toward you. If he'd been avoiding your camera, he'd have recognized your car when he showed up to shoot her. He wouldn't have given you the chance to act."

His theory made sense. I'd liked it when I thought of it last night, and I still liked it. I said, "Probably not. Of course, if he's killed before and gotten away with it, maybe he's getting overconfident."

"It's possible," Pat admitted. "We'll know more when the police finish analyzing the bullet they found in the tree."

"They will. I won't. That bullet will match the gun that killed Mrs. Woodbury. I'm sure of it."

"What if the cops say it doesn't?"

I knew Pat was playing Devil's advocate, but I considered my answer carefully.

"If they do, then there's something really fishy here. Somebody's lying big time, probably more than one somebody."

Pat stood up and walked around the desk. He was grinning ear to ear as he walked to me and put his hand on my shoulder. "I'm so glad to hear you can come up with a conspiracy theory to explain the facts even before you hear the facts. I think you're going to love your new boss."

"What new boss?"

"I told you I'd help you find a job with another agency, remember?"

"Of course, I remember, but that was for when you shut this place down at the end of the year."

"I might shut it down sooner, if I get everybody placed. You've got an opportunity I don't think you're going to want to pass up."

"I do?"

"You do. Carl and Freak want you to go work for Pegasus."

Pegasus was fast becoming the premiere detective agency in Dallas. I'd never had the heart to mention that to Pat, but it was a fact. I'd also never dreamed of leaving Secure to go work for them. I'd have never done that to Pat, but if he was shutting down Secure, I couldn't think of any reason not to go.

I asked, "When do they want me to start?"

Pat smiled, "Now. But I told them you couldn't start until tomorrow morning."

"You don't want two weeks notice?"

"It wouldn't matter. You'd still be working on the same case."

"I guess so, but at least it would be billable for you."

He shrugged, "I'm going out of business, Jeff. That doesn't matter now. The good news is they're going to match your salary."

I laughed, "Why exactly is that good news?"

"Because I told them I've been paying you what you're worth, not what I could afford."

50 Employee Orientation

"It's official. I'm no longer the newest employee of Pegasus Investigations. Welcome aboard." April's smile always lights up a room, but her smile this morning seemed more contented than designed to impress.

I'd arrived at Pegasus Investigations at nine in the morning and spent twenty minutes filling out employment paperwork. I was now the new employee. I'd seen no sign of Freak or Carl.

I asked April, "Where are the bosses?"

"Carl's in Colorado looking into things. Freak's on personal business; he'll be back in a little while. He wants you to review the case notes before he gets back."

She showed me to an office and I started reading the case notes. It didn't surprise me that Carl's notes were detailed and organized, while Freak's were more like a personal journal. It did surprise me that by the time I finished reading everything, I was convinced that Woodbury had nothing to do with the murder of his wife.

I walked back to the lobby. April was sitting at her desk looking sexy as she always does. I was thinking about what a lucky man Freak was to have her, when it occurred to me that the early case notes were dated on the day after their wedding.

"Did ya'll even have a honeymoon?"

April looked up, "Not really, or at least not yet. We're detectives. We don't always get to decide when we work and when we play. You've been a detective for a long time; you should know that."

"I guess I thought there might be some exceptions for the guy who owns half the agency."

She laughed, "Maybe, but not this time. Let's just say he was inspired by staff to prioritize this case."

By staff, I knew she meant herself. I didn't know of any connection between her and Woodbury, but I knew April could inspire her husband, or any man for that matter, to do or not do almost anything.

"I see," I said. "What inspired you to make the case a priority?"

She smiled, "You're a detective. You'll figure it out. Did Pat tell you what's going on with my husband?"

As she asked, she looked very worried. Nothing Pat had told me would cause her to be worried.

I answered honestly, "No."

"He's sick. He and Carl have long planned to try to hire you away from Pat, but his illness made it a priority."

186

"Is it serious?" As soon as I asked it, I realized it was a stupid question.

"Yes, it's serious. He's getting a kidney transplant this weekend. I have to be with him. Can you handle things here until he's up and around?"

I didn't really know how long it took to get up and around after a kidney transplant. If it were anybody else, I'd assume it would take a long time. With Freak, it wouldn't surprise me if he were running through fire again the day of the surgery.

With as much confidence as I could muster I said, "I'll handle it."

She pretended to share the confidence I was pretending to feel. "I need to be with him. Before I go, let me show you how to work the doors and windows."

"I know I'm the new guy here, but I've been working doors and windows for a long time, April. I think I can handle it without a training session."

She smiled the smile that once made her the most popular bartender in Dallas, "Not these, Baby. I promise you haven't worked anything like these."

She opened a desk drawer and pulled out a remote control. "The first thing you need to know about working the windows is where they are."

She hit the remote and the painting on my right quickly slid away revealing a window to the waiting room at the top of the stairs.

I said, "Nice. Maybe, I do need a training session."

She slid the remote across the desk to me. "It won't take long. The button marked 'W' opens or closes that panel. If it's open, that button closes it. If it's closed, that button opens it. The button marked 'U' unlocks the door from the waiting room to the lobby. The button marked "L" locks the same door."

I looked at the remote. It had six buttons. "What do the other three do?"

"This office and the windows are all bulletproof and thankfully explosion proof as long as the shields are up. The button marked "R" raises the shields over the windows. The button marked "L" lowers them so you can look out the exterior windows."

"I've heard people call this place a fortress. I didn't realize they meant it literally."

"They do. It is. Carl and Freak both say it's saved their lives a few times. It's important, though, not to let everybody know about it. Strangers and possible enemies should never see its features. Always cover the waiting room window before letting anybody into the lobby."

"I understand. What's the 'S" button do?"

"I can't tell you."

I smiled, "Why not? Am I still a stranger?"

April smiled, "You've never been a stranger here, Jeff. I don't know what it does. I know Freak doesn't know either. I don't think Carl even knows."

I doubted that, but I let it slide. April spent another ten minutes showing me features of the security system. After she left to be with Freak, I spent ten minutes playing with the remote control. After I put the remote back in the drawer, I sat at April's desk and returned to the case notes. It took me three minutes reading the case notes to realize Freak had forgotten to do one important thing.

It's not like Freak to forget things. His illness had affected him more than I thought it might. Maybe, he really isn't a superhero. Either that or maybe a bad kidney is a form of Kryptonite.

I started reviewing the case notes more thoroughly trying to see if I'd missed something. I was rewriting Freak's notes in the manner that Pat had taught me, which was apparently the same manner Carl uses, when I heard somebody climbing the outer staircase. April told me with the shields down, I'd hear it before anybody reached the door, but I hadn't realized it would be this loud.

I picked up the remote as I watched Mistress Caroline walk cautiously across the waiting room to the lobby door. She hesitated briefly, and reached for the buzzer. As she rang it, I covered the secret window, and then unlocked the door.

I hit the intercom button on the desk and said, "It's open; come in."

She walked confidently across the lobby with none of the hesitation she'd shown in the lobby. She held her head high and barely glanced down enough to see me still seated behind April's desk.

"I demand an explanation. Rachel tells me you had people watching my building without my permission."

In her parking lot, she'd intimidated me without even trying. Now on my first day as an employee of Pegasus Investigations, she was trying to intimidate me in our office, and failing completely. I smiled, but it was wasted on her, as she was still trying to intimidate me by not even looking at me.

"Actually, I didn't have people watching your building. I was watching your building. It's a free country. I don't need your permission to watch it."

That got her attention a little. She looked me in the eye and said sharply, "You might want to watch your…"She stopped in mid-sentence.

Her tone softened when she continued, "You? You were the one watching my building? You told me you were a pizza boy."

"I lied. It's an occupational hazard. I was afraid somebody might try to hurt Rachel, so I watched your building in case they did. I'm glad I did. If you're not glad, I'd love to hear why not."

She sighed. The wind was out of her sails and she sat down in one of the chairs opposite April's desk. "I'm glad you did. She'd probably be dead if you hadn't."

I asked, "Probably?"

"Okay, she'd be dead. Why?"

"I don't know. Somebody took a shot at her. That's all I know."

Caroline looked puzzled. "I mean, why were you worried about Rachel? Did it have something to do with Gertrude Woodbury?"

I didn't know if I was prepared to handle the office for a little while. I sure as Hell wasn't prepared to handle this. Without saying anything to Caroline, I reached for the phone on April's desk. I don't know what I'd have done if Carl hadn't answered.

Part 6 – American Heroes

"If you plead your pleading's come too late,
Like glory paid to ashes.
The reward is not on earth, you say,
But I promise you the cash is.

Think of what they'll say,
When justice sees the light of day
Some might think I'm crazy,
A suicidal play."

Long Sword Spectacular
'The Glory & The Cash'

51 Another Question

I was sitting outside Sheila Tobias' house at 9:30 Denver time on Friday morning when my cell phone rang. A glance at the caller i.d. showed it was the office. I wasn't sure if it would be Freak, April or our new hire, Jeff, so I answered professionally. "Pegasus Investigations, this is Carl."

"Mr. Jennings, I'm glad I caught you; it's Jeff. Rachel's boss, Caroline Smart, is sitting across the desk from me, and she just asked a question I can't answer. She wants to know if our concern for Rachel's safety has anything to do with Trudy Woodbury."

"Indeed, what did you tell her?"

"Nothing, I don't know the answer and I didn't want to guess. That's why I called you."

Jeff knew we were working the Woodbury case, but we hadn't really discussed if Rachel was a part of it.

I told Jeff, "Honestly, I don't know. Until we learn if the bullet that was fired at Rachel matched the one found in Trudy's head, we won't be sure."

He didn't answer, and I realized that he was reluctant to say anything in front of Ms. Smart. "Put me on speaker."

"Sure," he said. There was a slight pause. "Maybe April didn't cover everything this morning. How do you put a call on speaker on this phone?"

I walked him though the process, and made a mental note to ask April if it was time to upgrade our phone system. When I heard the sounds of ambient noise, I said, "Ms. Smart, I'm Carl Jennings, the co-owner of Pegasus Investigations. Jeff tells me you have some questions for me."

"Are you the reason Jeff was spying on my building?"

I don't like to lie. "I was paying him to be there. It was my business partner's idea."

"Why?"

"You do know somebody took a shot at Rachel, right?"

Ms Smart sighed, "Yes, and I know Jeff saved her life. I like the girl. I'm glad he was there to save her. I have the right to know why you thought that something like that might happen. I have other girls."

Her voice trailed off. I knew she had more to say, and I also knew that she was hoping not to say it. I knew I would remain silent long enough to give her time to continue. I hoped Jeff also would.

He did. The next voice I heard was hers, "Was it something to do with Trudy? If my girls and I are in danger, you need to tell me what's going on?"

I heard Jeff start to say something, but he stopped himself immediately. I'd always liked the kid. I was starting to like him even more.

I said, "Of course, we do. We're professional detectives. We'd be glad to protect all your girls. At very reasonable rates, I might add. But I don't understand why you think any of this has anything to do with Trudy Woodbury?"

"Aren't you investigating her murder?"

"We are." I admitted. "But we do sometimes work on more than one case at a time. Protecting Rachel was a side job we took on as a favor to a friend of one of our employees." It wasn't the complete truth, but it was close. April was an employee and her friend and husband, Freak, definitely wanted it done.

Caroline wasn't happy with my answer. "That doesn't answer the question, Mr. Jennings. I'm not here to hire you. I'm here to find out if somebody shot at Rachel because of something in her past or something in mine."

I was suddenly very interested to know about her past. I decided to quit being cagey. "We won't know for sure until the police finish running the ballistics, but it's likely that the gun that fired at Rachel is the same one that killed Mrs. Woodbury."

"How sure are you?"

"I'm not sure, but it's likely. You wouldn't be sitting in our office talking to us, if you didn't think it was possible. If you'd tell us why you think it's possible, that might help us know for sure."

She hesitated. As always when I talk on the phone about anything important, I wished I was talking in person, so I could read body languages and facial expressions. When I heard her sigh, I knew how her face must have looked.

"You're right. Trudy was my partner. We opened our first dungeon together many years ago. I'm the one that suggested she propose to her husband. I think I may have made a terrible mistake."

I tried to sound comforting, "Maybe not. I'm convinced he didn't murder her. We're going to find out who did."

I heard a commotion and Jeff's voice saying tensely, "Hold on. Don't go."

Then I heard Jeff again. "She's gone, boss. Do you want me to go after her?"

"No, we can find her again if we want. Call Sam and make sure he's with Rachel just in case. I'm going to make arrangements to get back as quick as I can. I don't know exactly what's going on, but it's happening in Dallas, not Denver."

"What should I do in the mean time?"

As he asked the question, Sheila Tobias came out of her house and walked to her SUV. I started the rental as I answered, "Why don't you see what you can find out about the bullet. If they seriously think Rachel's shooting might be related, they've run the tests already. They won't be rushing to let us know first thing, but somebody might tell you something."

"I'm on it, boss. Do you mind if I ask Pat to help. He's got more contacts over there than NASCAR has lug nuts."

I assured him that would be fine, as I again followed Ms. Tobias out of her neighborhood and onto I-25. I had forgotten how often new employees tend to ask for permission, instead of just doing what they think is the right thing to do.

As I followed her toward Ft. Collins, I called the airline to book the quickest flight to Dallas I could arrange. As soon as I was booked on a 4:20 flight to Dallas, I lost interest in following Ms. Tobias to Wyoming again. I took the next exit and turned back toward my hotel. On the way, I made two calls. The first one to Emily letting her know I was heading back to Dallas went beautifully. She was just as excited to hear I was coming home as I was to be coming home.

The second call didn't start out nearly as well.

52 Phone Calls

"How much did Tequila Sheila pay you to not find anything?"

I don't know how I expected Detective Paul to react to the news that I was flying back to Dallas without having found anything incriminating. I know I didn't expect her to accuse me of taking a bribe.

"I think you're overestimating my ability as much as you're underestimating my integrity. Did you really expect me to solve your case for you in a couple of days?"

She scoffed, "No, I expected you to spend more than a couple of days on it. When you came to my office, it seemed important to you. Now, it isn't. That bitch either threatens or bribes her way out of any situation. I assume it would take longer to threaten you than this, so I want to know what she paid you."

"Why, so you can demand a finder's fee?"

"That's harsh! I want that bitch in jail. I don't want her money."

"Unless it's illegal to drive to Wyoming in a gas-guzzling SUV, I didn't see her do anything that can land her in jail. If it is, I'll gladly testify in court that she drove there every day I followed her."

"Wyoming? What the Hell would she be going to Wyoming for?"

"I don't know, but it wasn't the fresh air. She drove to an old Steak and Ale in Cheyenne and went inside for several hours. Then she drove home. If that's really the life of an arch-criminal, include me out. Even by my standards, I was bored following her around."

She laughed, "Okay. Maybe I was wrong. Do you have the address?"

After I gave her the intersection, I asked, "A little out of your jurisdiction isn't that?"

"I don't plan to visit it officially. But the powers that be can't tell me what I can do in my off time in another state. Call me if you find anything in Texas that might interest me."

"I will. Let me know if you find anything in Wyoming of interest, too."

The call ended better than it had began, but I still didn't like her quick accusation. It made me wonder if she had a guilty conscience or a history with co-workers which had jaded her. If I were staying in Colorado, I might spend some time looking into that, but I wasn't.

I was back in the hotel room packing when my cell phone rang. It was Jeff and he sounded excited, very excited.

"It's official! Okay it's not actually official, but it might as well be. One of my sources and three of Pat's have confirmed that the bullet that was fired at Rachel came from the same gun that killed Mrs. Woodbury."

I'd been expecting that, but I still didn't know how to react. To us, it was enough evidence to clear Woodbury. But we already thought he was innocent. The D.A. would probably look at it as a coincidence if we couldn't find something other than the gun to connect the two shootings.

If we did connect them, he might decide it was a cover up. Knowing district attorney Dougie Kenth the way I do, I could easily see him making a case that Pegasus Investigations got the location of the gun from 'our client' and staged the second shooting to create reasonable doubt. McCoy could shoot that down for a jury if it got that far, but I didn't want it to get that far.

And if it did get that far, would McCoy even be the one trying the case? He was going to be giving Freak a kidney soon. I'd been assured that the surgery itself was safe for donor and recipient, but I read the news. There's no such thing as a completely safe surgery.

"So even employees get the famed silent act," Jeff said. "I'd been wondering about that."

"Sorry, I was just thinking about where this leaves us regarding Woodbury."

"It doesn't clear him?"

"I don't think so. It didn't clear Darryl Ray Robinson when it was used again to kill Mrs. Woodbury. I think our services are still needed."

"Hey, speaking of the gun, did anybody go and get the books from the property room? Freak's notes say that the clerk had agreed to copy them, but I don't see them or any indication that he picked them up."

Jeff had obviously studied our case notes much closer than I had. I think I liked that about him, too. "Freak's been a little indisposed lately. Do you want to go get the logbooks?"

He hesitated, "Well, the notes say the clerk wants April to come with Freak when he picks them up. I understand she's not planning to leave the hospital until after Freak's transplant."

It wasn't hard to guess why the clerk wanted April to pick up the log. The thing about having legendary beauty is that it becomes legendary. I told Jeff, "Sit tight, I'll see what I can work out."

One call to April's cell phone followed by one call to Blake Harrison was all it took to work out the logistics. Fifteen minutes later April called me back.

"I just got off the phone with Rachel. She and Sam The Man will watch Freak while I go with Jeff to get the logbooks from the Perv clerk. If Rachel lets anything happen while I'm gone, I'm blaming you."

"First off, wanting to trade an asset for a look at the legendary April Rose doesn't make him a pervert, it just makes him a man. Secondly, Rachel's damn near as tough as you; she won't let anything happen until you get back."

"She's nearly as tough as me, but not nearly as mean, but I won't argue. Freak called Crawford and he'll be there all day Monday. I'll call Jeff and we'll work out the plan. Are you coming home soon?"

"I am. I'll be back tonight."

"Good, Emily will be happy."

She hung up before I could ask if anybody else would be happy. It didn't matter; Emily being happy was what I cared about. I finished packing and headed for the airport. I was cautiously optimistic that we could solve this case without me having to leave Texas and Emily again.

I had one more call to make. I didn't look forward to it, but it had to be done. I dialed the number of the Office of Norfolk Commonwealth's Attorney. I held for eight minutes before Samantha Martin answered..

"Please tell me you've found something, Carl."

"I wish I could. I just wanted to let you know that there's been a new development in Dallas that makes it unlikely that my case is related to yours. I know you were hoping I'd find something related to T-Money's murder, but I don't think I'm going to find anything."

"I guess it was crazy for me to hope, maybe a little selfish, too. Are you at liberty to tell me what happened?"

"It's not public knowledge yet, but I'll tell you. There was another shooting with the same gun that killed Trudy."

Samantha interrupted, "Another victim? Damn, now I really feel bad."

"Don't, there's not another victim. The shooter missed this time, but the girl he shot at has no connection at all to T-Money or Virginia. I don't see how it can be related."

"How are you so sure?"

"She would have been seven when T-Money was killed and she's never lived anywhere but Texas."

"Okay, I believe you. Thanks for letting me know. I might have been happier if I thought there was still a chance to nail 'Seven' for something, but I appreciate you calling."

"You're welcome. If something else comes up, you'll be the first person I call."

"Thank you."

I'm really good at keeping my promises. Technically, though, that wasn't a promise.

53 Distressed Mistress

Rushing back to Dallas on Friday night had cost an extra hundred and three dollars and seventeen cents, but it gave me the weekend to be with Emily and work on the case. Time spent with Emily is never wasted, but the time I spent on the case pretty much was. Except for confirming what we already knew, I accomplished very little.

On Monday morning at 8:07, I sat in the office at April's desk reviewing the recent developments again. The gun that shot at Rachel was the same one that killed Mrs. Woodbury. District Attorney Kenth didn't think that meant Woodbury was innocent. In fact, sources indicated he was planning to have Lisha McDonough questioned as a person of interest in the shooting.

Seventeen attempts to talk to Caroline Smart again had failed. Rachel tried to help us, but also failed. Ms. Smart had told her to take a week off, with pay, to clear her head after her ordeal. Rachel thought she was being nice, but I didn't trust her. Jeff and April were going to go get the property room logbook.

I planned to leave the office at nine-thirty to go park outside The Castle to try again to talk with Ms. Smart. It seemed like a good plan, but it wasn't necessary. At 9:27, I heard footsteps on the outer staircase. For a small woman, Caroline Smart has a loud walk.

I suspect that has something to do with her choice of career. I wasn't sure which was the cause and which was the effect, but I guessed it didn't matter.

As she wordlessly approached the client chair, I said, "How nice to see you, Ms. Smart. May I get you cup of coffee or something?"

She glared at me. It was a look that Woodbury would have been proud of back in the day, but I didn't wilt. I looked back at her impassively.

"You may not. You do not need to get me coffee; nor do you need to harass me or try to suck up to me. I'm here because I'm going to talk to you. Do you record conversations in this office?"

I answered easily, "Sometimes, but never without permission. If you want me to record this I will. If you don't, then I won't. I should warn you, though. I have a very good memory."

"I know you do. I also know you have a reputation for complete honesty. I checked you out quite thoroughly before I decided to do this. Your reputation suggests that if comes down to your word against mine, you will win. I'm very much hoping it doesn't come to that."

"I see no reason why it should." Her clipped tone of voice was apparently contagious.

"You do not. I know that. You might, though if I tell you what I came to tell you. I need a promise from you."

I smiled, "Of course you do. You had me checked out. I guess your friends at city hall told you how I feel about promises."

"You underestimate me, Carl. You should not do that. You also underestimate yourself and your own reputation. I will not do that. I know that you will do what you feel you have to do with any information I share with you. Will you promise me to let me know what you decide to do, before you do it."

"What are you afraid I might do?"

"I fear nothing."

She said it in the same terse, confident voice she'd been using, but I didn't sense the same confidence. She feared something. I really wanted to know what.

"Of course you don't. People fear you, not the other way around. I would promise to tell you, but I don't know why you want me do so. Is it so you can kill me if I plan to do something that you do not like?"

She laughed. Surprisingly, it was a soft pleasant laugh. "I do not kill people. I know you think I might because you know my career. You must understand that as a Dominatrix, I only hurt people who want me to do so. Some people need to be hurt as much as a diabetic needs insulin. My staff and I provide a service."

"I understand that. It's not my place to judge you or your business. It's supposed to be a free country. If I ever feel the need to be whipped, I'll look you up."

She laughed again, "Oh, I'm sure Freak or Rachel can hook you up with somebody to do it for free. Rachel has quite a knack for it; maybe you can persuade her to do it. Back to business, will you promise to let me know before you act on any information I provide you."

I wanted the information, and I figured between the security of my office and my own survival skills I could protect myself from any threat she proved to be.

"I promise."

She breathed a sigh of relief. She'd tried not to let on at all that she'd been afraid that I wouldn't, but she obviously had been. I chose not to gloat.

"I'll be right back," she said.

"Seriously, you're leaving after all this build up? You can't tell me what you came here to tell me?"

"I am going to my car. I did not actually come here to tell you something. I came here to give you something. If you wish you may come to the car with me."

I didn't want to insult her by going with her, but I also didn't want her to change her mind. "I could use some fresh air. If you don't mind, I'll join you."

We walked wordlessly down the stairs and across the street to the parking lot. Her car was a late model blue Thunderbird. A chauffeur stood beside it stiffly. I've seen chauffeurs standing stiffly beside a lot of cars, but this was the first time I've ever seen a chauffeur for a two door sports car.

She walked up to the chauffeur and held out her hand. He handed her the keys and she walked to the trunk. She opened it and pulled out a black leather suitcase. It looked expensive and heavy. I went to take it from her.

"I will hand it over to you in your office." She closed the trunk and handed the keys back to the chauffeur. "You may wait out here."

We walked back to my office in silence. She didn't speak until we were once again seated at April's desk.

"I told you last week that I made a mistake. The mistake was not encouraging Trudy to marry. I do not know how the marriage worked out for Mr. Woodbury, but it served its purpose for Trudy. My mistake was not following her instructions when she died."

She paused and looked at me, so I asked, "Instructions?"

"I've known Trudy for years and years. She owned this suitcase when I met her. Shortly after she married, she asked me if she could trust me with an important favor. I said yes, of course, but I guess I lied."

"Maybe you were wrong. That doesn't necessarily mean you lied."

"You do not need to try to make me feel better. In fact, it might be better for you if you don't. I am giving you her suitcase in a probably futile attempt to make myself feel better. If you do it for me, I might change my mind."

"I presume there's a reason why you think I should have it. What's in it?"

"I do not know what it contains, nor do I want to know. She asked me to give it to her husband if anything happened to her. Obviously, I did not do as she asked."

"I guess I know why you didn't."

"You do. I saw no reason to give her suitcase to her killer."

"So why exactly are you giving it to me?"

She hesitated. She was a strong, hard woman. For a split second, she looked defeated, but she recovered quickly. "I hope that something in it will lead you to the person who did kill her."

It's not a good idea to look a gift horse in the mouth, but I had to ask, "Why not the police?"

She laughed derisively and for the first time spoke in an informal tone, "So they could screw this up, too? I'll take my chances with you."

She stood to leave, and I passed her on the way to the door. As I opened it, she said, "You will remember your promise?"

"I will."

"Please let me know immediately if you even suspect that her death or the attack on Rachel has anything to do with the incident."

"What incident?"

54 Accidental Deaths

Ms. Smart refused to discuss what she called the incident. Instead, she simply gave me a name and assured me that with my talents I'd be able to learn all I needed to know. The name was Kendall Crawford. My talents were not unduly tested in the quest for information about the incident. It took only two minutes on Google and one trip to Blake's office.

Kendall Crawford died of asphyxiation last August. The tragedy occurred in a private loft near the intersection of Cedar Springs and Oak Lawn. No charges were ever filed, and the official cause of death was listed as an accident. The internet offered little more than that. I called Blake to see if he could provide more.

"Why are you interested in the Crawford case? I thought you were travelling the country chasing Mrs. Woodbury's skeletons."

"That's the thing about skeletons. You never know where they may turn up."

"I guess not. Why don't you come down here? You may hear something interesting if you do."

I locked the suitcase in the safe, secured the office, and walked straight to Blake's office in the George Allen Federal Building. His admin, Ana Marie, smiled as she saw me enter. Smiling hadn't always been her reaction to seeing me, but she'd finally decided I probably wasn't going to get Blake fired. I hoped she was right about that.

"He's expecting you, go on in." She said as she nodded toward his open office door.

He was expecting me, but I wasn't expecting he'd have company. Detective Teresa Randall stood as I entered. "Blake said you wouldn't mind if I stayed for this. The Crawford case was mine. You don't mind, do you?"

I smiled and shook her hand, "Of course not. I'm grateful for your help."

She laughed, "Don't stop me if you've heard this, but I'm actually hoping for your help. I'm not happy with the official decision, and I'm hoping you'll find something."

"Your friend, Annette, might advise you not to get your hopes up. She's not happy with how little I found out in Denver."

"Actually, she is. That's why I was sitting here talking to Blake when you called."

I'd wondered how Blake had gotten her here faster than I could walk from my office. As usual when I couldn't think of anything to say, I said nothing. Detective Randall looked from me to Blake; and then from Blake to me several times. Blake showed no expression.

Finally she said, "Are you going to tell him or am I?"

Blake answered, "Weren't you told not to discuss the case with anybody?"

She simply nodded.

"Maybe you should leave and Carl and I can talk baseball and make lunch plans."

She immediately recognized that Blake was trying to protect her. She looked a little relieved at first, but then her resolve steeled.

"Screw that. I'm through paying for mistakes from long ago." She gave me a hard stare. "I trust you guys and I'm grateful for all that you've done for me. But I trust myself now, too. I know Annette and I aren't wrong. If we are, I'll take the consequences, but we're not. "

She turned back to Blake and said softly, "Thank you. I appreciate it. I really do."

Blake continued for her, "But?"

"But, I'm all in on this one. Somebody's getting away with murder, and my job is to prevent that. I'm going to do my damn job; the hell with the consequences."

Blake coughed, "I've heard this. I'm going to go check on my staff." He smiled at me, "Don't steal anything while I'm gone that I might miss."

He closed the door behind him. I'd seen him do that many times; usually when he was letting me use his computer to research something he shouldn't let me use it to find. If he had to now, he could swear that he had no reason to think that Detective Randall had told me anything she wasn't supposed to tell me.

Despite the fact that the door was closed, Teresa spoke softly. "Annette went to Wyoming and checked out the place you told her about. She saw Tequila Sheila go in; then she saw several other people go in and out. She couldn't make anything out of it. So she took a bold step."

"That doesn't surprise me."

"It shouldn't. She decided to follow a car with Colorado plates. It drove to Denver, and she pulled him over. He admitted what he'd been doing in Wyoming and insisted it wasn't illegal. He also offered her a nice bribe to let him go without his wife finding out."

She paused. I said, "The bribe is definitely illegal. Was what he was doing in Wyoming illegal?"

She smiled, "Probably not. Even if it was, it was out of her jurisdiction. You want to take a guess what he was doing in Wyoming?"

I thought about the people I'd seen going into the old restaurant site in Wyoming; compared it with what Jeff had written about the people he'd seen going into The Castle, and smiled.

"I'm not sure it would count as a guess. I'd rather you tell me about Kendall Crawford. As far as we know, nobody's died in Ms. Tobias' Wyoming dungeon. I'd like to hear about the man who died in Ms. Smart's Dallas dungeon."

"How'd you... Never mind. You're good. I knew that. Kendall Crawford was a regular client at The Castle when it was located off Cedar Springs. During a session last August, he choked on his own drool while hogtied and gagged during a role-playing scene."

"What type of scene?"

"Does it matter?"

"I don't know. Sometimes you don't know if a question is important until you know the answer. Is there any reason you shouldn't tell me?"

"I guess not. We never released the details, but I can tell you. Mr. Crawford was dressed as a high school cheerleader, complete with short skirt and pompoms. The suspect, Melissa Kendra, wore a man's suit and tie. The scene was that 'the girl had violated the school's fraternity rules by sleeping with a star basketball player and the principal was punishing 'her'."

She looked at me, obviously expecting me to be shocked. Since I've met Freak and his circle of friends and acquaintances, I'm not as easy to shock as I used to be. Instead, I said, "Not my cup of tea, but it sounds like a good time if you're into that sort of thing. What caused this innocent little fantasy scene to end so tragically?"

She was the one who looked shocked, "Innocent? a good time?" She calmed quickly. "Oh, I get it. You're 'Mister Open Minded' now, because your business partner is the king of freaks."

"Actually, he abdicated his throne. But, yes, I've seen stranger things than a guy in a cheerleader costume. How did he end up dead?"

"He was gagged. He choked to death on his own saliva. His whore swore that it was an accident and that she did everything she could to prevent it."

I noted her use of the word 'whore,' but let it slide. "What did the technicians say?"

"That's the part I don't like. At first they said it looked like homicide. Then the official coroner's report ruled it accidental. I asked to be allowed to continue the investigation."

"But you got told, 'no.' Why?"

"I don't know. But this is Dallas."

Her implication was clear. She thought corruption was involved. Considering that the FBI had spent the last few years investigating and occasionally filing charges against high level government employees and elected officials, she probably had a valid point. She also had a friend in Denver who was convinced that the same thing had happened to her investigation.

"Maybe we can find something to change their mind. I should talk to Melissa Kendra myself."

"You can't do that."

"Why not? If y'all aren't pursuing charges against her, there's no reason I shouldn't talk to her."

"You should, but you can't. She overdosed on prescription meds."

I asked, "Suicide?"

She stood up and walked to the door. As she opened it, she turned to me, "Accident. Let me know if you learn anything interesting."

She closed the door behind her before I could answer. I had a suitcase to open, but obviously that would have to wait. I walked behind Blake's desk to read about two deaths which had been ruled accidental.

55 Matching Luggage

"Open the son of a bitch; burn the damn thing or throw it away. I don't give a shit what you do with it."

Woodbury obviously had no interest in his late wife's suitcase. That didn't surprise me, but I didn't want to open it without his consent. Mistress Caroline's instructions had been to give it to him, not to a detective working for his mistress.

"You should care at least a little," I said. "It may contain evidence that will clear you."

"So? McCoy's taken the case. I'll be cleared. His guilty clients don't get convicted. I didn't kill her, so it's just a matter of time."

Obviously, Woodbury didn't know about the kidney transplant. I saw no reason to tell him about it. "You're probably right. Since you don't care, I'm going to open it. Even if you don't, I'd like to see the killer punished."

"Of course you do; you were never married to her," he said. He set the phone down and turned to let the guard escort him back to his cell before I could respond. I was starting to notice that people often didn't wait for my response. I noticed it, but it didn't bother me. As I walked back to my office, I wondered briefly if it should.

Rachel and Sam The Man were waiting in the lobby when I got to the office. They followed me in without saying anything.

I asked, "What's up? I thought you kids were going to stay with Freak at the hospital."

Rachel answered, "We were, but I couldn't take it any longer. As soon as April got back, we left. We decided to come here."

If April was back at the hospital, I was surprised Jeff wasn't back at the office with the logbook. "Other than the fact that it's a hospital, was everything okay?"

Sam The Man answered, "Yes. Freak's convinced it's no big deal. I'm the only man on earth who can tell when he's fronting, and he's not. His confidence is contagious."

"That it is. How's Larry Joe?" I was surprised as anybody to hear myself call McCoy 'Larry Joe,' but nobody commented on it.

"He's fine, I guess," Rachel answered. "Does he not have any friends or family?"

I thought about it. "Honestly, I don't know. Obviously, Freak is family. Other than that, I don't know. Maybe we should visit him."

Rachel said, "No need. They've moved him into Freak's room. I wouldn't call it the social event of the season, but he's got company."

I had a suitcase to open. I didn't want to send them away, but I wasn't sure I wanted to open it in front of them. I turned on the computer at April's desk. When I was logged in, I checked email as I thought about the suitcase. Rachel and Sam held hands and said nothing as I did.

Some silences are awkward, some aren't. The three people in the office that morning were all used to silence, so it wasn't awkward. At least, it didn't strike me as particularly awkward.

As I closed out of AOL, Rachel said, "Should we leave? We don't want to bother you. We're just really curious about any progress."

Sam added, "You know, really curious, since somebody took a shot at Rachel. I'm not saying I plan to go vigilante on his ass, but I'd like to know who did it if I decide I should."

I think I'd already made my decision, but if not, Sam's reminder clinched it. "If there was any progress to report, I'd report it. There was one interesting development. Let's check it out together to see if it's progress."

I locked the office door with the remote control. Sam recognized the significance of me locking the door, even if Rachel didn't.

"Do Rachel and I need to swear an oath of secrecy or sign a blood oath?"

I laughed, "I don't know." I unlocked the safe and pulled out the suitcase. "Let's see what's in this and then we'll decide."

"Where'd you get that?" Rachel shouted.

Her tone surprised me more than the question. I put the suitcase on the desk and took the lock picking kit out of the file cabinet where we keep it. "It was Mrs. Woodbury's. I take it you've seen this before."

Rachel looked surprised. "Sort of, I thought it was mine. Caroline gave me one just like it when I started at The Castle. What a strange coincidence."

"Actually, it's not a coincidence. Let's see what's in here."

I picked the lock and opened the suitcase. When Rachel gave me the impression the suitcase was standard issue Castle equipment, my hopes for finding anything interesting dwindled. On first inspection, I was right.

Rachel looked into the case, "Tools of the trade: whips, crops and paddles. Why would Mrs. Woodbury have a case like this?"

Sam laughed, "Because you were right at Fogo de Caio. Trudy worked at The Castle. I should have known as soon as Freak got nervous. That cat is scary."

"But that was just a joke."

I emptied the suitcase. There were many leather items other than whips, crops and paddles. There were also at least twenty padlocks in various sizes and colors, including black, red and pink. Some of the other items I could identify; some I didn't even want to identify. Nothing seemed the type of thing that Mrs. Woodbury would want to leave to her husband in the event of her untimely passing.

"I don't know what you were joking about, but I know Trudy Woodbury worked with Caroline at The Castle. She told her to give this suitcase to Woodbury if anything happened to her. What I don't know is why she did that."

Rachel laughed. Her laugh turned into a giggle. She barely managed to say, "No, you don't. But I bet we will soon." She stood up and zipped the suitcase closed. Then she turned it over and set it back on the desk. Five seconds later, the back of the suitcase popped up. Rachel opened it all the way to reveal a small storage area with a red spiral notebook in it.

"I take it Caroline didn't mention the secret compartment," Rachel said smiling.

I nodded. "I guess she figured a professional detective like me would be smart enough to find it on my own."

Sam laughed. "She doesn't know you well enough. She doesn't realize you're so smart you let other people find things for you. Let's see what's in the notebook."

I picked up the notebook. It was a five subject notebook like the ones college freshmen used to use back when note taking was a big part of the college experience. A notebook like this was a big part of my college experience for the one year I was in college. I looked at the subjects written on the divider tabs.

Eastfield Junior College didn't have classes in the subjects written on the tabs back then. They don't have classes in them now, either. However, law enforcement personnel in at least three states were going to want to see everything in this notebook.

If I told them about it, that is. I put the notebook in April's desk and locked the drawer. "I need to be alone when I look through this."

56 Five Subjects

Rachel and Sam weren't happy about leaving, but they were polite about it. As they stood, Sam said. "Do what you have to do with that notebook. I trust you and I trust you have reasons. Don't leave us out of this, though. We're in it, now."

"You are." I told them both, "I won't leave you out. I promise."

That satisfied them and they left. As soon as they were gone, I secured the office and called Jeff and asked him if they got the logbook.

"Yeah, we got it. April had the dude eating out of the palm of her hand in two seconds flat. Does that girl know how dangerous she is?"

"She does. Fortunately, she's sworn to use her power only for good. Have you looked at the logbook?"

"No, I left it with April. Did she not drop it by?"

"Not yet, she may have decided to look at it with Freak at the hospital. I guess mostly, I was checking in on you."

"I guess I should have called in. I guess I thought April would tell you what I found. If she didn't, you're not going to believe it."

I didn't bother to tell Jeff how many times I'd been told I wasn't going to believe something on this case. I also didn't tell him again that he wasn't expected to check in while working for Pegasus. I knew Pat was pretty O.C.D. about checking in and filing paperwork.

Instead, I just asked, "What did you find?"

I could almost hear him beaming as he answered, "A red Saturn Sky with a damaged front fender on the driver's side."

"You think it's the same one?"

"I don't know. The plates don't match, but the Sky is a pretty uncommon car with a pretty devoted following. Very few owners leave them in disrepair for long. I thought I'd hang around and take a few pictures of it, and whoever gets into it. If it's a dude who looks like the guy I took from the back, it'll it be real interesting to have a few shots of him from the front to go with it."

"I like that plan. Just in case, give me this one's plate number and I'll have it run."

He gave me the number and I called Blake. I had to hold for three minutes before he came on the line. While I waited, I reviewed case notes hoping for an epiphany. I was still hoping when Blake came on the line. "I've got about two minutes, buddy. What do you need?"

"Can you run a plate for me?"

"Sure, do you need it right now? I'm due in Commissioners' Court in five minutes."

I saw no reason to rush running a plate that might not even impact our case. I told him to get back to me when he could and gave him the plate number. I then turned my attention to the notebook. I didn't expect to like much of what I was about to read, but it had to be done.

Reluctantly, I opened the notebook. As I'd noticed earlier, the five subject tabs were labeled 'Aunt Sheila,' '7 Seaton,' 'Courtney Remington,' 'Melissa Kendra' and 'Kendall Crawford'. Not having a better plan, I decided to start at the beginning. I hoped to find something in the first two sections that might keep me from having to read the third.

What I found in the first section made me want even more not to read further, but also made it obvious that I wouldn't have a choice. The first twelve pages had header lines above the blue line followed by details below it. The header lines were the same on all twelve pages:

Name	Start Age	Start Date	End Date	Phone

The first line was similar to most of the rest:

Name	Start Age	Start Date	End Date	Phone
Thi Nguyen	16	9/14/86	11/27/89	801-###-####

The lines were in chronological order based on start date. The phone numbers were a mix of area codes, mostly Nevada, Colorado and Kansas. Very few of the start ages were 18 or higher. The oldest start age was 20; the youngest was twelve. If this list was what it appeared to be, I wanted Miss Tequila Sheila in jail every bit as bad as my friends with the Denver police did.

Several of the numbers were written over white-out. On the second page one line most caught my attention. It was the third line from the top, and it read:

Name	Start Age	Start Date	End Date	Phone
Tammy Chang	14	10/7/87	11/13/88	none

Lamont Allen and Annette Paul had told me that a girl named Tammy Chang had committed suicide in her jail cell after her arrest. If I'd had any doubt what this list meant as I started reading it, I didn't once I read her line. Chang may be the Asian equivalent of Smith or Jones, but this couldn't be coincidence.

Sheila Tobias had indeed been prostituting underage girls. She might still be. I turned to the twelfth page of the notebook. The last line read:

Julie Jackson   16   3/14/09   05/22/09   307-###-####

Julie apparently hadn't stayed in the business long, but she'd definitely been in it recently. Or maybe, she was still in the business, but no longer working for Sheila Tobias. Since The Castle in Dallas is a legit business, Ms. Tobias' dungeon in Wyoming might also be legit.

This list might have nothing to do with underage prostitution. Even if it did, nothing I'd read so far would count as evidence. I'd learned something, but I wasn't sure what. I wasn't eager to read the rest of the notebook, so I read every line of the 'Aunt Sheila' section. One more name stood out as I read the eleventh page.

Melissa Kendra   19   7/21/03   09/11/08   214-###-####

When I read that name, I was tempted to skip forward in the notebook, but I decided against. I flipped to the second tab to read about James '7' Seaton. Fortunately, as I flipped over I noticed pages filled near the back of the first section, also. Again it turned out to be lists. The header lines in this section were simpler and the first few lines made it clear what was being documented:

Date	Amount	Bank	Check #
1/24/99	$300	First National	2259
7/24/99	$300	First National	3543

Based on the dates, she'd started this part on the back page and continued toward the front. It didn't take a genius to figure out that this was a record of blackmail payments. If this notebook had belonged to anybody other than Gertrude Woodbury, I might have been shocked, or at least disappointed, to learn she had blackmailed her own aunt for years.

I looked over the rest of the entries. In June of 2004, she had quit writing the name of the bank, and started using bank routing numbers instead. The payments generally occurred about six months apart and the amounts steadily increased. The last entry dated 01/17/2009 was for $2000.

In addition to having something tangible to give Annette regarding Sheila Tobias criminal activity, I also had a plausible suspect in the murder Richard Woodbury was accused of committing. I expected to have four more suspects once I'd read the rest of the notebook. I hoped it would only be three, but I wasn't optimistic.

57 Guilty Bystanders

The second section started out much like the first. Instead of underage prostitutes however, this list appeared to be a list of criminals. At the very least, it was a list of crimes.

Name	DOB	Charge	Where	Date	Phone
James Seaton	7/4/76	Murder	Norfolk	1/8/96	415-###-####

It didn't surprise me that the murder of T-Money was first on this list. It did surprise me that a phone number was listed, but not that it was written on top of a thick coat of white-out. I resisted the urge to call the number immediately, but only barely.

I also resisted the urge to call Letot and ask him if he'd mind if I flew out to San Francisco to interrogate a suspect in the murder of Tasheika Monroe. Instead I read the rest of the list. The eighth line caught my eye.

Jessie Jones   4/7/78   Prostitute   Baltimore   6/7/01   410-###-####

The phone number matched the one Letot had given me for Courtney Remington. I knew she'd been a prostitute, but I was disappointed that Mrs. Woodbury would include that on her list of crimes. I chided myself for even allowing myself to be disappointed. I briefly wondered why I was worried about the recent relationship between the supposed childhood friends.

I put it out of my mind and read the rest of the list. There were twenty-four names in all. Of the other twenty-two, all but two had area codes in the Norfolk, VA area. Most of the crimes listed were misdemeanors, the two exceptions being an aggravated assault, and a grand theft auto.

The only other name on the list I recognized was the last one.

Sal Perlini   10/23/68   Forgery   Dallas   4/5/04   214-###-####

Sal Perlini was the previous tenant who had turned my office into a fortress. He'd done a damn good job of it, but nobody had ever told me why. I knew he'd been a commodities broker before he left town in a hurry.

He was also the reason that Maurice Letot and I knew each other so well. If Letot knew I had a notebook in my hand with Perlini's phone number, he'd probably be in my office now demanding that I give it to him. I didn't want to give this to him, so I decided not to let him know.

I turned the page expecting to see more columns and lists. Instead, I found descriptions of various crimes with enough detail to make Ann Rule proud. The crimes themselves were less major than the serial killings Ann Rule writes about, but the detail left little doubt that the unsolved crimes were committed by the people on the list.

James Seaton's section started by repeating what I'd learned in Virginia. It included the witnesses who had testified that he'd been in Virginia Beach and listed the reasons they'd lied. The details of the murder were described in great, almost loving, detail. These details took up most of four pages.

On the fifth page was the one line bombshell. "James '7' Seaton was paid $1000 for the premeditated murder of Tasheika 'T-Money' Monroe.' This sentence was written in big block letters quite unlike the small letters used in the rest of the notebook.

Underneath was taped a returned check showing that Gertrude Lund had paid James Seaton one thousand dollars on January 2nd, 1996 'for services to be rendered.' The check had cleared on the sixth. T-Money had been murdered on the eighth. Even McCoy would be hard pressed to convince a jury that murder wasn't the service to be rendered.

Only one page was dedicated to Courtney Remington's career as a prostitute. It included a copy of a personal advertisement and case numbers of two arrests, both dismissed. It wasn't as damning as the dossier on James 'Seven' Seaton, but I doubted if she'd want her husband to see it, either. I didn't plan to let that happen.

Sal Perlini had bounced a check to a Fort Worth excavation company in 2004 for $2,541. A copy of the returned nsf check was taped to the notebook. The address of the firm and the FWPD case number finished that page.

The rest the section contained varying degrees of detail and various levels of crimes. The common thread thoughout was that nobody in this section would want Gertrude to go public with what she knew. As a blackmailer, she had a gold mine. I checked the back of the section to see if there was a list of blackmail payments and dates. There wasn't. This section was apparently about protecting herself from James 'Seven' Seaton, not making money.

That made me wonder why she'd instructed Caroline to get this to her husband. Did she want him to continue the blackmail or did she want to know justice would be served after she died. She probably figured somebody in here would eventually kill her and wanted revenge. She was probably right.

I didn't want revenge, though. I wanted James Seaton and Sheila Tobias in jail. It was clear they both deserved to be there. Good honest cops also wanted them in jail, and I had a notebook full of information that should help make that happen.

But I couldn't take the chance that putting those two in jail would hurt my goal of freeing Richard Woodbury and reuniting him with my client. I'm a private detective. Sometimes it's important to remember that the clients pay the bills.

Reluctantly, I turned to section three to read how Gertrude Woodbury planned to use her childhood friend Jessie Jones' transformation into Courtney Remington to her advantage. I needn't have worried. The entire section consisted of her phone number and a single line. 'Call Mrs. Remington and tell her she can open the envelope.'

I wondered if I needed Woodbury to make that call or if Courtney would rather hear it from me. I decided I'd make the call myself after I'd finished the notebook. I skipped ahead to subject four, Melissa Kendra. Not surprisingly, this section contained no mention of her death by overdose.

In fact, this section contained very little writing at all. Instead, it consisted of twenty photographs taped to the pages with a date written underneath. The dates were chronological dating from 2001 to 2007. The pictures all contained one or more girls doing things that would not make their parents proud. One blonde girl was in every picture. I presumed her to be Melissa Kendra.

The acts ranged from the relatively benign tipping of a beer bong to a completely disgusting act that might be considered sexual by some, but not many. In between, were some drug usage, some sex and two pictures of her passed out on a canvass of empty liquor bottles. The last picture reminded me very much of something I read in Freak's case notes.

The girl was on all fours in what appeared to be the ladies lounge of an upscale nightclub. Two women were using her back as a foot rest as she stared straight down. In front of her was a familiar black suitcase. It was open and displayed about the same bondage tools that we'd found in Gertrude's bag earlier.

In the picture, she was naked. The women using her as a footrest were cropped out, but I pretty much knew who one of them was. I wondered if the gag the girl wore was in the suitcase locked in our office safe.

I also wondered if it was possible that the girl submitting herself in this picture was the same girl who'd accidentally killed a client while working as a dominatrix. I looked through all the pictures and scanned the remaining pages of section four and found them all empty.

I called Sam The Man. When he answered, I asked, "Is Rachel with you?"

"Of course, she's here and we're both fine. What's up?"

"Can I talk to her? I have a professional question for her."

When Rachel came on the line, I asked. "Is it possible to go from being a complete submissive to a professional dominatrix in a couple of years."

Rachel laughed, loudly and mirthfully. She was still laughing when I heard my cell phone ring.

58 Personnel File

Rachel eventually quit laughing long enough to explain to me that the career path to professional dominatrix starts as a submissive almost as consistently as the career path to NFL quarterback starts as a college quarterback. I learned a long time ago not to ask questions I didn't want answered so I left it at that.

The call to my cell phone had been from Jeff, so I called him back without checking the message.

"Dude, you are not going to believe this!"

Again, I saw no reason to argue with his statement, so I just said, "Try me."

"I just saw a guy get into the Saturn Sky and drive off. I got some great pictures, but we don't need them. It's the property room guy who gave us the logbook, Robert Crawford."

I looked down at the fifth tab on Gertrude's five subject notebook. Crawford is a common name, but it's not Smith or Jones. It could be a coincidence, but I doubted it.

I told Jeff, "I believe you. Are you following him?"

"Yes, but it's rush hour. We're not really moving."

"Stay on him. You've probably stopped him from killing once. You might need to do it again."

"If I do, I will. I'm in a rental now. If he tries anything, I may damage more than the Saturn's fender."

As soon as he hung up, I called Sam. "How fast can you get to The Castle?"

"Twenty minutes, fifteen if I have to. What's up?"

"Jeff's following a red Saturn Sky that may be our killer. They just left downtown. If he heads to The Castle, it'll be nice if we're waiting for him instead of chasing him."

Sam's laugh can be pleasant or jovial. This one was neither. "We will be. Can I give Rachel the first shot?"

I tried to calculate the odds of somebody who had nothing to do with the shooting driving to The Castle in a red Saturn Sky. I quickly concluded that the odds were approximately zero.

"Sure, just don't let him get the first shot."

I hung up the phone as Sam's laugh again echoed in my ears. If Robert Crawford drove to The Castle today, he wasn't likely to live long enough to stand trial. I wondered if the D.A. would want to prosecute Rachel. Since Larry Joe would almost certainly represent her, I doubted it.

I turned my attention back to the notebook. Kendall Crawford's tragic, allegedly accidental, death while visiting The Castle was not mentioned. Instead, I was treated to an in-depth description of a scam he'd allegedly operated out of his car dealership in Massachusetts.

Sixteen cars were listed. The first one was a 2004 Mazda Miata, sold in 2008 for $15,500 by Trusty Motors in Somerville. The license plate and vehicle identification number were included. Taped below the note was a classified ad, 'For sale: 2004 Mazda Miata; all power; 45,000 miles.' Beside the ad, she'd written 'Roanoke Times, 04/19/08.'

Taped below that was a repair bill for a 2004 Mazda Miata. The bill was dated 09/14/2007 and showed the vehicle with 96,000 miles. The other fifteen vehicles followed the same pattern. Only fourteen different repair shops were listed because two had been used twice. All the cars had then been sold by Trusty Motors.

It's not unheard of for a repair shop to get the mileage wrong. For fourteen different repair shops to get the mileage wrong on sixteen cars all later sold by the same dealership was uncommon enough to be laughable. The fact that Gertrude Woodbury had documented this evidence against Kendall Crawford made it also impossible to believe his death at The Castle was a coincidence.

I had another coincidence that probably wasn't a coincidence to check out. I called Detective Randall. I had to hold for twelve minutes before I reached her. I'm not a patient man by nature, but I can be when I have to be.

When she came on the line, I said, "You asked me to let you know if I found anything interesting regarding Kendall Crawford's death. I have. What do we do now?"

"Since you're asking, I presume you don't plan to simply tell me or bring it to me in a nice little gift wrapped box. Should I come to your office, or would you rather come to mine?"

Normally, I like to have home court advantage. Of course, normally I don't have a notebook full of evidence regarding crimes in four states in my office. I told her I'd meet her in her office. She invited me to come right away. I locked the notebook in the safe and walked to her office.

"Where's this evidence you promised me?" She asked as I entered her office.

I pointed to my temple and smiled.

"I'm not sure that'll be admissible in court."

"I'm not sure it will matter. You want to hear what I've got or not?"

She did, so I told her. When I was finished she asked, "So you think the two Crawford's are related? We talked to Kendall Crawford's parents in Massachusetts. They didn't mention a relative here in Dallas. They also told me he was an only child. I can see why you like Robert Crawford for this, but we can't arrest him based on what you've got. It's not illegal to drive a wrecked Saturn Sky or to have the same last name as the victim of an accidental death."

Her point was valid. The fact that Kendall and Robert had the same last name could be a coincidence, and Robert might not be the shooter that Jeff prevented from shooting Rachel. General Motors' Saturn division had probably made many Sky sports cars. A good percentage of them were probably red.

I admitted to her that I'd need more and stood up to go. As I walked to the door, she said, "Sorry. I appreciate your help, but I can't do anything based on this. Keep looking. Let me know if I can help. I'll do what I can."

I thanked her and left. As I was walking down the hall, I had the epiphany I'd been hoping for earlier. It started with a disturbing image of Kendall Crawford shortly before his death crossing my mind. That led to the thought that not everybody with the same last name was born with the same last name. Some were married to each other.

I walked back to Randall's office. The door was still open and she was sitting behind her desk. When I entered the room, she looked up, "Yes?"

"Did you mean it when you said you'd do what you could?"

"Of course" she answered way too casually. "Why?"

"I'm interested in Robert Crawford's personnel file."

She answered immediately, "I can't do that."

"Sure you can, you're the investigating officer on an attempted murder that may have been committed by a gun that disappeared from the property room he's supposed to maintain. That's not enough to arrest him, but it has to be enough to let you pull his file."

"Probably, but that doesn't mean I can show it to you."

"I don't need to see it. I just need you to tell me one thing about it."

"What?" she asked curtly.

"I want to know if there's a spouse listed."

"You're kidding, right?"

I wasn't kidding, but I also wasn't interested in arguing with her. "Will you do it or do I need to ask somebody else?"

"I'll do it, but I think you're insane."

I didn't reply. I just walked away wondering if she was right. I know almost nothing about the state of gay marriage in America, but I know that it's legal some places. I could go back to the office to see what Google had to say on the subject, but I had some things to do before I headed to the office.

I knew somebody who could tell me what I wanted to know, so I pulled out my cell phone. Bobbie Jo Nottingham answered on the third ring.

I asked, "Do you know which states have approved gay marriage?"

"No, but I guarantee Mandy does. She's right here; hold on."

59 Served Cold

"Massachusetts was the first state to legalize it five years ago on May 17th of 2004..." Mandy's knowledge of the gay rights movement and legal gains and losses was extensive, as Bobbie Jo and I knew it would be. The first sentence was the one that most interested me, but I let her continue her discourse until I got to the hospital where Freak and Larry Joe were convalescing.

I got to the room they were still sharing as Mandy started getting really warmed up on the subject of California's Prop 9. I'd tried a couple of times to politely end the conversation, but when Mandy gets on a roll, Mandy is on a roll.

As Mandy said, "... like muff diving is more dangerous than pot smoking or something. What a bunch of hypocrites," I closed my phone and put it back in my pocket. Eventually, she'd realize she'd lost her audience and calm down. Bobbie Jo would apologize for me.

I walked into the room. Larry Joe appeared to be asleep. April was sitting beside Freak holding his hands in hers with both their hands and her head resting on his chest. If I'd interrupted a conversation, I didn't notice it. April didn't even look up. I stayed silent, in case Freak was also sleeping.

He wasn't. "What's up, Boss? You know who killed the bitch, yet?"

When he spoke, April raised her head and turned to me and smiled. She didn't let go of his hands.

"No, but we're getting there. April, do you have the logbook?"

"Of course, it's on the table." She pointed with her eyes; then turned her face back to Freak. Larry Joe stirred, but he didn't say anything. I suspected he was staying quiet until he had time to reload his fake Texas accent.

I picked up the logbook, opened it and pretended to read it. "What did you think of Mr. Crawford? Jeff said you had him eating out of the palm of your hands."

April looked back at me. "You're good, but you're not that good. You're not chatting while you read the log book. You're pretending to read the log book while you investigate. What are you hoping I can tell you?"

Freak said nothing, but he stared at me intently.

"One of the things you bring to this agency is your beauty and the effect it has on men. But your greatest talent is your ability to read the men who react to your beauty. Mr. Crawford specifically told Freak to bring you to get the log book. Jeff says he reacted when you two went to get it. Tell me about his reaction."

She hesitated. I've never seen April blush. I doubt if anybody ever has, or ever will. She came as close to blushing as I'd ever seen, before she answered. "He didn't react. He fawned. He gushed. He even leered."

Freak grinned and said, "That's sounds like a reaction to me. When I get out of here, I'm going to kick his ass."

April gently poked him. "Save the Superman act. Crawford wasn't reacting, he was acting. I didn't even need to be in the room. He could have played that scene out with one of those blank screens they use in Hollywood."

I no longer needed to know what Crawford's personnel file said. If April didn't affect him, my hunch had been right on target. "Of course, he could. It's a scene he's rehearsed many times."

I brought them up to date on what Jeff and I had learned recently. Some of it, April had already shared, but some of it she hadn't known. I went through it all if for no other reason than to make sure it was clear in my own head.

When I finished, Larry Joe asked, "Is Ms. Randall going to pull the personnel file?"

'She said she would. I doubt if she'd lie about it."

"Probably not," he agreed. "If she doesn't get to it quick enough for your tastes, I can make some calls."

My cell phone rang. When I answered, Teresa Randall said,

"Okay, you're not crazy. I don't know if you're just lucky, that good or you're playing me for a fool, but you're definitely not crazy. Robert Crawford's personnel file lists his spouse as Kendall Crawford. That can't be a coincidence. Douglas Kenth is working on the arrest warrant."

She asked me for a few details, some of which I could provide and some of which I couldn't. When she hung up, I looked at Freak and April. "That was Detective Randall. She pulled the file. Kenth is working on the warrant."

Larry Joe raised his bed into a sitting position. "Has my client been released, yet?"

"I don't know. I'll call Randall back and check on that."

He reached for the phone. "The Hell you will; this is gonna be more fun than shootin' varmints with a peashooter."

Larry Joe was tired of being on the sideline. I couldn't blame him. I chose not to consider how much fun shooting varmints with a peashooter might or might not be.

Instead, I stood to take my leave. "I've got some promises to keep. April, you're in charge of getting these boys back on their feet as soon as possible. We've got another successful case to celebrate."

I kept the first promise as soon as I got back to the office. Caroline Smart answered my call on the third ring. I told her what I'd learned, and what I planned to do about it.

"Of course, it has to be done. Did this man also kill Miss Kendra?"

"I don't know, but Detective Randall told me the case has been re-opened. She never believed it was an accident."

"I'm glad to hear that. She was a troubled girl, but she had a good heart. If she was killed, justice should be served."

"I agree. Assuming he killed them both, why do you think he shot at Rachel? She wasn't even working there at the time of the incident."

"I wondered about that, too. I think that might have been a case of mistaken identity. Rachel didn't have her own uniform yet, so she was wearing Trudy's old one. Crawford may have noticed that and assumed she was one of the four mistresses on staff when the incident occurred."

I'm not a mathematician, but I did some quick addition in my head. "Melissa Kendra and Trudy Woodbury are dead. You're obviously fine. Who's the fourth and where is she now?"

"After the incident, Miss Georgia quit. She told me she was going back to Atlanta to reconcile with her ex-husband. At the time, I suspected that the stress of the police investigation had been too much for her."

I asked, "What do you think now?"

"I don't know what to think. I'm going to learn more. Are you sure Trudy blackmailed those people?"

"Sure enough; it won't go to trial, so it doesn't matter."

"No, I guess it doesn't. I wish I could say I didn't think my friend could do that, but I can't say that. Do you think she had anything to do with the incident?"

"I don't think so. According to the police report, she was at the DMA when it happened."

"I know that. The police report of the incident is primarily an account of the worst week of my life. I know its contents better than I know my own diary."

I doubted seriously that Caroline Smart kept a diary. I knew that it didn't matter. She knew the police report like she'd know her diary because like a diary she wrote it. At least, she wrote part of it.

I asked, "What's not in the report that I should know?"

"That's not it, at least not exactly. If this man killed Trudy and Miss Kendra, I was obviously on the list. You may have saved my life.

You definitely kept your word to me. I owe it to you to let you know what I find."

I thought about asking her to promise, but I decided against it. Instead I thanked her for her help. Every question I answered was creating a new question. That's the nature of this business. I spent a few seconds reflecting on that before I picked up the phone.

I still had promises to keep.

60 Grave Danger

"Please tell me you found something on Tequila Sheila!" Annette Paul didn't bother with pleasantries. She got right to the point, which didn't disappoint me in the least.

I did the same. "I found something. I don't know how useful it will be. I have no intention of telling you where I got it and I'll probably deny it if you tell anybody it came from me."

She laughed. "I doubt if you have enough practice lying to pull off the last part, but that won't matter. You're not the only one who can be discreet. What do you have?"

"I've got a twelve page list of names and phone numbers. I think it's all girls who worked for Sheila Tobias."

"You think? Do you even know if you have anything?"

I spent enough time with my former attorney, Daniel Leeds that I channel his attitude when I so desire.

"It is my professional opinion, based on my wisdom guided by my experience, that this list is comprised of women who at one time performed sexual services in exchange for financial compensation in the employ of Ms. Sheila Tobias of Aurora, Colorado."

"Okay, I get it. I'm sorry. Can you fax it to me?"

"In the interest of maintaining plausible deniability, I shall not. I will however read to you as many as you wish to hear."

"I've got as much time as you do."

I started reading. I read only the names and phone numbers. The rest should come up in her investigation. She typed as fast as I read, so it went quickly. She gasped slightly when I said, "Tammy Chang, no current number".

Other than that, it was straight dictation with no sound from her end other than the sound of her keystrokes. I skipped the name Melissa Kendra since I knew it wouldn't help her.

When I finished, she said, "Thank you."

"Good luck; if she was in fact prostituting underage girls, I'd like to see her punished for it as much as you would."

"I doubt that, but I won't debate it. By the way, how do you know I didn't record this conversation?"

"I don't know that, but I do know you won't share it?"

"How do you know that?"

I smiled as I answered, "By using my wisdom, guided by my experience."

224

I hung up without waiting for a response and called Samantha Martin. I had to hold for seven minutes before she came on the line. "Hello Mr. Jennings. How is the weather in North Texas?"

Very few calls can be completely without pleasantries. I wasn't really disappointed that this wasn't one those few. My computer shows current time and temperature in a box on the right hand side of the screen when I'm logged in. I glanced at it, 103 degrees. I said, "A little warm, but we're used to it. How's the weather there?"

"It's dreary and overcast, but if you're calling because you found something useful, it might be sunny in this office very soon."

I couldn't resist, "What if I'm not."

"Then the forecast for my bedroom might be improving. But I know you're a happily married man. If you've found something, tell me. If you need something, ask."

I didn't know whether to be flattered or wonder why her background check on me had been that thorough. I decided not to worry about it.

"I found something. I know why Gertrude Lund committed perjury at James Seaton's trial."

"Interesting; will it be helpful?"

"It might be. She paid him one thousand dollars to kill Tasheika Monroe."

"Do you have proof?"

"I have evidence. These days I'm never sure what constitutes proof, but I have convincing evidence. There's one problem with it, though."

"Isn't there always? What's the problem? Will it not be admissible?"

"No, it will be admissible when I give it to you, but I can't give it to you, just yet."

"If you're not going to give it to me, why did you call?"

I know what a woman sounds like when she's angry, but doesn't want you to know she's angry. I'd expected her to be angry about this, so I was surprised that she'd try to hide it. I suspected she wasn't completely convinced that I was happily married.

"I didn't say I'm not going to give it to you. I said I couldn't give it to you right now. I am going to give you some related information that I'm sure you'll find interesting."

"I'm listening."

"I have twenty-two names of people who have committed crimes for which they have not been punished. Along with that I have explicit details related to those crimes. The details leave little doubt about their culpability."

"And this affects me, how?"

"I believe some, if not all of the perpetrators, have evidence related to Ms. Monroe's murder which they either kept to themselves or lied about. Most were probably afraid of either Gertrude Lund or James Seaton. Those who were afraid of Ms. Lund may be more willing to talk, now."

"They may be. It's a long shot, but it's a shot. I'll take it. Can you fax it to me?"

"I can, but I won't. I'll give it to you over the phone if you promise not to record the call."

She promised, and I did. I left out Jessie Jones and Sal Perlini, but I gave her everything else. It took longer than it could have because every time she recognized a name, she immediately checked her computer to see what she had on him. When we were done, she asked, "Are you going to tell me where you got this information?"

"You don't want to know," I said jokingly.

She replied in kind, "If you told me, you'd have to kill me, huh?"

I looked down at Sal Perlini's page in Gertrude's notebook.

"I'm not a killer, you know that. Good luck; let me know if anything good comes out of this."

"I will…" She hesitated before she continued. "Hey, Carl, thank you. I know you didn't have to call me with this. I appreciate it. Does your wife know how lucky she is to have married the one good man in America?"

"I've never asked her, maybe I will. I'm not, you know?"

She asked, "A good man?"

"No, I'm not the only one."

"Then why don't I ever meet any?"

"I don't know. Could it be because you're a prosecutor for the Commonwealth of Virginia?"

She agreed that could be an issue and we ended the call shortly after that. I didn't feel guilty enough that I felt the need to call my wife and apologize for flirting with Samantha, but I called Emily anyway. I didn't ask if she knows how lucky she is. Like always when I talk to her, I was too busy basking in how lucky I am.

My last call was to Courtney Remington. When I identified myself she said, "Mr. Jennings, how nice to hear from you again."

She sounded like she meant it, but I doubted her.

"I have a message for you from Gertrude Lund."

"Indeed? Has she come back to life or is this a message from the grave?"

226

"I think it's a message from somebody who expected something bad to happen to her and wanted to cover her bases."

"I'm listening."

"She says you can open the envelope."

She laughed, "Of course, I can. Does she also say I should tell you what I find?"

"No, actually she left the message for her husband, but he didn't want it. It ended up with me. Obviously, I'm interested in the contents of the envelope, but she didn't say for you to share it."

"I admire your honesty. I guess I'll repay you with some of my own. I opened the envelope years ago. I can't share the contents with you because I don't have it. There was nothing in it but paper; paper that was useless to me. I didn't have any use for it, so I got rid of it."

As she spoke, I flipped through the notebook. I was back on the first page of the James Seaton section when I figured it out.

I asked her, "How many sheets of paper?"

"Three or four; does it matter?"

"Not really; I just wondered if her last list of people who know James Seaton is a killer is longer than the one she left with you."

She shrieked.

"You have another list? You can't have that! It's not safe."

"I can handle danger. I'm a trained detective. Seaton doesn't scare me."

"It's not you that's in danger. Promise me you'll guard that list with your life."

"I'll guard the list, but I've already given the information to the proper authorities."

She shrieked again.

"Oh God! You don't even know who the proper authorities are. I've got to make a phone call. Please don't do anything rash with that list."

I always seem to act rashly when people ask me not to act rashly. This was no exception.

"Give my regards to Letot. Will you?"

She shrieked again.

It occurred to me that genetically born women aren't the only women who could be overly dramatic. If I'd known what I would soon be discussing with Maurice Letot of the Department of Homeland Security, I'd have been far less cavalier about Ms. Remington's reaction.

61 Ice Cold

"I don't know how to thank you enough. I thought my life was over and now it's just beginning."

Woodbury and Lisha were sitting together in one of the client chairs in my office as he spoke. They looked good together, like they should have always been a couple, or like they always would be a couple. I knew they hadn't always been one, but I hoped they always would be.

I picked up the check Lisha had dropped on my desk when they came in. "You've thanked me enough."

Lisha said, "No. We haven't, but we get your point." She stood up and Woodbury stood and followed her.

He turned to me, "We're going to Vegas for a couple of weeks. We'll be leaving on Tuesday or Wednesday. If you need anything, call me."

"I will. But I doubt if I'll need much this weekend."

"I don't mean this weekend. I mean forever."

Lisha turned to him and pulled him down to kiss her. "You better mean forever when you say forever."

When the kiss eventually ended, he said. "I mean forever, baby. I know what forever means and I mean forever."

Lisha looked back at me, "See you tonight."

I agreed as they walked to the lobby. Lisha and April exchanged a hug before they left. Woodbury kept his eyes on Lisha the whole time they were in the lobby. That bodes well for the future of what I expect will soon be Mr. and Mrs. Woodbury.

After they left, April poked her head in my office. "Everything's set for the party tonight. We've got a table for ten at Nick and Sam's."

"That's great. Are Freak and Larry Joe both going to make it?"

"So they say. If you don't need me here, I'm going to run home and check on Freak. I can be back by two or two-thirty if you want to leave early to get Emily."

"Go ahead and take the afternoon off. I'll stay here. Emily's working until five. She's going to pick me up here."

After she left, I went to her desk and used her computer to pull up the Morning News' website. Robert Crawford's confession wasn't the top story, but it was on the home page. I read it thoroughly, but as expected, I didn't learn anything I didn't already know. Crawford had killed Melissa Kendra and Trudy Woodbury to avenge the death of Kendall Crawford.

Either in keeping with its reputation as the 'Morning Snooze' or because the police had been discreet, the article contained no mention of what Kendall had been wearing when he died. It did mention that Ms. Kendra and Ms. Woodbury had been professional dominants, and that Robert Crawford insisted that Kendall would have never paid for that kind of professional service.

The article also quoted District Attorney Douglas Kenth. 'Committing multiple murders in an act of retaliation is a capital offense. His confession will not keep us from pursuing the death penalty. Two innocent women were murdered in cold blood. In the great state of Texas, the law demands that justice be served.'

I hate it when I find myself agreeing with Dougie. The office phone rang as I read about Robert Crawford's comment that his only regret is that 'two of the whores who killed Kendall are still alive.'

I answered, "Pegasus Investigations."

"Carl, this is Samantha Martin. We need to talk."

"Okay, let's talk."

She paused before asking, "Confidentially?"

I didn't hesitate, "If you wish."

"I do. My daughter just called me about Robert Crawford's confession. There's something accurate about what he had to say. KC wasn't the type of person to hire a dominatrix."

"Casey?"

She answered, "K period C period. KC is what everybody called Kendall Crawford."

That wasn't what I expected to hear. "You knew him?"

"I didn't, but Erica dated him briefly in college."

"Uh, Samantha…"

She anticipated my concern, "I know. KC's gay. He and Robert got married before they moved to Texas. He was a sweetheart. He was the equipment manager for Erica's team. She described him as really cute and really sweet, in hindsight, maybe too sweet. They dated for about a month before he broke it off."

"He broke it off?"

"Yes; she asked him why and he admitted that he was gay. She'd been around so many gay people by then, that she accepted it easily and they stayed friends. In fact, after they broke up, they became even closer as friends than they'd been as a couple. I suspect KC and Robert moved to Dallas because she did."

"Were they close enough that Erica might have told him about T-Money's murder?"

"I don't know. If she had, would he have pieced it together enough to go after Gertrude?"

"He could have. Robert Crawford worked for the police department with Trudy's husband. They very well might have attended a function together at some point. Gertrude isn't a common name. Even if he only learned her name and her reputation as a complete bitch, he'd have suspected. How many people named Gertrude can be that much of a bitch."

"Probably more than you think, but you have a point. I need to call Erica."

"Do you?"

"What do you mean?"

"Kendall and Trudy are dead. Robert is in jail. If Kendall really died trying to avenge T-Money's murder, will it be better for Erica to know that?"

She hesitated a long time before answering. When she did, she spoke deliberately. "I don't know. I really don't know."

"Maybe you should wait. It can't be undone once you tell her."

"No, it can't. Thank you. By the way, I have some other news for you. We've reopened the case on T-Money's murder. We've found three witnesses who will testify that Seaton and Gertrude weren't together at the time of the murder. That got us a warrant to arrest Seaton on a perjury charge. We're still checking to see if we can try him for murder for hire, since it's a different crime than murder."

We discussed the likelihood of that working out and other details of the case against Seaton for five minutes before we ended the call. I reread the article on Crawford's confession a couple of more times. We had a celebration planned tonight. We always celebrate when we solve big cases, but I wasn't sure about celebrating this one.

I heard the hard, familiar sound of Caroline Smart's boots climbing the outer staircase. She entered the office with her usual confident walk, but without the air of confidence that usually accompanies such a walk. She had made it clear that pleasantries aren't needed on her last visit, so I just waited as she sat down opposite April's desk.

"What do you know about 'justifiable homicide'?"

"That's more of a question for a lawyer than an investigator, but I think the state's current position is that homicide is only justified if the state executioner performs it after a trial, five appeals and a ten year waiting period. Why do you ask?"

"Robert Crawford killed two of my friends, and tried to kill an innocent young lady. If he gets away with it, he'll almost certainly try to kill me. I do not want that to happen."

I thought about what she'd just said: two friends, one innocent young lady. The implication was clear, but I don't like to make assumptions.

I said, "Of course not. Are you going to tell me what you found out?"

"I don't know, maybe I should talk to a lawyer."

"If you need a recommendation or a referral, I know the best."

She hesitated, "No thanks. McCoy could convince a jury that Jack the Ripper should get a probated sentence. I'm looking for a long sentence, not a short sentence."

I noted that she chose to use a serial killer known for killing prostitutes as her metaphor, but I didn't comment on it. Not commenting is often my best option. We looked at each other without saying anything. She appeared to be thinking seriously about something.

After a few minutes, she decided. "I'm going to tell you. I promised you I'd tell you if I found anything and I did. I think Gertrude murdered Kendall Crawford in my dungeon."

"I thought she had an alibi."

"I've decided to tell you. Perhaps, you should let me before I change my mind."

I nodded.

"Most professional dominants are just that, professionals. The sub pays the check and sets the scene. Like your friend Rachel, we're basically actresses playing a role for a small audience. Gertrude was always different. She liked to see how far she could go. She was always experimenting with new and wilder ways to do her job."

She paused and looked toward the kitchenette. "Do you have anything to drink over there?"

I stood quickly and walked over to the kitchenette. She followed and when I opened the mini-fridge, she helped herself to a Guinness.

Once she had it open, and had taken a swallow, she continued. "One of Gertrude's gadgets was an ice lock. It creates a timed experience, like self-bondage fanatics enjoy, but with more control. Freeze the lock for two hours and it absolutely can't be unlocked for an hour, freeze it for four hours, and it's locked for two."

"There's nothing in the police report about that."

"No, there isn't. Gertrude's early models were clunky and useful only for handcuffs and leg cuffs with wide openings for the locks. I talked to Mistress Georgia. She says she saw Gertrude freezing a pink ice lock that looked just like the lock in the gag Melissa used on Kendall. If she's right, it's probably in the bag I gave you."

"If it is, what does that mean?"

"It means that when Kendall Crawford started to choke, there was nothing Melissa could do. She couldn't get the lock off and she had no idea why."

"She told the police she must have panicked."

"She did, and she passed a lie detector test about that. I think she did panic, but only after the key wouldn't work."

"I understand the lie detector test results were a key factor in the decision to rule it an accident."

She paused. "It was important. Mostly because they didn't ask the one question she wouldn't have been able to answer honestly."

I waited silently.

Ms. Smart continued, "After the incid… after he died, she went through his stuff and found a pipe bomb in his bag. She was coherent enough to know that would look bad, so she took it."

"Where is it now?" I asked.

"I don't know."

I knew she was lying, but I saw no reason to mention it. "So what do we do now?"

"Are you going to look in the leather case for the lock?"

I thought about several things before answering. I thought about Samantha Martin's daughter telling Kendall Crawford about the murder of her high school teammate. I thought about him later carrying a pipe bomb into Mrs. Woodbury's house of domination and dying for his effort. I thought about his lover Robert getting revenge less than a year later by killing two women.

I thought about the entire convoluted chain of events that led to so many dead bodies. I thought about Robert Crawford taking a shot at Rachel. I thought about Sam The Man and Rachel holding hands at Freak and April's wedding. Lastly, I thought about Crawford saying his only regret was that he hadn't killed two other whores.

I made my decision. "I am not."

She briefly looked relieved, but quickly returned to her natural austere state. She asked, "Why not?"

"The leather case now belongs to Richard Woodbury, both as her heir and in keeping with the instructions you promised your friend that you'd carry out. He specifically requested that it be burned. I'm faster than you at keeping promises."

She smiled and stood up. It wasn't a sweet smile, but I suspected it was the most pleasant one she had displayed lately. "Thank you. I knew I could trust you."

"If she killed him, she paid the ultimate price for it. Crawford killed two people and planned to kill others. The state will make him pay for that."

She finished the rest of the Guinness and sat it down on the desk. "I hope so."

Knowing what Sam The Man might do to Crawford for shooting at Rachel and how the state would then treat him, I told her honestly. "I hope so, too. It would be a bad thing if Kendall's pipe bomb turns up before the state executes Robert Crawford."

She smiled. If I ever doubted that there could be such a thing as a purely evil smile, those doubts forever vanished as she said, "It will not. I promise!"

As she left, I also smiled. I never told her that I hadn't promised Woodbury that I'd burn the case. I'm sure if Freak ever decides to return to his unique version of performance art, his troupe will find many uses for the contents of the leather suit case.

62 Surprise Visitors

Nine minutes after a smiling Ms. Smart left our office, the phone rang. As usual, I answered, "Pegasus Investigations."

An electronically disguised but vaguely familiar male voice said, "Check your email. You have an email from Reuter's news. It is not spam. You should read it as soon as you can do so in private."

I turned to April's computer to open up email. The message from Reuter's was the newest. It had been sent by 'You should know.' The note read, "this can't be traced to me, there is no reason to delete it." The headline of the article was to the point. "Two Dead as Sniper Fire Ends Special Forces Mission."

The article was slightly longer than the headline, but provided very little more detail.

"Two Green Berets were killed by sniper fire in Afghanistan. Second Lieutenant Robert Kilgore and Private First Class James Seaton were on a mission near Kabul, Afghanistan when sniper fire erupted and both were killed instantly. Army spokesman Jill Banyon declined comment regarding the nature of the mission or the details of the attack, except to say that friendly fire is not suspected."

I was reading the article for the eleventh time when I heard Maurice Letot ring the bell in the waiting room. I shut down the computer and buzzed him in. He waited until he'd settled into one of the client chairs to speak.

"You've been a busy man, Mr. Jennings."

He calls me Mr. Jennings when he's upset. "Have I?"

"Don't be that way. False modesty does not become you. You've somehow managed to solve crimes in three states in less than a month. You should be proud of that."

"I just do my job. I'm trying to make a living the best I can. I'm not looking for reasons to be proud."

"Of course not," he smiled. "You should also be ashamed. By ignoring my warning, you also jeopardized the security of the county you love and indirectly caused two damn good soldiers to die."

He smiled at me the way he always did when he hoped that he'd rattled me. During our first few meetings, he was always right about it. Lately, he'd been wrong more often. This time he wasn't even close.

"So I gathered. James Seaton got what he deserved. Give my condolences to the family of Robert Kilgore."

Letot looked rattled in the exact same way I think he'd hoped to rattle me. "How do you know about that?"

"Homeland defense is needed to protect us as a free country. A big part of that freedom is the free press. When a military spokesperson tells the media that friendly fire is not suspected, I tend to think it was friendly fire."

Letot relaxed. "Of course, you do. You also think the KKK killed Marilyn Monroe and that Jim Morrison is still alive."

He was only half right, but I didn't correct him. It's not his business which conspiracy theories I choose to believe. Saying nothing has always been a good idea for me. I decided to do it again.

Letot eventually tired of the silence and stood. "I guess you did what you had to do. It probably worked out for the best. We won't need to discuss this again. Don't forget your promise. If, make that when, you hear from Sal Perlini, I expect you to call me."

I watched him walk to the door. Just before he got to it, I asked, "Were Seaton and Kilgore killed by friendly fire?"

He turned to me. "There's no such thing as friendly fire, Carl. You know that. If it'll help you sleep, know that Kilgore deserved it just as much as Seaton, maybe more."

"I thought you said they were both good soldiers."

"They were good soldiers. They were not good men. Speaking of good men, how's your partner. I stopped getting updates once he checked out of the hospital."

"He's fine," I smiled. "You know he's going to outlive us all, don't you?"

"He just might at that. And how's Cowboy McCoy?"

"Also fine, are we still talking about good men?"

"I'm not sure, but he's one hell of a lawyer. When the devil comes for me, I hope the old boy's still around to take my money."

Letot was out the door before I could mention that McCoy didn't like defending guilty clients as much as he once did. He'd only been gone three minutes when another visitor arrived. He was a tanned, wiry man about six feet tall, maybe forty years old. He had the familiar, worried look that I'd always been happy to see on a potential client when the agency was struggling.

"You're Carl Jennings," he said as he sat down in one of the client chairs. It wasn't a question.

"I am." I admitted. "And you are…?"

"John Doe."

"Pleased to meet you, Mr. Doe; may I call you John?"

He tried not to smile, but he couldn't help himself. "Mr. Doe will do for now."

He immediately proceeded to tell me a story about an inheritance and a missing heir, complete with big talk about large finder's fees. As he spoke, his worried face became less worried. It also became more familiar. By the time he finished talking, I knew I was talking to Sal Perlini.

I agreed to take his case, and he stood as if he was ready to leave. We shook hands, and he held my hand a little longer than normal. He sat back down.

"Before you call Maurice Letot, there's something you should know."

I tried to look confused, "Maury Leppert? Who's that?"

He smiled. "You're good. I knew that before I arranged for you to have this office. If I didn't already know how good you are, I'd probably believe you don't know who I am. But I'd still know that you know Letot. He just left your office."

I simply looked at him without saying a word.

"I know you're the master of the silent treatment. I also know you promised to call Letot when I showed up. I have no problem with any of that, but before you do, there's something you need to see."

"I'm interested," I told him honestly.

He pointed to the remote control sitting on the desk.

"May I?"

"You paid for it. Help yourself."

He secured the office and then walked into the smaller office. I knew it was smaller because Freak had pointed that out to me one day after circumstances had left him cooped up here with nothing to do. That day seemed like ages ago as we walked into the office Freak still uses. Perlini pointed the remote control toward the back wall.

"Let me show you the secret stair case."

I let him. He also showed me some tunnels and some doors. He showed me many things that I had no intention of sharing with my partner or with Maurice Letot, at least not in the immediate future.

When he left, I decided to spend the night at the office. I called my wife. As always, she understood.

After a short conversation, she said, "I love you. Sleep well."

It would be a mistake to say that I slept well, if, in fact, I even slept at all.

ACKNOWLEDGEMENTS

First, I'd like to thank the many fine people involved in Dallas' fetish communities who kindly answered every question I had and many I'd have never thought to ask. All they ever asked in return is that I treat their scene with dignity, respect and a sense of humor. Since many of these ladies and gentleman own whips and know how to use them, I hope I succeeded.

Also, I'd like to thank the Dallas County Community College District for once hiring a professor so universally hated that she helped me realize there are no limits on how despicable a fictional character can be. In a related note, I should thank the University of Phoenix Marketing professor who reignited my literary aspirations by telling me that my papers were hard to grade because the writing was so exceptional.

Lastly, as always, I thank each waitress who served me a beer or two while also serving as a muse, a motivator, a sounding board or the inspiration for a character. I especially want to thank those who have moved on to other careers, but continue to take interest in my writing and my life.